the
LOST LOVE
LETTERS
of
HENRI
FOURNIER

the

LOST LOVE
LETTERS
of
HENRI
FOURNIER

ROSALIND BRACKENBURY

Text copyright © 2018 by Rosalind Brackenbury
All rights reserved.

Published by Lake Union Publishing, Seattle

www.apub.com

Amazon, the Amazon logo, and Lake Union Publishing are trademarks of Amazon.com, Inc., or its affiliates.

ISBN-13: 9781503902879
ISBN-10: 1503902870

Cover design by Faceout Studio, Lindy Martin

Printed in the United States of America

In memory of Edith Sorel

"I love you. On the night of the Rite of Spring, on my way home, I realized that one thing in my life was over and another was beginning—wonderful, more beautiful than anything, but also terrifying, and quite possibly fatal."

Henri Alain-Fournier to Pauline Perier, née Benda
Sunday morning, June 8, 1913

August–September 1914

In the slow train that crossed the hexagon of France from southwest to northeast, the men leaned against each other in the corridors and pressed up against the windows. There wasn't room to sit or move. Henri felt hunger growl in his stomach. Leaving the station at Auch, there had been that moment of exhilaration—At last, we're off!—but it hadn't lasted. A time like free fall, he imagined, when you plummeted, tugged by the earth's gravity, no need to open your parachute yet.

If only he had flown more. If only the aeroplanes he loved could have carried him high above the earth, to look down and see it all, the earth spread out beneath him like the body of a woman you made love to, all graceful hills and valleys, with little hidden rivers, clumps of trees, broad plains, and forests. He'd so wanted to fly. If he came back from the war, he would become a pilot. But he would not, most probably, come back. He felt it deeply, and it was why he took so long to get organized to leave, why he left it till the last minute, although Jacques had told him irritably that last day in Bordeaux, Henri, man, it's now, you have to get moving. *Why he lingered with Pauline, why he couldn't get out of bed, why he dreamed, his eyes open, beside her in the mornings, as sun moved across the room and the blue day awaited them and she was warm and sleepy at his side. Tasting life, taking his time, because it was all there was: this glimpse, this vivid intense beauty of everything, like the moment when you came inside a woman and knew that this cry of life that escaped you was all surprise and pleasure and intimation of mortality, because the moment couldn't be prolonged.*

They were told to report for duty at Mirande on the first of August. He'd arrived on the fourth. He'd been nearly late for the war. And she'd still been with him, yes, but essentially he'd already departed. Once you were in uniform, your head shaved, feet booted, weapons prepared, you had already gone. He thought of her face at the station in Auch as the train pulled out, so slowly that the women on the platform could walk alongside it and only at the end had to run; a cruel slowness, a long-drawn gradual departure, faces blurring, hands waving handkerchiefs like small white birds. Her face, sharpened almost to ugliness with despair. He had stopped saying to her, "It will be all right, I'll be back soon, the war will be over, we'll have a life." These words that were repeated all around them were just empty promises made by men to women in tears, men whose own hearts were breaking.

The train moved like a sluggish river through country stations and past fields in which corn still stood, unharvested. At the stations, women rushed up and pressed holy pictures and medals on the men, held out rosaries, even pinned homemade corsages on their chests—pictures of the Virgin, blue, white, and red rosettes for France. The few old men left guarding their farms stood at roadsides and level crossings, watching the train pass, their caps held to their chests as if they were already at a funeral. Shouts, scraps of La Marseillaise *floating in their ears, there, and then gone. The rations were miserable. After Bourges, where they got out and stretched their legs at the station, a deeper hunger ached in Henri's guts. At Saint-Florentin there was a Red Cross truck parked at the station, and some women stood up on it to hurl what he suddenly realized were hard-boiled eggs—eggs!—and they all flung out their open hands to catch them as if it were a game. He reached as if to catch a high ball, and an egg landed in his open palm and cracked as he grasped it. The men who caught them peeled them with trembling fingers and ate them—that dry, slightly sulfurous taste, the yolk crumbly, the white slippery and firm. The soldiers who hadn't managed to catch an egg watched them, but didn't ask for any; there was a sort of respect, as if the men who'd caught the eggs had won a prize.*

Outside the station at Brienne-le-Château he saw a crashed aeroplane in bits, its fuselage torn and flapping, among some wrecked trucks. These were the first casualties of the war any of them had so far seen; and they were only things, not men. They reached the camp at Suippes. In the middle of the wide plain of the Argonne, they heard the first cannon fire; at first it seemed like distant thunder, but too sharp and hard. The sky was black, the sun almost eclipsed by smoke, the trees blackened too. They were entering a place that hadn't existed before, a place stripped and poisoned by war. He tried to remember what he'd imagined only days, weeks before, in that other life—that war would be glorious, that they'd be marching in sunlight, their weapons glittering, selves forgotten in the beauty of the crusade. But he couldn't. He was just a hungry man with his gut churning and hands shaking, looking out on the ruins of his country. Until now, they had been children. Now, they had to be men. And none of them had a clue how to change so fast, become warriors, fighting machines. None of their training—even in all those long maneuvers in the sleepy countryside, their practice in ditches and fields and behind trees, the bright formations, even the fatigue and discomfort and hunger of those days—nothing had prepared them for this.

He wanted to write to her, to tell her. But there was no time, no space. In his head he spoke to her, tried for the words of love, but they were out of reach.

Verdun, under what looked like an eclipse. The sun shrouded by black rags. The summer trees, leafless. The whole flat plateau of the Woëvre filled with milling soldiers, guns, trucks, vehicles of all sorts, as if this were a maneuver taking place in hell. One of the men said to him, "There's bound to have been some hats blown off over there." They had no news. The railway line to Étain was deserted, and all the houses, including the crossing keeper's and stationmaster's, were barricaded, their windows blind. They'd have to march to Étain. It would take nearly a week. He had the new serviceable *boots that he'd bought with Pauline, and they'd carry him well, but already he and every other soldier felt his guts like water, his stomach flapping against his backbone. Why couldn't they at least feed them? Watery soup, hard corners of stale loaves, potatoes, meat that had been boiled so long it looked and tasted like rags; he began to dream of butter, cream, roast lamb the way his mother cooked it. He marched at the head of his men. They salivated as they walked, their legs marching in time, their minds floating and cloudy. His head pounded; hunger gave you a headache. It was hard to focus when you were this hungry; it felt as if the enemy had already moved inside them, weakening them from within. Napoleon's army, coming back from Moscow, had fallen apart with cold and hunger. The Russians had hardly needed to attack them. They collapsed from inside, in the entropy of the body.* He thought, A man is this easily destroyed.

Their first battle was on August 24, their battalion in the second line at the Bassin de Briey. They knew what to do, it turned out—their train-ing had worked. The years of maneuvers had conditioned him. Once you were in it, you simply reacted, like reciting lines you have learned, over and over. It was less hard than the waiting, than the train journey, than having the time to look around. All through the last days of August and through September, around Verdun, they struggled for control of a few meters of their own territory. It became like a game, like football even—taking all your time and attention so you never had time to think or wonder. You moved, fell to the ground, fired, advanced, hid, fired again. Men fell around you. Germans and Frenchmen died. There was no time to notice, to feel, to fear. He had become a fighting machine, all the tender parts burned away in the fierceness of the great game of war.

In the morning, on a day in late September, his party reached the Calonne trench, which zigzagged between lines of sentries. They crossed it a little to the right of the road between Vaux-lès-Palameix and Saint-Rémy. They fell into formation, four at a time, and saw a figure run out from behind trees and apparently jump into a hole.

"Come on, let's get some Boches," said his superior, Captain Grammont.

Suddenly a crack of fire and puff of smoke came from the trench. The captain leapt forward, his revolver in his hand; Henri and the other lieutenant followed him. He glimpsed two men carrying a stretcher behind trees. Who was he about to shoot at? Surely not a stretcher party? But it was suddenly marvelous to be in action, to be running, firing, engaged. It was as if he were about to score a goal out there on his own, no other choice or action possible. Feeling the stock of his revolver in his hand, he leapt and ran over small bushes and twigs, darted between trees—they were at the edge of a beech wood—heard the shout as the captain fell, and then was suddenly belly-down on the earth, his weapon still in his hand, there on the open ground. Dirt in his mouth, twigs and grass before his eyes. Nothing happened for a moment. Everything else was a long way away.

He sat up against a tree and felt a dull ache in his lower stomach, as if his body had decided it wanted to shit. I want to shit, therefore I'm still alive. This is what it comes down to? *For a long moment there was silence, unless he had gone deaf. The earth he sat on smelled of leaf mold, beech mast. Birds rustled in leaves. Crisp leaves of September, turning color. Must have rained recently: this fresh loamy smell. Mushrooms, truffles even. His fingers in earth, feeling for it through grass. Should stand up. Movement didn't come. A man stood in front of him. A uniform he didn't recognize—*Not one of ours. German? *Strange, to be in a war with them and not know what they looked like. The man wore a helmet. He pointed a gun at him. A small animal scuttled in the undergrowth close by: rabbit, squirrel, stoat? Henri lifted his face to the man, as if to ask him the question,* Why?

A gun barrel, like a single eye. You sat under a tree and someone came and stood in front of you and wanted to kill you? You, a man who had a book to finish, a man who was loved, who had a life?

I.

1.

September 1975, Paris

When she opens the door to him, the shock of his young face is nearly overwhelming. Henri? No, of course not. She is too old, Pauline thinks, to be made to feel like this. She almost wants to shut the door in his face. But she holds it open to him, shaky and out of breath as she is.

He sticks out his hand, a long wrist beneath a too-short cuff. He's tall, skinny, his dark hair ruffled. He wears a black jacket, jeans, and he's carrying a leather bag. But it's the face that threatens to stop her heart.

It's September, another autumn. She's at home, in Paris. Then, she remembers. It's the young man from London. It's today, and he's here. She forgot it was today, that he was coming. Perhaps she can keep this visit short, offer him an hour or so of her time, then be rid of him.

"My name is Sebastian Fowler. You were expecting me, Madame?" He's nervous, jittery on her threshold, like someone delivering unwanted news.

She wants to reassure him; he looks so uncertain. "Oh, yes. Of course. Come in." Only, she had no warning that his arrival would revive such memories. A copy, a spitting image. Isn't that what they say in English?

She leads him down the corridor toward her salon, where today's newspapers lie about and it looks, with another person here, rather a mess. He follows her closely as if eager to get into the room. The photograph of Henri on the wall looks down at them both.

"Do sit down. Can I get you something? A glass of water? Coffee? I'm sorry the place is such a mess. My cleaning lady wasn't able to come this week."

He looks about him as if the concept of untidiness mattering is new to him. He puts down his worn leather satchel and produces a little cassette recorder that he sets on the coffee table. He sits down on the edge of the sofa, opposite her chair.

"You don't mind?"

"Is that a tape recorder? It's so small."

"Yes, isn't it? Saves a lot of heavy lifting."

She sits up, opposite him, brisk. "So, Mr. Fowler, you are writing about Henri Fournier?" Talk covers her agitation. She has had his letter from England with its black spiky handwriting open on her desk for at least a week. Did she answer it? She must have, or he wouldn't be here.

Sebastian thinks, *Now I'm actually here, I don't know what to say.* The tape recorder sits between them like an obstacle. What was he thinking, asking this ancient woman to talk about her long-ago lover? He's read about the actress whom Fournier loved, the woman called Madame Simone, with whom he had a passionate affair before the First World War. But how to bridge the gap? It's all very well reading about it, but how do you go about asking intimate questions of a stranger?

Seb got the address by mail from the Comédie Française. He found that the living Pauline, still in Paris, was a real woman, surprisingly present and of this time, and so here he is. Baffled. Too young to know what to say.

He doesn't want to tell her it's his first live interview. He clicks his pen, recrosses his legs, glances around the room as if it may help him. Sitting in his room in south London, with the chimneys of Battersea power station to remind him that he was nowhere near Paris, it wasn't hard to write that letter. But to be here, now, with someone who not only knew Fournier but had been in love with him . . . well, it feels as if he's overstepped the mark. It would almost have been easier if she had died, if this were just a matter of history. Yet, she did write back to him. She did say that she would be delighted—yes, delighted—to talk to him. He remembers this. And she's smiling, waiting for him to speak.

"Yes. I'm writing a book about him. A biography. Well, I hope I am."

"And you wanted to meet someone who actually knew him, rather than rely on secondhand gossip?"

"Well, yes," he says, the polite boy his parents raised. "Madame Simone, it's really good of you to see me."

"You can call me Simone. Madame Simone sounds too much like a concierge. Don't you think? You know my real name is Pauline? Simone started out as my stage name."

"Oh. All right. And I'm usually called Seb."

"Seb, like the pressure cooker?"

"What?"

"Just a stupid joke. There is a pressure cooker called Seb. Kitchen utensils."

"Oh."

She thinks, *Oh, God who does not exist, get me through this panic. Jokes about pressure cookers, what next? He is not Henri. He isn't even all that like Henri. He's a young Englishman, come to do an interview. Get a grip on yourself, idiot. Just answer his questions, and be done by lunchtime. But, start by putting him at ease.*

"Tell me about yourself," she says. Always ask about the other person, especially if they are younger than you, which means everybody these days.

Seb is thinking, *Jesus, she's so old, and what on earth can I ask her that isn't going to be desperately intrusive? Tell me all about your love affair of sixty years ago? I want all the details. This is, after all, 1975, we talk about such things. And, she looks like she's sharp as a tack, as my mother would say. She'll disappear back into her shell like an old tortoise if I start off too nosy.*

But she's asked him about himself. He looks around him at the table with the blue cloth, the lamp—must be art nouveau and worth a fortune—the pictures on the walls. What did he imagine? Her letter to him was, after all, on headed writing paper, in an antique but perfectly legible hand, hardly a tremor, a clear signature. Formal, but friendly enough.

"Where are you from? Who are your parents?"

"My dad's English, my mother's American. I grew up on both sides of the Atlantic, but we came back to England when the war in Vietnam began, so I wouldn't risk being drafted. I read Modern Languages, at Oxford, did my doctorate on early twentieth-century French writers— Claudel, Péguy, Rivière, Fournier. Then I decided I wanted to do a book on Fournier. I love his writing. It's extraordinary. And, it was tragic that he died so young. And then, well, I found out about you, that you existed. Exist, I mean."

"Yes, I exist. Just about. I'm ninety-eight, did you know that? And he, poor man, only got to twenty-seven. Tell me, what do your parents do?"

"My father taught at Berkeley, where he met my mother. She was in the theatre then, she still is, on and off. She does more stage design now. Dad's attached to New College, Oxford. He teaches American history."

"And they didn't want you to be sent off to the war in Indochina."

"Right."

"Very sensible. Nothing worse than having a son go off to war. Or, anyone one loves."

There's a silence in which she wonders, as she often does these days, if she has actually said the words that exist in her head.

"You know, it's amazing to meet you. To be actually in the same room with—"

"His lover? I've aged a bit, you know. It's quite a surprise for me, too, but then I don't get many surprises these days. I have to be grateful for them." She thinks, *I can't tell him; it will make him too self-conscious. Poor boy, he doesn't want to hear an ancient woman tell him he's the spitting image of her lover of more than sixty years ago.* So she simply smiles and pulls herself up by the chair arms to hobble to the kitchen to pour coffee for him, while he gets up and walks around her room examining the paintings on her walls and the books in her bookcase, as if this is how he always makes himself at home.

She sets down the coffee, watches his roaming. He makes the room seem smaller. It's so long since anyone has been here who doesn't already know its every detail, who bothers to look.

"Moravia. Fuentes. Woolf. Hemingway. Genet. You have a pretty eclectic collection."

"Well, I'm a pretty eclectic person, I suppose."

"Is that really a Chagall?"

"Yes, it is."

"He signed it to you!" He's standing in front of the drawing, staring thoughtfully.

"It was after a performance. It was my birthday. So, you like the beaux arts too?"

"Well, yes. Yes, I do." He pauses. "But I mean, Chagall!"

He stops before the photograph of Henri. "Was that when he was in the army?"

"Yes, on military service."

"Amazing. He looks so young. Younger than anybody does now, somehow. You know what I mean?"

"I'm surprised that anybody looks young to you. But I suppose it's relative. Perhaps what you are seeing is a certain innocence. Now, what was it you wanted to ask me?"

The pain of it lives still in her body like an old injury; most days she doesn't feel it anymore. Henri departing that day: his face already drawn with fatigue, the last touch of a hand through a train window, then the last sight, that hand waving. You looked, long after the train was gone. You couldn't tell, in the end, one hand from another. A soldier waved from a departing train; a woman stood on the platform. Multiply it by a thousand, even a million. You saw it later in so many films; it became a cliché of war: men departing, women staying. You buried the anxiety deep inside yourself and hurried away to try to be useful somewhere else, but part of you, the part that mattered, was still on that deserted platform, waving as a train disappeared.

Seb is fiddling with his machine, so luckily he can't see her face as she tries to compose it. She's shuffled all the objects on the sofa to one end—newspapers, library books, her magnifying glass, her shawl. "Are you in a hurry?"

"No, no. In fact I've several days in Paris; my flight isn't till Thursday."

She thought, *Well, perhaps it could take an hour or so, and we might have lunch afterward.* But he's planning three days with her? Surely not.

"So could we chat for a minute first?" she asks. "I'm not keen on interviews. They make me nervous, always have. Sit down, have your coffee. You do like coffee? I'm afraid I'm still an addict." Too bad, it will speed her heart, but she needs the energy.

He sinks down in the sagging leather armchair in which she usually sits to watch television. He exhales, as if it's all been a physical effort. She observes his long legs in the blue jeans that everyone seems to wear these days, as if whole generations were at work on construction sites, his black corduroy jacket, his shirt white and open at the neck. His brown eyes, in clear light the color of coffee sugar. His cup clinks in its saucer. He's anxious; she can feel it coming off him like sweat. *How hard life is for the young,* she thinks. *They care so much how they are seen.*

He says, "Well, interviews make me nervous too. It always seems like too much to erupt into people's lives and ask them questions."

"Particularly about old love affairs, eh? Still, it's what you're here for, isn't it? Now, I've asked you a few questions, so it's your turn. Fire away."

He glances through the high windows to the slate roofs of the buildings opposite. A pigeon walks the iron railing. It's like being lost in time. *Chagall. He signed it for my birthday.* "Have you always lived here?"

"A long time, now."

"It's great."

"It used to be better, before all the traffic on boulevard Saint-Germain, and before all the shops turned into fashion boutiques and shoe shops. It's getting hard to buy a baguette even."

Silence. His spoon rattles against his saucer. She thinks, *He's used to mugs and Nescafé, most likely.* He looks up again at the photograph on the wall, Henri in his military cap, his eyes points of light.

Has she imagined or remembered that quick upward thrust of the head, that suddenly dreamy gaze? Seb flicks his hair back from his eyes. Men are wearing their hair longer now; it makes them sweetly androgynous. He picks up a tiny spoon to stir sugar into his coffee. He has such big, young hands.

She waits for him to speak.

"I know I shouldn't, but do you mind if I smoke?"

"Well, I'd rather you didn't. I like the smell, but it makes me cough."

"Of course. Sorry, I shouldn't have asked."

"Feel free to go and smoke in the courtyard, whenever you like. Now. You can ask anything. As long as I have the right not to answer."

"Shall we talk about the book? Lots of people are reading it in England, you know; it's had quite a renaissance lately. Some critic said he thought Fitzgerald must have got his idea for *The Great Gatsby* from reading it in translation. Though you can't exactly imagine Gatsby having a baby, can you?"

"Not really. No. But you say it's having a renaissance in England? I'm surprised. People here find it rather old-fashioned. Tell me, why do you want to write about Henri? What does he mean to you?"

He takes a breath, blows out his cheeks, as if after running. "Well. He writes about adolescence and adult life, both. He joins them—as if, well, it seems to me—as if we remain the same person, caught in a sort of dream, for our lifetimes. Only the life around us changes, and challenges us. Not only that, but there's a mystery at the book's heart that never really gets solved, or explained."

"And you think it should be solved, or explained? Or, that it can be?"

"I don't know. I'm just rattling on, it's probably nonsense."

"Relax," she tells him. "I have absolutely nothing else to do today except listen to you, and tell you what I can. If you live to your nineties, you'll find that's true of most of your days. I'm delighted you're here. Now, if we can entertain each other for an hour or so first, I'll send out for some lunch. There's a very good restaurant down the street, and I just have to telephone, they deliver. I find talking gives me an appetite. Don't you?" *At least,* she thinks, *I can feed him. Poor boy, he looks half-starved.*

"Well, yes."

"Don't mind the dog. He doesn't like men, but you can push him down if he annoys you."

The Pekinese sits up, his face like a black pansy, his fawn body and curled tail tense. He is a dog bred to sleep in the sleeves of princes.

"No, he's all right." The young man's hand lies on the dog's loose ruff, rolling it between his fingers. Henri always got on well with her dogs.

His tape recorder is running now, and she takes a deep breath, hand on her chest.

"Life," she says. "It's so all over the place. There's an order to it, perhaps, but it certainly isn't obvious. Well, maybe it's not like that for you; you're still young. But I find I can plunge in anywhere, and the details come to life, and at the same time it's as if it all happened to someone else. Everything shifts about. Like a kaleidoscope, you know? I had one when I was a child."

"Kaleidoscopes have definite patterns, don't they?"

"So they do. Or is that an illusion, created by the eye? Do we simply have such a need to see patterns that we create them in spite of ourselves?"

He doesn't know. "Any way you want to tell it will be all right."

"Well, I was his lover, as you know, and he was killed in the first months of the Great War, and he wrote this one book that everyone found extraordinary, and it has never I think been out of print. It has something that fascinates people. It's like a puzzle. And yet it's also very clear and precise. You know, one line of a book can change a life? Have you felt that?"

"When Meaulnes walks into the schoolroom and you know that something is going to happen."

"Exactly. When I first read it—and I was his first reader, you know—it gave me a frisson. Because it is what we all want. To have our lives transformed, and preferably for someone to walk in and do it for us. No?"

This boy with the miraculous face. He would have been born well after the Second World War, brought up in a postwar England that only slowly freed itself from austerity. Or, luxurious, gadget-ridden America. He lives in London, where the IRA is blowing up mailboxes and the garbage lies piled in the streets. There have been strikes, miners' strikes, she's heard, and three-day weeks, people sitting by candlelight, threats of government collapse. Perhaps nobody in any generation has it easy.

Seb feels the furniture crowding him, the piles of stuff getting in the way of any movement he may make. As if he may be stuck here forever. All these glasses of water and boxes of tissues, these piles of books, these shawls thrown about, these little tables. Yet what she has just said has made them equals.

She asks, "So, what do you want to know about Henri that you don't already know?"

"Well, what he was like, really. It's different, finding out about him from books."

"Did you ever see the film with Gérard Philipe, *Les Grandes Manoeuvres*? About the first war?"

"No, I don't think so."

"You should see it. He reminded me so much of Henri. They had the same-shaped face. The same heartbreaking smile." She pauses. She thinks, *Yes, Gérard Philipe and now you. Why else would I be indulging you?* "Well, the first thing is that he wasn't a saint. He was an extremely complex person, and he was only twenty-seven when he died, so who knows how he would have turned out. How old are you?"

"Twenty-five."

"That was the age he was when we met."

The tape whirrs in its little box. The sun moves across the room. She goes to pull a blind down, raise another. Light flashes up from glass in a car window below.

"You know, you're the first person I've agreed to talk to about all this for years? I did a filmed interview a few years ago for French television, and the interviewer suddenly asked me point-blank what effect Henri's death had had on me. I couldn't speak. I just said to him, I can't talk about it—so he got the point and moved on to something else. It was very crude."

"Why did you agree to talk to me?"

"Something about your being English, perhaps? Or because you're young? Or because I saw from your letter that you love the book. Who knows? Perhaps because it's time I told somebody." It is, after all, pleasant to have him to talk to—and to look at.

"Well, I'm grateful that you agreed to see me. I'm a beginner at all this."

"You can't help that! You're twenty-five. You're a beginner at everything at your age."

The tape recorder is running.

"I'll just plunge in, shall I? He was my husband's secretary—my second husband that is—and when we met I was already in my thirties. I had had no experience of real love, in spite of two marriages. I loved his mind, the way he thought, the way he saw the world. We became lovers—to make a long story short—and then in 1914 he was killed. We had less than two years. His family covered up our love affair, because they were very Catholic and pious and I was not only half-Jewish but an actress and a divorced woman—three counts against me. It wasn't surprising. So, they cleaned up his act for him after he was dead, and I was vilified and then left out of the story. Everything that contradicted their version was suppressed."

"You aren't in his book, are you?"

"Not in *Le Grand Meaulnes*, no. He had nearly finished it when he met me. The heroine of that book, Yvonne de Galais, was based on a girl he saw in Paris when he was a teenager and followed home. He fell in love with her at eighteen, and longed for her for years, the way young people do. Nowadays, people would see that she was an anima figure for him—a projection. His family made out that she was the love of his life—the real Yvonne, I mean—and that he died a virgin, just loving her from afar. It was simply untrue. He had women before me; he even wrote about it. But they wanted to present him as a sort of saint. But the other book, *Colombe Blanchet*, I was in that, if you like, as the love interest—at least, she was based on me. I was with him when he was writing the first draft. Then he went to war and it was never finished, and the manuscript was lost."

"I didn't know there was another book."

"Nobody did. It was only a first draft, the way he left it, but I know he'd have finished it and published it, if he'd come back from the war." She leans her head back against the chair, and looks exhausted. As if the strain of telling it is too much. And he, with the tape recorder still running, forgets to turn it off, while silence, the silence between them, is recorded.

She wonders what, from these scraps of conversation, history, memory, gossip, will survive in coherent form. What matters here?

She looks up at Sebastian—Seb Fowler—bent over his little machine. She could, she realizes, tell him anything and he would believe her. But this is her truth, her life she is giving him, and if it drains her, then so be it; she will not tell it again. It matters to her, to be honest with him, to tell it, show it just this one time, what she carries inside her. Our stories are what create us and let us live: they are the engines of our lives.

The kaleidoscope was a present from her father, that last Christmas, when she was twelve. She was amazed at how it turned everyday objects into marvels of dazzled geometry. She took it away from her eye and looked at the plate on the table, the curtain behind it, the windowsill, the geranium, each one a separate entity, shaped for use; then she flashed back to the kaleidoscopic vision and saw the separation disappear, the colors join and shrink and spread outward to the edge. As if everything could be re-created simply by the act of looking through this cardboard tube. Geometry and light were what ruled matter. Anything could be transformed. For days she had wandered like an explorer in the new world she could look into simply by raising this object to her eye. The kaleidoscope made a concentric world. Everything coalesced and sharpened and was drawn into it. The very center was a vanishing point; everything else was shards of light.

Robert, her older brother, had told her on the day their father died that there was no God. She remembers him sitting at the dining table, his schoolbooks spread around him as if nothing had happened, at their house in Paris, as she tried to make sense of it all. No God. God, if He'd existed, would have been at the center of the kaleidoscope, the bright point that vanished and grew. But if it were not God, it was something else. It was a gift that Papa had given her, as if to say, *Look, Pauline. Look and keep on looking.* Notice that nothing stays the same, that there is a pattern in everything; the angle of vision is what counts. When Robert said, "There isn't a God," she thought, *So, that, too, has gone. So, I will have to live without both Papa and God, with one brother who mocks me and trips me up in corridors and another who wants only to go back to sea, and a mother who hardly notices that we exist.* She gave up, then, on consolation. She sat outside her father's room, where she had seen him die. She dangled her legs in their black stockings. All the mirrors had been covered and the windows closed.

She'd walked about with her kaleidoscope, that spring, because he had given her this way to see things, and it was all she had left of him, her dear Papa. The dazzle and the focus, both. But the focus today is once again Henri Fournier, and the boy opposite her with the dazzling face, who wants to know about how she and Henri first met. Time travel, now. Yet after three-quarters of a century, the time and place exist inside her, intact. She takes a sip of water and shifts in her chair.

"So, do we want to get back to the book, or my all-too-short love affair?"

"Do you think—can I ask you this—that you'd have loved him even if he hadn't written the book?"

She looks amused. "Well, one doesn't have to fall in love with every author who writes an original book! But it did seem to encapsulate him, somehow. Can you imagine, reading it for the first time, before anyone else? I helped him get it published, through a friend of my father's. It was as if it were our book, then."

Le Grand Meaulnes, that untranslatable title. In English they call it *The Lost Domain*. She's right, he loves it. He loves it like a private possession, this novel. He's been reading and rereading it since he was a teenager himself and first met the teenage Augustin Meaulnes on the page, and glimpsed—what?—a story that can live at the heart of a life, and inform it. The possibility of a life lived at different levels, the day-to-day and the imaginary. A way through the world that involves going to the source of a mystery, and living there, and letting everything after that be transformed. Meaulnes walking out of the schoolroom that day to embark on his solitary adventure is surely every adolescent who has longed to do the same. But Meaulnes coming back with his adult secret, his love for the girl he meets at the lost château in the forest, affects the lives of everyone around him. There's something—he says, Fournier says—that exists hidden at the heart of the world; and you can go there, and find it. It is both beauty and danger. Each time Seb reads it, it seems to be slightly different. As if the words shift on the page when he isn't looking; as if the story changes and remolds itself when the covers are closed and the book back on the shelf.

He's also thinking—being twenty-five, being restless—*It's time for a cigarette,* and *I'm hungry, what about lunch,* and *I really do have to get out of here, move about, breathe some fresh air. I'm in Paris, for God's sake, and the sun is out.* And, being the student he is, *I'm really privileged to be here, she has an extraordinary store of memories,* and *Does anyone ever really know a lover as the public person he or she is?*

He hears the quiet slipping of the tape and her whispery voice, her throat clearings, her pauses; he glances through the high windows to the buildings opposite, across the street—iron railings, shuttered windows, stone parapets with strutting pigeons, the way the light falls, making the walls pale yellow, then suddenly gray—and his stomach rumbles noisily. And then his thoughts quiet, he relaxes as she has told him to; he breathes out, flexes his toes inside his boots, feels time pass in a way that's easy, all at once, that he doesn't have to fight. It is as if she has taken charge of him, of what happens next, of the direction of this book he wants to write, even the direction—way into the distant future—of his own life.

2.

Early May. She—the woman of more than a half century ago they are both conjuring to life—was going home after weeks playing in *The Detour* in London. (The Henri Bernstein play, you know? No?)

The day had begun far too early in the Savoy hotel, with terrible coffee and leathery triangles of toast. (You know they offered us fish for breakfast? Kippers! Haddock! It was unbelievable.) Rain spattered the street as she stepped into a cab to go to Victoria, for the boat train. But now, seen from the train window, it was all sun and wind with the hawthorn blossoms turning the hedgerows white. The South Downs, with their swells and curving chalky hollows. Like large sleeping animals. All the little low red houses, their curtains drawn. Other, unknown lives.

In Newhaven, a breeze came off the sea. That bustle and stir of ports—boats with water slapping up their sides; men at work, coiling rope, tightening knots, testing engines. (Perhaps this—sniffing up the air, feeling the focused activity—was the closest women ever came to being sailors?) She stood on deck, watched the white wake lead all the way back to the vanishing coastline. France emerged out of a thin horizon as England disappeared. It fattened, took shape. The buildings of Dieppe grew. You saw water between you and the land, and then it was gone. You came smoothly, or bumpily, alongside. Land. France. Square wet cobbles and men in blue; gulls hanging screaming above the fishing boats; slick slate Normandy roofs; the familiar size and scale of it all.

She leaned on the rail and looked down at the men catching the lines and making them fast, the strutting gray-backed gulls. Six years ago she'd come back here from London, perhaps on this same boat, with Claude, who was now her second husband. It had been a mistake, of course, from the very beginning, but how good the mind was at deceiving itself; how different life would be, if you only paid attention. She had seen their luggage piled together, being wheeled away down the quay by porters, and felt wild alarm: *But those are my trunks, my valises, what are they doing all mixed up with his?*

She'd married Claude Casimir-Perier because he had pursued her for years after her separation from her first husband, Charles le Bargy, and she had given in. He'd come to her dressing rooms with flowers, taken her to Maxim's for oysters and champagne; he was madly in love with her, he'd said (you should never trust such phrases), and he would love her forever. Immediately after their marriage, she'd known about the women; all she was to him was a mistress for his house, a trophy when her name was up in lights and he could boast about her to his friends. He had given her a status, mistress of his house, and that was it. Now, there was the woman she called *la belle dame sans merci*—a certain Fernande—who needed his time, money, and constant attention as well as an apartment and incredible numbers of jewels.

She could ignore this, because essentially she didn't care—after the initial sense of insult—any more than she had cared about le Bargy's infidelities. They played their games, these men, they had their little friends, they spent their money on them, they impressed them, no doubt. Her life was about work. She had decided this at an early age, appalled by the lives of frivolous women like her mother. Since the very beginning, when le Bargy had pushed her out on the stage that night in Reims as an understudy—"If you don't become a serious actor after this, my dear, you are crazy"—she had, to her own surprise, never doubted, and never felt stage fright. Even that first time, playing Camille in *You Don't Fool Around with Love*. Acting was simply, surprisingly, what she could do well. While life was chaotic, the rules of the stage held you upright and in place. Obedience to them was a necessity. Life let you down; the text of a good play, never. She'd watched Sarah Bernhardt, the great actress, over and over, studying how she moved and spoke, and then her friend Réjane. She'd learned. You filled the space available, you walked the narrow way laid down for you by the play itself, and then, only then, could you allow yourself to spread out. Your art was in full obedience to a text; and then, paradoxically, it flowered. Each night, the same play; each night different. The first actor onstage was able to come backstage and tell them all how "they" were tonight. You felt it in the darkness, the attention of invisible people; you spoke the words, and the response came back to you, warm or cold, attentive, moved, distracted, silent, breathing. In London, with that English audience, she had felt the breath of their respect, even before the applause.

After the play, you needed people, you needed a drink, to make the transition back into ordinary life. People came to the stage door; people waited for you. But what you had done, what defined you, was the alchemy that had taken place in the theatre, in the span of the play's time, in the breathing dark. It was in the best sense a *métier*—a loom on which thread became solid cloth. It had become the loom of her life, on which she discovered, in play after play, the growing resonance of who she had become.

She went alone to the cemetery in Montmartre, that next day in early May, the anniversary of her father's death. She walked the narrow paths between granite monuments. The hill behind the cemetery with its vineyard and few remaining windmills was almost like the country; the salt-white bulk of the new Christian basilica loomed at the top of the hill, workmen hanging like trapped flies from its dome.

She walked past Stendhal and Zola to find him. He wasn't here, of course, but she could at least place a stone on the grave, to honor her Jewish father.

Papa, I'm here for you. Life is good, I'm working, it's not at all what I imagined, but it's all right.

"Eugène Benda, beloved husband of Anne-Marie née Canet, father of Robert, Sigismond, and Pauline. Eternal rest."

The plain headstone was neither Jewish nor Christian; he had been an agnostic, trying to assimilate into French society. Poor dear, ever since his marriage to her mother, he had been ostracized by most of his family for marrying a working-class dancer from Marseille. Anne-Marie, her mother, had danced half-naked, wearing butterfly wings, on the stage at the Opera. She had found the photograph, a white upside-down square that must have fluttered out of his pocket to the floor of his study, and turning it over, had seen that this woman, very nearly bare of all clothing, was actually her own mother. The name scrawled across it: Anaïs. She must have been seven or eight when she found it, and the next time she was in his study, it was gone.

Papa, I am here, even if the others are not.

Robert was probably gambling at the racetrack today, Sigis would be at sea, and Maman, forgetting the date, would no doubt be out buying something expensive with her second husband, the appalling Alfred.

Papa, I remember everything about you. Your chestnut hair, your moustache, the boxes of dates with African boys on the lids that you brought back from Madagascar. Your question—"Well, now, darling, how are you getting along?" The day I brought you my birthday present to you, my painting of a peach on a plate. Our visits to the Louvre together. The way you marched me past naked ladies and bulls to look at Dutch paintings. You see, you said, the way they painted the things around them? They loved their own towns, their lives, and the times they lived in.

Thinking of him alive brought an ache to her throat. She was once again the frightened child who had watched the life in him sink like a boat going down as he slumped to the floor in his dressing room. It was unbearable that there was nobody else here today to mourn him. She thought of that last evening of his life, when her parents had been out to Fouquet's to celebrate his birthday; how handsome he had looked, and her mother, twirling down the staircase, gloves to her elbows, in a cloud of perfume that had reminded her, the child Pauline, of cats.

Then she placed the white pebble she had brought from England, and straightened her back. *Goodbye, Papa. I still miss you. Au revoir.* The gravedigger went by, saluted her as he went. Clouds in the sky of May, and the lilac out, the hill of Montmartre green with spring.

At quai Debilly, the house seemed to be empty, and her traveling trunk, sent on ahead from London, was still only half-unpacked.

She called out, "Claude? Are you there?" No answer. He must still be out. She went up to dress for dinner: a black silk dress, tonight, and a rose-patterned shawl in honor of Papa. There was a deep loneliness in this house, as there had been in her parents' house when she was young, as if nobody really lived within these polished rooms. Then she heard men's voices in the hall and leaned over the banister to look down. They must have just come in. There was her old friend Charles Péguy's quick, light voice, then Claude's, then an unknown voice, speaking slowly. She came downstairs looking down on the men's heads—brown, bald, dark—bunched close together under the light. The men looked up. The little group moved to include her.

"Pauline, how good to see you. May I introduce Henri Fournier?" Péguy said.

"My dear, welcome home. This is my new secretary, the brave man who's going to stop me from going mad over the Port of Brest." Claude's eyes narrowed, his voice tinged with sarcasm.

Henri Fournier bowed slightly and came forward to take her hand. A very tall young man, with brown hair and a moustache. Dark eyes, long eyelashes. She felt the size and warmth of the hand.

"He's just the person we need," said Péguy to nobody in particular. Fournier stood there, introduced. They all waited for him to say something, but he simply smiled. He let go of her hand, murmured at last, "Madame," and looked down at her through his thick eyelashes; she thought, *Who are you?* Beside the other men he was tense with energy. *A secretary? Really?*

3.

Her message appears on his screen among others full of condolences. It's strange, he thinks, how people don't find it necessary, these days, to write their sympathies out on paper. He rereads it. It isn't about Annie, or anything that has been happening to him since Christmas, during this bleak winter of her death. It isn't from anyone he knows, but a French woman who has somehow found him online. It doesn't mourn the past, Annie's extraordinary goodness and beauty, the shocking suddenness of her death; it isn't about how he is going to cope, or how long he will be likely to mourn her, or what he is going to do with the dog; it doesn't suggest websites for lonely people, systems of mourning, hierarchies of suffering, stages along the way of bereavement. It points in another direction, reminding him that he has a life, as well as a disaster to cope with.

Isabelle de Giovanni is apparently Isabelle Fournier's granddaughter. So, Henri's great-niece. She has written to him to say that she has discovered some papers in her house in rural France that she thinks might interest him. They seem to be parts of an unpublished novel that her great-uncle was working on just before his death in the Great War. Might he be free to travel to France to take a look? She's Googled him, of course, to discover his whereabouts and recent occupations; she has read his early book on Fournier and the love affair with the actress, and has looked up some of the essays and articles he has published since. She would be delighted to welcome him to her house in the country this summer, if he might care to come. All these subjunctives, these unsettling French verbs that always seem to posit an uncertain future. But Seb finds that he cares very much to come—if only because here is one person in the world who seems not to know that his beloved Annie was felled by an aneurism on the kitchen floor in their house in Oxford, only days after Christmas. As she was putting a plastic bowl of turkey soup into the freezer, to be exact. The Christmas decorations all still up around her, and her body as he found it spread upon the quarry tiles among the viscous puddles of soup that he had stepped through, horrified; inside her brain, he hadn't known, hadn't guessed, an artery and a vein had taken their time over years to grip each other invisibly and at last implode, cutting her off from him suddenly and forever.

Isabelle de Giovanni's e-mail comes after months of winter that have seemed interminable, living as he does in his cold house, deprived of his wife and all the warmth she created around her. He sits with his computer at the table in this same kitchen where Annie fell, from where the ambulance men—stretchers, red blankets, straps to hold her in, and that damn soup still underfoot—took her to die in the old Radcliffe Infirmary less than a day later. A cold time he's had of it, and a miserable one, though he takes care not to let people see it as far as he can. His crying is done at night, or occasionally in his shrink's room, the one he found the way you find spies, or private detectives, he imagines, no plaque on the door, down a back street in Jericho. Giles's suggestion, that was, as they strode together across Port Meadow for a beer at the Perch one early evening, cows driven home, horses with frost on their breath, the vast skies streaked before winter sunset over placid land and water, the familiar tracks, bridges, towpaths, sodden undergrowth. It was all too familiar, worn by memory, aching with her absence. "I know someone, they say he's good, if you should feel the need, they do say it helps."

But this Isabelle doesn't know any of it. She knows him as a success-ful writer, an expert on Fournier and his contemporaries, a man whose photograph was once in a Sunday paper, years ago when his book came out, whose Google life goes trundling on, like a parallel train track, beside his actual one. People have several lives, these days, not just the public and the private, but invented lives, in which they put photographs of them-selves and their friends on view on Facebook and on blogs, in which they are Googled and their houses and streets are made visible to an eye from space. He marvels sometimes at the way other people, especially young people, live with all this. His one life, the one he struggles to maintain, seems too much to deal with at present. He tries to keep to his rituals—getting up, shaving, making breakfast; his work hours, his meetings with students; walking, shopping in the market, getting dinner. It all used to seem doable, even easy, when Annie was there with him, dashing in and out, bringing a new coffee machine home for him to be amazed at, trail-ing her samples for the shop, scarves woven in India, a new line of flowing silk robes for Christmas. But what he does alone seems to have no point, no real resonance. There is no one to tell, in the careless, intimate way you tell a spouse of forty years, how your day has been. A day is a day. It passes, slow and thick as—well, cold soup. Hours pass, and the clocks hardly move. He buys absurd amounts of food in the market, more than enough for two, and lets it go to waste. He thinks of lighting a fire, but lets the thought go: Why would he sit beside a wood fire without her? He goes to bed at midnight, lies awake till four. Mornings, he's groggy, needs coffee more than ever, drags himself to his desk. His children worry about him, but have, as people say, their own lives, of which he is obvi-ously not a central part. People all say it will pass. But why will it pass? And, how do they know? And why should it damn well pass? He has lived for nearly forty years with a woman who remained interested in everything, a woman who cared what happened to him, who was alive as few other people seemed alive and who loved her own life. Who has been killed off by something like a time bomb, an unfair booby trap, a physical conjunction of blood and tissue that remained invisible until its moment of combustion. He is angry that this has happened. To her, above all. That it has deprived her of the holiday in Croatia that they planned, and of a return to Italy, and of who knows how many other holidays, and of her children and possible grandchildren. The simple deprivation of a day of her life, an ordinary day, a waking and a return to sleep, is enough: that she can no longer see the sky, drink wine, do the *Guardian* crossword, go to a film. The anger feels justifiable on her behalf, if not his own. It's possibly better, if less manageable, than the entropy of sadness.

He also minds—yes, is even angry—that she had no last words for him. Why should last words matter, any more than the first words spoken? She died without speaking to him about last things. Her last words like her first—"Seb, what on earth are you doing down there?" as far as he remembers—were banal: "Seb, could you run out and get a loaf of bread?" It was the words spoken in between that had to count now, the words of a lifetime together, of forty years of conversation. She left him with no final message; although he hung above her bed where she lay in a coma in the hospital, willing her lips to part, her eyes to open, speech to come, it did not. The last thing she had said to him was about a loaf of bread, and that was that.

So he writes back to Isabelle de Giovanni, in French, taking care to put in the accents. He is delighted to make her acquaintance. *Enchanté.* He will finish up his teaching commitments in June. Can he come for a few days after that, and see the papers she has found?

She writes again, quickly. He can stay for as long as he needs; she has plenty of room. France. Where he and Annie have had so many good holidays, over the years; where they lived for a year when their children were small. He thinks of that early time in Paris, the first time he met Pauline, when she changed the course not only of his professional life, but his love life too. He feels energized, more so than at any time for months. He buys Eurostar tickets, and then TGV tickets, online. He waits for June, for the end of teaching, as he used to wait for the end of the English school term as a boy, longing for the freedom and release of the summer holidays.

4.

Isa wakes at five. She has only one more day to paint; she mustn't waste it. Tomorrow she will drive south to open up her house in time for the English writer to arrive. Yesterday was the hottest day of the summer so far. In the south, they call it *les grosses chaleurs*, the big heat. Here in Paris, people die in weather like this. Grandmothers left alone in attics, when their families go off on holiday to breathe sea air. When she goes out to cross the courtyard, after coffee, after a shower, the sky is already a hard, carved blue above the rooftops. The air smells of the traffic on the boulevard. Little rivers run in the gutters to clean the streets. Isa crosses the cobbled courtyard, unlocks her studio door. She climbs the steep stairs into the smell of oil paint and white spirit, up into her good north light. She turns the window lock and throws the window open to let in what little air there is. The walled space of the courtyard outside holds a small freshness where someone has chucked water over a row of geraniums, a tired hydrangea.

She's back among her canvases, her invisible people. All except the one she's working on have their backs turned, so what she sees first is like a row of children facing a wall. It makes it slightly alarming to turn any of them to face her. The one on the easel shows a wrapped head swathed in white, like a beekeeper's. She mixes up the Chinese white and a little touch of burnt sienna and begins again.

When her phone rings, it's still only nine. She fumbles to pull it from the depths of her bag with paint-wet hands. The beekeeper looks more like a ghost, now. Chloé. Isn't Chloé safely incommunicado somewhere in Spain with her friends? She's supposed to be on the medieval pilgrimage route they call the French Way, where surely people will not be talking on cell phones.

"Chloé? Are you all right? I can't talk now."

"Maman, you're always making excuses."

"Listen, I'm in the studio, and I want to get on with painting, can this wait? I've only just started."

"I wanted to talk to you before you leave. It's important."

"I'm not leaving till tomorrow. Could we talk later? Call me tonight."

She'll have to paint over. The surface is too smooth; she'll have to roughen it up with something, to give the feeling of layers. Sometimes a slice of raw potato works. If not, a pumice stone. Otherwise the veiled look is lost.

With one hand, she tips the canvas to the light, the head outlined, no features yet, a swirl of white paint like sea fog. Perhaps the bandaged effect is one she should stay with. In spite of the reminder of mummies, even corpses. Accidents, burned faces, victims of explosions. The surface that covers what has to be hidden, in order to heal. Sweat runs down her neck and she pushes back her escaping hair.

Now, looking at her painting, as she half listens to Chloé, she can't remember what she saw in it yesterday or even a few minutes ago. It definitely needs to be painted over. If you paint on too smooth a surface, it will not last. That gray-white won't do. And no, she does not want to remind anyone of burn victims, let alone corpses. She has been letting these heads appear on her canvases like people emerging from—what, the smoke of a recent disaster? But she wants them human, wants them alive. Her daughter is still talking, even though she has said she is busy.

"Where did you say you are?" Isa asks, still of the generation that wants to know where someone is when talking to her.

"I'm in Spain, Maman. Are you paying attention? You can talk on a mobile from Spain, you know? European Union, euro, twenty-first century? When are you going to Les Martinières? For God's sake, don't let that manuscript out of the house. And don't do anything about selling the house. Maman! Promise? I'm coming up, I'll be there sometime next week."

"Call me tonight?"

She hears Chloé's annoyance. She can't promise. She turns the canvas, sees a delicate halo where a few minutes ago she saw only gray fog. The shape of the face turned toward her is not corpse-like at all but waiting to be given its unique human stamp. If she roughens the surface of just part of it. Perhaps even a scatter of sand? She takes off her shirt and prepares to paint in her bra and pants, her hair tied up high.

It's the house of childhood; no wonder Chloé wants to keep it. We all want, don't we, to hold on to the places where we were loved, where the days were long, where meals came on time and all you had to do was play by the river and in the long grass between poplars, build huts and houses, play shop, play brigands, play at life?

The last time Isa saw her daughter was when Chloé came to leave a heap of her belongings at the apartment in Paris before she set off to Spain.

"Maman, the house, it's everything we are going to need, don't you see? We'll all have to grow food, the vegetable garden there is huge, and there's water from the well, and clean air. We won't be able to go on living in Paris. Look what is happening to the climate, *la canicule* every single summer now. People are going to die here like fish."

Isa's Paris apartment is not large, not grand at all, but sufficiently solidly built in the nineteenth century to allow her some coolness even in a summer like this. And when, she wants to know, is this apocalyptic time going to begin? When are we going to start gasping, dying, heading for the country, living off cabbages and pulling up water from wells?

"It's happening now, this is reality," Chloé has told her.

Isa knows there's no point in arguing. People believe what they want to believe, and many people agree with Chloé that it's already too late. The ones who don't remember the era in the last century when they were all supposed to head for the country, live in communes, eat carrots with earth on them, draw water from wells, not shave their legs, or, worse, go to the Pyrenees to raise goats and make cheese, as some people she knew then did. The goat-raisers in the Pyrenees believed in free love and letting the goats come into the kitchen, and as far as she knew, never returned to Paris. They were probably still wandering in the woods naked, scrawny, and brown in their sixties, and the goats were probably still in the kitchen.

Now, here is Chloé threatening to return early from Spain, and there is the house that she must sell by the end of the summer, and an unknown Englishman is coming to stay.

Not for the first time, she lectures herself in her mind for taking on too much. But what is the alternative?

In her apartment, at the end of the day, she opens all the windows to let the air move through. She makes herself a salad with the remains of cooked green beans and some olives and walnuts, sits at a corner of her table beside the open window, and eats, with a glass of chilled red wine left over from yesterday. There's a heel of cheese, and an apple in her green bowl. She's left her painting, the latest veiled portrait, unfinished. Tired with the heat at the end of the day, she's stopped herself from going on. She likes the raised, curious tilt of the face, the way the eyes seek the light and hold it. The head has eyes now; the bandaged-accident-victim look has quite gone. The questioning air, the aura around the head, the contrast of the rough with the smooth—it will last till she returns.

5.

You have to love the time you live in, Pauline thinks, *however much it may scare you.* Her father was right. You have to be in the present, or you have already died. It's what you learn as an actor: night after night of sheer presence, you in the role onstage, you in the immediacy of the present.

The church clock at St. Thomas Aquinas across the street strikes the hour. It's one o'clock on a September afternoon in the ninety-ninth year of her life. She feels time swirl around her like rising water; if she is not careful, she will drown in it. Marcel Proust devoted his life to past time, and died early, in his room on rue Hamelin. When she was eighteen, he and his friend René Blum came and threw pebbles up at her window at Charles le Bargy's house on rue du Cirque, nearly opposite the Prousts' family house; the three of them ate bread and butter and drank chocolate at the kitchen table at one in the morning, and talked till dawn. It feels like yesterday.

So many moments, when you have lived a long time; memories themselves like pebbles thrown against windows, striking and then falling back. What happens when you leave this world? Do they all just disappear? She wants, quite urgently now, to tell someone, to have one other person know.

She goes to telephone for their lunch. "*Quenelles de brochet* and a beetroot salad, will that do?"

"Anything, great." Young men are omnivores. He probably lives off fish and chips and that awful sliced bread they have in England. It's the least she can do.

"Ten minutes? Fifteen minutes? Yes, somebody can come down to the door. Thank you."

The bell downstairs rings before either of them has thought what to say next. Seb goes down, as directed. The dog scuttles out of his way, whines, and then barks. There's a flurry of conversation at the base of the stairs, and fresh air rising.

Then Seb comes leaping back upstairs two at a time. Do all young men behave as if they have a train to catch?

"Thanks." She breathes, in, out. Her heart rocks in her chest, as if she herself has run downstairs and up again. Energy, that precious dying source. How it strands her these days, sudden as electricity switched off.

"Shall I dish it out?"

"Would you? This happens sometimes, I just run out of steam."

The idea of it alarms him, she sees. He busies himself, spoons sauce onto their plates. Then she breathes easily again and her heart quiets.

"Better," she says. "Sorry. Do begin. I'm just going to take a pill."

They eat at the table with the blue lamp on it. The dog comes and snuffles up at them, forgets to bark.

"You'll have some wine? I think it may do me good," she says.

"Mmm, yes. Just a glass, though, or I'll fall asleep."

"Well, I'm planning to fall asleep, anyway! I spend half my life asleep, these days." How lovely it is, after all, to have someone with whom to eat lunch. She has not expected this. They eat. She watches his hunger, his tasting of the food. "Mmm. Good!"

The interview that she had half dreaded, to the extent of forgetting it was scheduled, has turned into a pleasant connection, in the space of a few hours. Whether it's because of his youth, his sensitivity, the way he looks, or his evident enjoyment of everything—including his lunch—she doesn't question.

Later, as they sip coffee, she says, "Tell me, if it's not too soon to know, how you'll write your book?" She's back in charge, fed, watered, nourished by his presence, her body lulled back into its precarious harmonies. "You said you were going to write a biography. A biography is about the whole of a life, isn't it? Unfortunately, his wasn't very long."

"I'm not entirely sure. I've been going on a hunch, that what people have been saying about Henri wasn't the whole story. Then I came upon your name, linked with his. I actually found out about you from that book his sister wrote. It was so bitchy, I thought there must be something more to discover."

"Bitchy, it was for sure. *Méchante*, through and through. So you smelled a rat. Jealousy rarely makes for good writing."

She watches thought pass across his face like a breeze on water. When people are young, there is that transparency. He is so beautiful. She wants to tell him, but it would be crossing a line that even in your nineties can't respectably be crossed. *Come on, Pauline, don't go falling in love with a child, just because he reminds you of him.*

"Tell me, what is this really all about for you?" she asks. "This quest for Henri?"

"He made me feel something it's unfashionable to feel about a book these days. We're supposed to think of them just as texts, you know? New Criticism? Semiology? The author isn't supposed to exist anymore, that's the idea. It's all just language. Text. Signs. But I felt I had to follow where he led, to find out how he did it. And he led me to you."

"Via dear Isabelle. And here I am. Just. I've no idea why, but here I am."

"Did you know Isabelle?"

"We met a few times. Her husband, Jacques Rivière, was close to Henri. But she made it clear from the start that she wasn't going to like me."

"You know, I felt as if he'd written his novel for me, when I first came across it. I was sixteen, and we read it aloud at a sort of reading party we had from school, one summer. But it left me full of questions at the end. Like, does love necessarily include death, do you have to walk away from it toward some invisible great adventure? Do you ever really get back to the Lost Domain?"

She says, "You were his ideal reader. You were at the same point in life."

"He was very keen on pure heroines, wasn't he? Like Yvonne de Galais, the girl Meaulnes falls in love with."

Now, she can take a deep breath. Now, she can explain herself. "In fiction, if not exactly in life. All that about seeking a pure heart. But you know, at the time I didn't understand it. I thought he was talking about sexual purity. But, Kierkegaard said it—'To be pure is to want one single thing.' It was single-mindedness. Like Keats and Radiguet and maybe others who died young, he had time for only one single thing in his life. His writing. I couldn't see it. I was too much involved with him. You don't always see clearly with the eyes of love."

Silence. She begins to clear the cups; he blushes, gets up. "Let me do that," he says, and she lets him. Old age is letting go. Letting go, in the end, of everything; for now, letting go of coffee cups to wash and the risk, once again, of being misunderstood.

"Thank you, Seb. Just leave them in the kitchen. All right, no more questions for now. Or it will be *le vin qui parle*. Time for my siesta, and for you to see some more of Paris. Then, come back and we'll go on—it seems we've just dealt with the tip of the iceberg. Not a great metaphor, but you know what I mean? Till five?"

"Till five."

When he's left to go wandering in Paris, she thinks, did she dream him? Did a young man looking uncannily like Henri really come to see her? Did they really drink most of a bottle of wine and say the things that linger now in her mind? Henri and his quest for purity. Yvonne. Once again, Yvonne. And Isabelle Rivière, damn her eyes. That ugly book she wrote. She doesn't want to be reminded of Isabelle. It all revolves in her mind uncomfortably, this old story; he has reached in and stirred her depths with his careless, trusting youth. Perhaps she should not have let him in. But yes, she had to let him in; once she saw his face, she had no choice.

She wakes from a dream-ridden snooze. When you sleep lightly, dreams slide close to the surface like carp in a pond. You can't be sure what is real. Perhaps even she is not real. Perhaps she has already died, without realizing it. Perhaps this afternoon, autumn outside the windows, life dwindling for her into an apartment, two rooms, one bed, one armchair, is really all the afterlife there is. You just go on, perhaps, doing what you were doing before. Heaven, hell in a series of TV shows, meals, rare visitors, memories, slightly changing sky above rooftops. Then she wakes properly, sits up, and lets the old self-critical voice take over. *Pauline, you're really wandering. Talk about losing your marbles. Did you really think you'd died? My dear, I'm afraid it's all still to come, and it won't be nice. But thank God—who does not exist—that Isabelle went first.*

She drinks a glass of water, takes a series of pills—pink, white, yellow—drinks more. He's coming back at five. She feels like skipping through to the salon now, tidying up the place, plumping up cushions, throwing out the rather droopy chrysanthemums someone has brought her—terrible flowers, chrysanthemums, she can't bear their sour smell.

She wants to be ready for him when he comes running up her stairs again two at a time. Who would have thought? *So, life brings you a last gift, Pauline, and this is it. This is he.*

Seb, striding along the rue du Bac toward the river, is simply enjoying being outdoors and free to move. The river throws light up the narrow street; there's a rush of traffic, a scatter of leaves. People, all with somewhere to go; all Parisians, none of whom he knows.

Perhaps it doesn't matter that their conversation comes out in chaotic fits and starts; he can edit, organize it all when he gets home. He's the first person she has talked to; what's on his tape will be unique. He's arrived at the last possible moment in the life of the last person who actually knew Henri Fournier—more, who slept with him. It's hard to remember that old people were once young. There's something attractive about her still, with those bright eyes, that cloud of white hair that frames her narrow face; that slight flirtatiousness that maybe all old French ladies keep, he doesn't know. She likes him, he feels it; even if at first she looked horrified that he was there at her door. It's the way she looks at him, as well as her wine, that has warmed and stirred him. He turns the corner and walks fast along the Left Bank of the Seine, not knowing exactly where he's going, in the direction of those flashing golden wings that must be on the Pont Alexandre III, and the bright dome of Les Invalides. Past gallery windows with single paintings or sculptures in them, past a bar, an art shop, a stamp shop, then the National Assembly. Traffic flows in a steady stream, buses slowing and stopping, and down there, across the traffic—he crosses at the lights to look down on it—the actual stream of the river, ropy with current, gray-green, its surface glinting and the huge barges passing, laden with cargo, or sand.

He's being given more than he'd hoped for, filled in places he has not known were empty, that seem to have nothing, or little, to do with Fournier himself. He feels renewed, as if today were his birthday and someone unexpected has remembered it. It's so much better than hanging around London pretending to work and avoiding the agony of bumping into Giles and Annie at the World's End pub. At least on this side of the Channel he doesn't have to think about them all the time, or worse, risk running into them, laughing, arm in arm. He's dreaded to see her smooth bright head and easy stride coming toward him down a street, to see Giles's embarrassment. Really, these last months have been hell. But he's in Paris, and the world, or Pauline, has opened a door to him, so he walks fast and carefree into the sun and wind of today, kicking up the few fallen leaves of September as he goes.

6.

Their country house, the château de Trie, was a building she still found ugly, in spite of the ivy that tried to cover it. It looked heavy, its façade blank, its doors and windows too regular. They had bought it in 1909, a couple of years after their marriage. In this house there was little that was really hers. They lived in it uneasily, with too much room for the children who had not come. Only a happy couple, she knew, can make a house a home.

They walked the grounds that summer, she and Fournier and sometimes Claude and sometimes her old friend Charles Péguy or young Jean Cocteau, visiting from Paris. But most often, it was just herself and Henri Fournier, her husband's new secretary. Across the mown lawns and into the shrubberies. Round and round the vegetable garden. "Look, we'll have lettuces in a few days, if the slugs don't get them!" Up and down the walks that smelled of roses and jasmine, stronger on the night air each evening until the petals began to fall. She picked a white cabbage rose that fell apart in her hands. "Feel this! It's as soft as ash. My father loved roses. He used to buy flowers for other people because we never could have any in the house, on account of his asthma. Marcel Proust does the same thing. He's always sending people flowers though he can't be near them himself. My father used to say you can't let an illness keep you away from the lovely things of life."

"He was right," said Fournier, who had probably never known a day's illness.

Claude yelled from the balcony, "Fournier, I need you!" and Fournier ran in shirtsleeves across the grass to bolt up the stairs to Claude's study several steps at a time, to sort out the passages of transatlantic ships, the trains that could meet them, the tides that might hinder their arrivals. She didn't mind, because he always came back, pounding down again a few minutes later and running to find her under the yew trees at the edge of the lawn, or in one of the greenhouses testing the ripeness of a peach or fig. He felt his way past vines and espaliered apple trees, pushed aside branches to find her. He was always running; he jumped up at anyone's suggestion like a young dog at the word *walk*.

Another time, she looked out from an upstairs window and saw him sitting, leaning against an oak, as if he were alone in the country. Eyes shut, head tipped back, hands loose between his knees. A certain singleness about him. A certain privacy. A way of not caring what people saw, or thought. As if he had been shot by an arrow: a felled outlaw, a Robin Hood. Then he jumped up again, and strode on.

He was both bold and shy, this Monsieur Fournier. He had opinions. He chattered when he was embarrassed. He threw her tennis balls to catch, sent out underhand, with a spin. He played violent games of tennis with Claude, leaping in the air to hit a high ball on the baseline, slamming across the net. Claude ran and lunged to keep up with him, yet won his own sharp serves, low and fast. Afterward, Fournier flopped down suddenly on the grass between the two of them. He wiped sweat from his forehead with his sleeve. He was both dreamy and active, she saw, moving swiftly from one state to the other. The reader and the athlete. A man who, in many ways, was still a boy.

"Has anybody ever shown you how to stand on your head? You make an equilateral triangle. A triangle makes a firm base. Look." He jumped up, placed three pieces of paper for head and hands, and heaved his long legs skyward to stand on his head. She looked at his grass-stained tennis shoes waving in the air. She said, "You could be an acrobat in a circus, Monsieur Fournier."

Claude said, "Personally, I've never actually felt the need to try."

They talked about books, he and she. What they were reading. He liked Conan Doyle, Stevenson, Mark Twain, Fenimore Cooper: boys' books, adventure stories. Melville, Jules Verne, Hugo. Books that had heroes, books in which things happened. She talked about the Brontës. Yes, he loved *Wuthering Heights*. All the books she had read in English with her governess, Katy Brassington, were the ones he loved too.

"How is your novel going?"

"I'm nearly at the end, only I can't finish it, if that makes any sense. I've been writing it for years."

"What sort of novel is it?"

"Oh, a boys' adventure story."

"Should I like it?"

"I would love to think so."

He told her of his passion for machines, speed of all sorts. Races and flight. Aeroplanes, balloons, cars, even bicycle races. He'd been out to the Bois de Boulogne in '06, when Santos-Dumont had first lifted his dirigible off the ground for a record number of minutes.

"It went sixty meters," he told her. "Imagine that! You do know who Santos-Dumont is, don't you: son of the Brazilian coffee king, prince of invention in Paris? You do know about the Demoiselle, surely, and Roland Garros, he was one of the first fliers to go up in one? That was in '09. Did you know that Santos-Dumont's first and second dirigibles had De Dion-Bouton engines? Wasn't that astonishing?"

One day he would show her, take her to the Bois, to the open spaces in front of the Bagatelle gardens where young men flew up and came down again in aircraft built like dragonflies; and to Longchamp, to Le Bourget, where the astonishing flying machines bumped gently up from the ground to straddle the invisible currents that exist in air.

That summer she wandered from room to room, forgetting what she had come for. Where was she? Where was he? In the corridors of the house they met, exchanged glances, hurried on. His glance at her was explosive. He held himself in. She longed to put out a hand, to stop him, confront him, and say—what? In her mind, roses, cars, aeroplanes, a sky full of balloons and zeppelins like floating cigars, airy constructions that he had drawn for her on whatever came to hand. His drawing hand, the pressure on the pencil, the knuckles, the joints, moving as he drew, a precious construction in itself.

He carried a small notebook with him, to write in; he also drew on the backs of envelopes, scrap paper from Claude's study, even walls. He had a row of pens and pencils in his jacket pocket. He walked through the world leaving his mark.

They went into dinner together each night and ate at the polished table, the three of them, as if he were a member of the family. Claude and he talked about work planned for the next morning. She moved her cutlery about, crumbled her bread, refolded her napkin, sipped wine. Henri Fournier, probably not used to formal dining, threw her from time to time a look of comic desperation that of course Claude saw and pretended to ignore. Claude knew and didn't know, about the complicity between them. Claude was acting as much as she was, playing the husband-who-does-not-know. She bowed her head over her dinner plate, ate the soufflés, daubes, and roasts that were carried in from the kitchen, pressed her napkin to her mouth, saw how Henri laid his hands flat upon the white tablecloth, his fingers spread, as he talked. She heard the voices murmur on, his nervous laughter, Claude's prim responses; when Claude scraped back his chair and said, "My dear. Time to move I think?" and the two men stood aside for her, she was ready to go first out of the dining room, the muscles in her thighs trembling with a tension she could hardly control.

The nights grew shorter. It would soon be midsummer, the fête of Saint-Jean. The trees filled out, their leaves heavier, darkness thicker beneath them where gnats moved in clouds. Frogs creaked from the edges of ponds. She leaned out of her window before bed and heard a long trill of birdsong from the dark line of trees. They were all in their separate rooms. His room was down a corridor at the back, away from hers and Claude's at the front of the house. The moon shone on the greenhouse roofs, was briefly blocked by the tall elm at the edge of the lawn, broke free and sailed in darkness ringed with its own halo. None of them were sleeping well. The days grew hotter. They wore white; he had a green stain on his white trousers from lying in grass. He hit a ball about on the tennis court in the heat of the day. Six serves across the net, smashing into the far corner, and then back again from the other end. When she passed him, coming back from the courts, his face was taut. His shirt was stretched across his back, like a wet map.

"It's too hot, Monsieur Fournier. You'll be exhausted."

"But I want to be exhausted. That's the point."

Claude announced at breakfast the following day that he was off to a meeting in Paris. She knew that it would be probably to spend an afternoon with Fernande. On the gravel in front of the house the carriage turned, its wheels grating, the horses waiting between shafts. In the distance was a train that would take Claude to Paris and bring him back, but she did not know when—tonight, tomorrow?

A hammock was strung between apple trees at the edge of the orchard and Henri Fournier lay in it, one long leg dangling out, reading a book. He often picked herbs from the garden and munched their leaves. Today, it was a sprig of mint. She walked toward him, saw him raise his face to her. He stopped reading, smiled, smoothed a page flat, marked the place with a mint leaf.

"Claude's left," she said.

"Ah. So we can be children, can we?" The sense of freedom made them both laugh, a little wildly. But what would they do? Talk of books?

Pauline sat down on the nearest deck chair, closed her eyes for a moment against the blur of sun, and stretched out her feet. Henri, lying full length in the hammock, looked at her through his lashes, narrowly, under his hat. She looked, saw his young man's insouciance, his physical ease, his inaccessible self. With Claude gone, he was at nobody's beck and call.

Ah, but we are not children, she thought. *That is the problem.*

Each of them was waiting for what would happen next. It was a play with acts. They were still at the very beginning. Perhaps they were waiting for something to begin the action. Three knocks: a word, a movement, a shift in the progression of time.

II.

7.

June 2013, Paris–Touraine

Isa takes the familiar road south, singing in snatches, fiddling with the car radio, switching off the news, welcoming a burst of Chopin. South, the way they always drove from Paris: Orléans, Tours, Châtellerault, only now the road bypasses towns, so that they can exist purely in imagination. The autoroutes tell you with their little white-on-brown pictures that there's a church, a twelfth-century fresco, an abbey, a village worth seeing; but you, the driver, have built up such a momentum that slowing down to look at something, actually stopping to park and walk and look, would feel like a visit to another century. Yes, the signs say, it is all still there, and you can say you have driven past it. You don't have to stop and look, because no one will ever know.

But she is, in fact, nearly there. She slows to fifty to go through the village, sees that where the second boulangerie used to be there is now a sign up about a children's theatre, that fresh roses are piled up in the little graveyard outside the church—who has died?—and crosses the bridge, passes the plantation of poplars and the field with all the cows huddled at one end, slows at the long tree-lined drive that leads to her house. She turns and jolts the car down the track between the walnut trees, bouncing as it goes—the suspension must be nearly screwed, the earth bone-hard—and enters the courtyard to park beside the woodshed in the shade. She switches off the engine, opens a door, listens to the country silence that is in fact not silence but crickets, a blackbird, wind stirring leaves, the remote voice of the river.

She sits for a moment, not moving. Remembers other arrivals—as a girl, with her mother, visiting her grandmother, then with Hugo when they were first together, and all that mattered was to shove the big old key into the lock, open the doors, run inside, and fall onto the unmade bed, where he would enter her as quickly as he had pushed in the key.

Then, with Chloé in her baby seat and plastic bags overflowing with toys, jars, blankets, all the paraphernalia of travel with a small child. Much later, with Chloé and her second cousins, the boys Gilles and Pierrot from Lyon, and no Hugo. Hugo had found Marie-Pierre, who was blonde and twenty and would produce three more children for him, pop, pop, pop, one a year; she was either very Catholic or very fertile or both.

Her mother, in her last illness, used to bend to pick the wild strawberries that grew under leaves in the border. "Look, Isa, lots of them! Oh, how good. There's nothing, absolutely nothing, that explodes on your tongue like a wild strawberry." Her stretched face, as cancer nibbled at her from inside and chemotherapy weakened her, her thin hand cupping the wild strawberries. She would bend her face to her palm and eat them like that, like feeding a horse, only she was feeding herself, feeding all the goodness and delight of life into herself while she still could. Years earlier, the other Isabelle, her grandmother, standing in the doorway, frowning, shading her eyes. Grandmother, mother, daughter: all the generations of women in this house, thresholds, strawberries, a child kicking her legs up high on the swing that twirled from the lime tree, a child showing her knickers, soaring up screaming into the blue.

But now there will be no more children. Isa bends to look beside the bench outside the front door, as her mother would have done. She rummages through the low green leaves for strawberries, finds a few whitish early ones. The suddenness of felt solitude, when it pierces her at moments like this, is sharp as pain. You are alone here, alone as you feel for unripe strawberries under a leaf, as you insert a key into a lock, as you enter a house you have entered thousands of times, as you push down the electric switch, as you repeat movements you have made over and over again. Alone. You will die alone. If you don't do something about it, you will fall down one day in the space between the table and the sink and nobody will find you for days, because of the choices you have made, away from people, away from what you most need. She thinks, *Tomorrow the English writer will be here.* What was she thinking of, inviting him to stay? If solitude is alarming, then the sudden arrival of someone you don't know from Adam is yet more so. She will have to give him meals. But of course, he will be busy with the papers, he will stay in his room, she need hardly see him. The face she remembers from the book jacket will have aged, changed, as her own has; he will be a staid academic, fat, bald or gray, only here for Uncle Henri, only interested in the task at hand. Isa wipes sweat from her face with her shirttail and breathes the stale closed-in air that smells of old fires and dust.

Then she begins opening all the shutters and windows, as you have to, one after another, to let in the light.

8.

At last, Seb packs a small wheelie bag with his new ultralight Apple laptop in it. He closes his house up, having put the border collie Fingal in kennels with the bad conscience of someone sending a child to boarding school. He takes a morning train to Paddington, crosses London to St. Pancras in a taxi, and is on his way. He's told nobody, except his children—not even his friend Giles. Laura, his daughter, called from London. "You're going to France? Oh, good idea, Dad, good to get a change of scene. Have a good holiday. Take care." (Why does everyone say "take care" these days—as if it makes any difference? The catastrophes of life lie in wait, whatever care one takes.) He hasn't had time to say it isn't exactly a holiday; but perhaps it is. It feels like a treat, an escapade, this dash across to France—a sortie into the kind of life he is not supposed, as a recent widower, to have. But Annie herself would cheer him on, he knows it, and he imagines her waving him goodbye, till, damn, more tears come; and then he wipes them quickly. In his mind, he leaves her waiting at the station, as women once used to wave at stations when men left, waving their handkerchiefs, as the long trains pulled out.

He's slipped his paperback copy of Fournier's novel into the pocket of his suitcase. The pages are soft with rereading, and there's a stain on the front cover, but there they are, the mossy stone gateposts opening on to an alleyway that leads to a distant house. *Le Grand Meaulnes.* The Great Meaulnes, like the Great Gatsby? The most recent translation has been titled *The Lost Estate.* It's a hundred years since it was published. Some people say now the novel is sentimental, it's out-of-date; it has lost the popularity it suddenly had in the sixties and seventies; this is a harder, less romantic generation. The old Europe, the old France has very nearly been lost to the stridency of the new. (He's been reading Stefan Zweig, with fellow feeling, until it made him too sad.) But it's his passport, his way in, or way back: as he goes to meet Fournier again he takes it with him as a talisman. In your sixties, you can be foolish, even sentimental. You can still believe that this hidden place exists, outside of time and geography and even common sense. You can even—is it heresy or just human resilience?—believe at last for whole minutes at a time that life goes on.

At five o'clock, after the train journey south on which he has dozed, while various changes of countryside flipped past nearly invisibly, in his old jeans and linen jacket, a Panama hat on the back of his head, he steps out into heat and a dazzle of pale stone. He's the last to walk down the platform, trailing his suitcase, having been in the rear of the long train. Most of the other passengers have left, and the platform seems to rise toward him in its haze of heat when he sees a slightly plump middle-aged woman in an off-white shirt and trousers and a floppy straw hat hurry toward him.

Yes, they agree at a glance, they are indeed Monsieur Fowler and Madame de Giovanni. She seems embarrassed, or maybe only shy; he feels exhausted. He woke at four today, to stand in his kitchen gulping coffee, and crossed southern England and then France—Oxford to

London, London to Paris, across Paris to the Gare Montparnasse and now the effortless TGV south.

"*Bonjour.*"

"*Bonjour, madame.*"

She shakes his hand, gazes at him with her head tilted as if trying to remember what they last said to each other.

"It's not far from here, just twelve kilometers or so. Is this all of your luggage?" She speaks English with a strong French accent. *Kilo-meters. Lugg-age.* Her hat has a hole in it. She seems vague, welcoming, a little self-conscious.

A dusty old Peugeot sits parked in a patch of shade. She opens its side door, pushes papers onto the floor so that he can get in. It's stifling inside. She opens windows, turns on an inefficient fan, backs out without looking where she is going, turns an inch from a parked truck, and shoots forward into the street.

"How was your journey?"

"Fine. *Très bien, merci.*"

"You are not too tired?"

"I'm pretty tired. But okay. *Fatigué, mais bien.*"

She drives, sitting very upright and gripping the wheel, her profile turned to him, straight nose, messy hair, and soft raised chin. She's tossed her hat onto the cluttered backseat. "*Bon.* Now, we will soon be there."

There are shallow hills with crests of woodland, villages signed off the main road, and vast wheat fields with few divisions. She peers in the rearview mirror, turns sharply to the left, and drives between stone gateposts and down a bumpy drive. Tree shadow stripes the track. The car bounces over ruts.

"We have had so little rain this summer."

"Ah. It seems to have been the same everywhere. At home too." They have slid easily into French.

"Here we are. This is the house."

He steps out of the car, the fields of yellow corn and even yellower sunflowers all singing. Is this tinnitus, created by his fatigue and all the stress of the last year? But no, it stops as she leads him toward the house. Cicadas. The car, its doors hanging open, is left in the middle of the courtyard where hollyhocks stand tall as people. The house, three separate buildings on three sides of a courtyard, must once have been a working farm. It's closed and shuttered to exclude the heat. The window shutters and doors are painted sky-blue, and the paint has cracked. Vines grow up its walls and borders flank it, lavender and geraniums, marigolds, tall feathery grasses. Tin watering cans lie about, and a hose snakes across grass, attached to a tap over a trough. He follows her in, accepts a glass of water from a carafe in the refrigerator. Compared to the blazing day outside, the interior is dim. A stone house, with walls a foot thick, he sees from the sills and doorways. His skin prickles and cools.

"I'll show you your room. Then you can wash, shower if you like—the bathroom is just down the corridor. Forgive me, but I've said we'll go to a concert this evening, I have to go, really, and I thought you would be interested. It's not far from here."

She leads the way up a flight of curving stairs of dark polished wood and shows him a room at the end of a corridor, a child's room surely, with a bed, a chair, a table, and little room to turn around. He dumps his suitcase on the bed and is about to open it, when he hears that they will be leaving in less than an hour.

"I have to water the vegetable garden first. With this hot weather, I really have to do it every night, or we'll have nothing to eat. Do you think you can be ready by the time I'm done?"

He finds the shower, strips in a narrow space behind a plastic curtain, stands under the tepid trickle. Drying himself on a too-small towel, he peers out of the window to a view of sunflowers, their faces a mocking crowd turned toward him. Trembling poplars stand against the sky. Swallows rush past him like planes refused permission to land. He is still traveling, but unlike the swallows, graceless and perturbed. Why can't she let him settle in for at least the evening, for God's sake? Seb feels that he has aged in the last six months in a way that has nothing to do with travel. Everything feels harder than it did. People say that the six-month moment is the hardest, and it's only six and a half since Annie died, so perhaps this is the worst possible time to arrive anywhere. He is in this new era, the era of raw widower-hood, the one that nobody warns you about, rather as they never really told you about the real confusion of adolescence, or what it's like to have a new baby. He feels shaky, quickly exhausted, suddenly tearful; sometimes, for a moment even, mercifully forgetful of what has happened. But Isabelle de Giovanni seems oblivious. Well, of course, she is oblivious; you don't tell complete strangers about your private life by e-mail, at least, he does not. She needs only time to water her garden before moving on to the next thing. He shaves quickly, feeling his face with his hands, pulls a clean but rumpled white shirt from his bag and over his head. Here he is, in France, in a strange house with a strange woman who is insisting that he should go to a concert with her, somewhere miles away. Seb has avoided concerts, plays, and the cinema, as well as parties and, as much as possible, gatherings with more than a few people, since that day in late December. Annie's funeral—he and his children weeping, a small coffin that surely couldn't contain her (did people shrink in death?)— held at the local church of St. Philip and St. James, known in his family as Phil-Jim, had felt like a mistake. But didn't all funerals feel like mistakes? What one wanted to do was howl in the wind, at a cliff edge. The few people who were there, surely only a fraction of the people in the world who had loved Annie, were quite enough. Any more, and he would not have been able to stay there, in the pew, looking apparently like a normal—normal?—bereaved man. He would have run out, tearing his clothes. Or something. Since then, he has known to avoid places where people gather and where he might have to speak to them. "How are you doing?"—that peculiarly Californian-sounding question that has spread throughout the English-speaking world—only fills him with dismay. He doesn't know. He is surviving, he supposes. Almost worse is the heartfelt "How *are* you?" He has mumbled, and avoided people; until Giles, his old friend, who loved Annie even before he did, suggested the shrink in Jericho who might be some help.

So a concert is not what he wants, not at all; but being here in Isabelle de Giovanni's house as her guest seems to put him at her disposal, and she's shown no hesitation in telling him to get ready. Perhaps it will be better in French, all this. And here, the great advantage is of course that nobody knows what has happened to him. He can hide it inside him, his bereavement, carry it secretly like a stone in a pocket; he can even perhaps behave like everyone else. That is a thing to value about French formality, that there is a code, a way of going on; people are not allowed to trip you up with inappropriate questions, any more than they may clap you on the back, hug you indiscriminately, or ask you with that fascination that masquerades as sympathy, "How *are* you? How are you *really*?"

He takes a quick look in the mirror, straightens his shirt collar, thinks, *Hmm, not too decrepit, considering,* and goes down to meet his hostess. She is already waiting, wearing a pink linen dress, a small controlled smile deepening the corners of her lips. Neither of them has yet mentioned Henri Fournier.

9.

It's been a long time since Pauline last left her apartment on rue du Bac. Space has shrunk around her, as time has stretched. She used to walk, cross the Seine to go to the Palais-Royal, the Comédie Française, and to Gallimard, the publisher and bookstore on boulevard Raspail. It started by being an adventure, then became an impossible effort. Now, even the doctor comes to see her here, as do the hairdresser, the podiatrist, the masseuse. Each of them expresses polite surprise that she is as well as she is. Old body, old bones, old heart: but all still in working order. Perhaps, she thinks, this is the real adventure of life— not love affairs, not journeys, but simply staying in this world. With meals sent up from the restaurant downstairs, and the cleaning lady every morning, and an alarm to press if there is an emergency, she can keep this version of life going within her four walls. With books and videos she can keep her mind interested. With a dog, even, you still have something to touch. The cleaning lady, who is Moroccan, takes the dog downstairs with hardly concealed disgust; Arabs, she knows, dislike dogs. (She should organize a dog walker next.) With Seb, the dog suppresses his own disgust at being taken out by a male person, and goes studiedly bored down the stairs behind him, claws clicking on the parquet. But oh, with the boy here she realizes it more than ever, conversation is what she relishes, that and the whiff of the outdoors that comes in with him. You can't order up conversation as you can a meal, a massage, the video of a new film. What a wonderful idea, to order a film to watch at home, as you can now. The new Truffaut is delivered to her door. A case of the Bordeaux that she particularly likes. Library books: Claude Lévi-Strauss and a biography of Keats—what a pair. The cleaning lady, Latifa, brings her sweet pastries that taste of rosewater and remind her of her trip with François down the Nile. Everything tastes of something else: taste, as Proust knew, is memory. But if you have no one to say this to, no one to respond to you, the thought dies in midair like a butterfly too weak to fly. She knows, now, what she has been missing. Talk, real talk is what keeps you alive.

He comes in fresh with Paris, with what he has been seeing: the walk all the way up to the Pont Alexandre III and across to the Grand Palais, and then back down the Right Bank alongside all the moored houseboats, with the people living on them, the barges and converted cargo boats, with the chairs out on deck and pots of flowers and people sunning themselves the way they always have, and down past the shops that sell animals and birds, and back by the Pont Neuf, Henri IV on his horse, and Vert Galant, where the lovers sit to kiss and dangle their legs and the solitary drinkers tip their bottles to their lips. He brings her Paris, the streets and bridges and squares she has not seen for so long; he comes in with the light of it in his eyes, the smell of it on him: petrol, leaves, bread, river mud.

"You walked all that way? You must be exhausted."

"No, not really, it was great. But yes, it's nice to sit down. Can I have a glass of water?"

"You can have anything you want. Tea? Don't you English still stop everything for afternoon tea? Or are you more of an American?"

"I did stop for a coffee. Tea seems somehow too English for Paris. But what about you? Did you rest? Do you feel like talking? I don't want to wear you out."

"You won't wear me out. I have quite enough time when I don't speak to anyone except the dog, and he's not a great talker. No, it's a pleasure. I can't tell you what a pleasure it is. And I don't mean just talking about myself either. I want to know about you."

"I haven't done much, compared with you. Well, obviously. My life's been fairly straightforward: nice childhood, nice parents, two continents to choose from, school, university, now research, if I can call it that. I sometimes wonder if I should be doing something more, well, adventurous. You know, trekking across deserts or sailing round the world."

"What do you care most about?"

He hesitates for a moment. "Hmm. I think, doing what I'm capable of. Doing it—whatever it is—as well as I can."

"Do you know what 'it' is?"

"I suppose—living my life, whatever it turns out to be—as well as I possibly can. Does that sound awfully vague? Or maybe pretentious?"

"No, it sounds as if you are trying to put words to something that isn't easily expressed. As Henri used to say, words are everything, until they suddenly can't be."

"He thought there was a limit to language?"

"He wanted to take it as far as it could possibly go, and he did. But he knew, too, that there was a place beyond it. The body, the soul don't do well with words. And they have to have their say."

"It's as if we have to keep trying to say things, and then there's silence. Shakespeare said it, of course. The rest is silence."

"I think he was talking about death, though. This side of death, there's always conversation, talk, or at least communication. The joy of it's immense, don't you think?"

"Yes, I know. My parents always used to tell me I talk too much. Just quit talking, Seb, and get on with it, my mother says. She's a great doer. But I love talking."

She says, "So, we are two of a kind. Now, shall we talk about what you're here for? Shall we include Henri?"

"I do feel," Seb says, "as if he's here, listening. With the photo looking down on us like that. He looks . . . watchful."

"He was more alive than most people ever are. I wonder sometimes if that quality has to do with knowing that you haven't long to live. He couldn't have known it consciously—I don't think Keats did either, even though he was not well—but perhaps you get a feeling about it. And of course, with all the talk of war there was then."

"Do you have any feeling about your own death? Is that a terrible question?"

"No, of course it's not. I do think about it. I feel it there, like someone watching me, someone waiting. But you know, I always have. It's not new. I think I haven't died yet possibly because I still have something left to live for?"

He turns on the tape recorder, sets it in motion before her, then with a little nod for her to begin. But they don't record what she has just said. It seems that he has tucked it away in his mind, perhaps to consider later.

10.

"Fournier's certainly got the gift of the gab," Claude said, laying the sheets of writing paper down on the breakfast table at the house they had rented in Cambo-les-Bains. It was August. They were spending two months of the summer in the Basque country, near the border with Spain. Henri was with his family at L'Anguillon. "The pen of a true writer, don't you think? Here, you read it. I don't know why he thinks I'm interested in all this. I didn't hire him to write about his family."

She read and reread, and knew that all these anecdotes were for her. They were certainly not aimed at Claude. Aha, so this was to be their code. Letters: the letters he would write to her when she was away in America on her tours, letters to Claude that were obviously meant for her, letters written only minutes after they had left each other, letters to explain, letters to describe, letters that one day would speak, finally, openly, of love.

You could send a letter in the morning these days that would arrive in the afternoon, and send another in the afternoon that arrived before dark. You could send a *pneu* across Paris, a message winging along hidden tubes in the intestines of the city. You could send transatlantic letters that arrived in hotels spread across the continent, in New York,

Chicago, Toronto, letters that could be seized up from trays held out by liveried men and torn open in private, or cut with silver paper knives, the little envelopes with the curling handwriting across them and the blue mark made by the French post office, the French stamps, the American stamps going back, the mark of the moment and the place where they were mailed, letters in envelopes licked shut, sealed with the tongue of your lover, the folded paper inside, the marks of ink as it rushed across the page, darker where the pen was dipped again, hesitant where the writer hesitated, fluent where the feeling ran ahead of him or her and it mattered only to get it down.

"I think he just wants us to know about his life," she said. And Claude went back to *Le Figaro*.

At the end of August they all came back as usual to Paris. It was time for *la rentrée*. Everyone went back to work or at least tried to look serious about life. Men like Claude, who had spent two months lounging in flannels and straw hats, dressed in serious black again. Paris was ready for its next season, and Parisians came back from Deauville and Nice, Arcachon and Le Touquet and Biarritz, from all the beaches of France. Pauline had to visit her dressmaker and order the clothes she needed for her next trip abroad in October. The Americans always took so many photographs, and commented quite mercilessly on what one was wearing, even though they dressed so badly themselves. It was a long day of standing immobile while materials were snipped and pinned against her, fabrics of different colors held against her face, still as a statue under the hiss of falling silks, the click of the dressmaker's pins, the touch of cold fingers, while the traffic of the world went on outside.

"I think that will do for today, Madame Mathilde, don't you? Can you finish all this by the end of September? I must admit, I'm exhausted. You must be too."

"It's my work, Madame."

The older woman was on her knees with pins in her mouth. How one depended on other people's work.

"Yes, Madame, this is the last hem for today. We could perhaps have one more fitting? Then I can certainly finish all this before you go. What about the *crêpe de chine*, is that for America too?"

"Yes, please; it will be perfect for evenings on the boat. And if it's still warm in New York. Thank you so much." Thinking of Henri toiling over her husband's books rather than working on his own, she gave Madame Mathilde a few more coins than usual before taking a cab home.

When she got there, she found Claude and Henri working together, Fournier sitting at the desk, Claude standing over him. There were ledgers with inked columns open in front of them. She tapped on the half-open door. Henri looked like a boy having his dictation corrected. He jumped up, scraping his chair, bowed over her hand, looked away. Claude turned to leave. He already had his overcoat dangling from one shoulder. "I'm sorry, I have to go out; there's a meeting I have to go to."

Pauline shrugged, letting him go. She no longer asked him about his "meetings" or even stopped to wonder if they were really rendezvous with Fernande and other women. He had creditors, she knew that. Since his mother's death, he had inherited more money, but she knew it was being drained away already and that Fernande, with her apartment in Paris, her furs, her wines, her debts, was part of the drain. It hardly mattered. She was alone with Henri at last, the first time since before the summer. Tired, distracted, she turned to him and saw the look in his eyes.

He stammered, "Welcome home. I'm so glad to see you."

"How are you?" She thought, *Do we have to start all over again? Is this how it goes?*

"Fine. I've been working on my novel." That sideways smile, his sudden shyness.

"Bravo. Tell me about it?"

"It's to be called *Le Grand Meaulnes* after its hero, Augustin Meaulnes. The narrator is a younger boy called François Seurel. He's grown up in a school. His parents are teachers."

"You said it was an adventure story, I remember." She felt a little sick. Had she simply run up the stairs too fast? They were still standing in Claude's study. He was at the desk, looking down on the spread of Claude's papers. She hadn't even taken off her hat. Oh, God who does not exist, is this how it goes?

He closed the ledger, but not before she had seen the marks in red ink. "Yes, there is a strange adventure at its heart. But I haven't finished it yet, in fact, because I can't yet find its true ending."

She said, "Well, Claude keeps you pretty busy. Perhaps you simply haven't had time. Will you let me read it when it's finished?"

The Atlantic Ocean would stretch between them soon, not simply the whole countryside of France. Time, tides, distance. Whales and dolphins. For now, there were only the realities of Claude's charts, a clock ticking, a novel that both could clutch at as if it would save them.

"Of course. You really want to?"

"Of course I do. Don't forget!"

"I'll let you know when it's finished."

"Write to me."

"Of course. Do you want to see my little niece, Jacqueline?" Henri passed her a photograph of a dark-haired child with his eyes. "She's such a darling, isn't she? Children are so amazing. I saw her most days this summer, as I often went over to see my sister; Isabelle's married to my best friend, Jacques. We're very close. You must meet them. My parents too. I'd so love you to see our house, and all the country around it."

So, he had all this love for his entire family? Whatever Henri might think, they were hardly going to approve of her. So, was he that innocent, naïve to a fault, dangerously unguarded? Or was she perhaps being warned?

Just two days later she came to him to ask for a paper she had to sign giving him permission to forward all her letters to America and to take charge of her future appointments in France. He appeared out of Claude's study and there he was in front of her, leaning against a table on which a vase of early chrysanthemums stood. Someone must have brought them in from the garden, not knowing that she disliked their smell.

Neither of them knew if Claude was near. Henri blushed and flung out an incautious arm and knocked the blue vase to the floor just as she was about to give him the addresses of hotels in North America; the flowers, water, pieces of blue china lay all over the parquet floor and he looked at her boldly, not apologizing, with the mess on the floor around them. They both began to laugh.

"It seems that I cause damage wherever I go," Henri said. They were still laughing when Claude came in and said, "Well, isn't someone going to clear this up?" He looked at the broken china, wet carpet, and broken blooms, not at her, not at Henri, as if all he wanted to see was a small disturbance in his house, a mess that could be swept easily out of sight.

In America, in Canada, in the loneliness of hotel rooms, the Ritz-Carlton, the Plaza, late at night after the play, she wrote to him, telling him about her days. The blue-marked envelopes from France addressed in his handwriting arrived on her breakfast tray like tickets to a future that neither had dreamed of. He couldn't imagine her life in the theatre, he could hardly believe that America even existed; her life in all these hotels would have been a nightmare for him. Words, ideas, stories, memories, questions—all that could be allowed into letters spun this conversation between the two of them, between continents. She knew without either mentioning it that they both remembered that moment with the broken vase, when they had looked at each other, laughed, and implicitly admitted everything.

There are stages in all love affairs that flag their progress as surely as milestones on a road. You have, both of you, to recognize them. They aren't always happy, or easy, but they are points at which you can both say, *Yes, that was then, and I was there, we were both there, and knew what was happening.* The narrative of love stories depends on them. Once one of you forgets, or remembers differently, the map changes, endings proliferate.

The broken blue vase, the scattered petals, the laughter that escaped from both of them, that day—how that moment carried them through the weeks and even months apart. Once you have made a pact with another person to respect these signs and allusions, you have entered into a life together, no matter what the distance between you. That he was Claude's secretary, that his function in life was to make Claude's own go more smoothly and to order hers while she was away, gave them such excellent cover, it was as if some god or gods were on their side. Perhaps this was being in love, this finding of gods everywhere, in random events, in the weather, in clumps of trees that can hide you, in the mysterious processes even of the transatlantic mail. He believed in the Christian God, of course; but He was not a sly God, not one to play tricks for the benefit of lovers. He simply demanded everything of Henri, and she saw him suffer from not being able to give it. Her gods, if she briefly conjured them to life, were closer to nature spirits or Cupid or the god Pan. He prayed; she expected magic. He confessed; she felt no guilt.

His letters grew longer and longer, his handwriting evidently faster. He still wrote *chère Madame* and signed himself formally, *Henri Fournier.* The business of her future engagements in Paris that he'd undertaken to arrange, the news of her husband's comings and goings, the books he was reading, the news of his family, all this arrived punctually, followed her across North America. Yet there was, increasingly, another meaning, a hidden message, that was coming to the surface, almost in spite of his efforts to remain formal. She read his letters, and understood: his attempts to remain her husband's secretary, and her friend; underneath, in the margins, in the passionate scrawl of his writing, the longing to express to her everything that could not yet be said. She knew she was not wrong. Toward the end of her time away, she wrote to him *mon cher Henri, mon cher ami.* And signed herself simply *Simone.*

In November, she was in Chicago, a cold place at nearly any time of year, when he wrote to tell her that *Le Grand Meaulnes* was finished. "I have to tell you that yesterday Meaulnes abandoned, on their wedding day, the young woman he had searched for, loved, and pursued during his whole adolescence."

She reread this curious sentence several times. It was not simply about his finishing his novel, was it? It read more like something in code. In her high room in Chicago she paced, and looked out on gray skies and down into streets like chasms. In a few days she would sail home on the *Mauretania* from New York. This time, whatever happened between them next—and they were still calling each other by the formal *vous*—she would be coming home to him.

We have to go forward, don't we, wherever this takes us? The letters have brought us this far. They are like thumbprints, a whorl of meaning wound tight, waiting to be lived.

11.

Chloé is sweating in the summer heat. The air is full of the dust of grain. No breeze comes in through the opened top half of the stable door. The yard outside is silent. Then someone scrapes a table's legs across cobbles, and she hears voices and the clink of glass. The big doors of the old posting barn, now a concert hall, creak open. There are people out there now, laying tables, covering them with white cloths. The sun, as it lowers over the quadrangle made by stables and the house and the big barn on the northern side, lights everything so that even the horse's skin has a yellow tinge. She climbs down off the box, caresses his neck, talks to him. His nostrils black and soft, their few hairs like a cat's whiskers. The soft fumble of his mouth as she feeds him a sugar lump from her pocket.

"There, we're nearly done." She stands back from him, appraises him, the gleam of his pale flesh, the ears that prick up as he munches, chasing the tiny sweetness through his mouth, the row of little knots she has made that stand up now like a row of tied onions on his neck. Her mother will be out there, almost certainly, and even that Englishman she has invited to stay. But she need hardly speak to them.

At the quarries in Triacastela in northern Spain, only weeks ago, she picked up a stone as pilgrims have done for centuries, to carry it in her pocket all the way to Santiago de Compostela. What difference do one person's actions make? One stone is a stone as one person is a person. You do what you can.

She lifts the oiled saddle from its wooden tree and slides it down his back. He hardly flinches, the sweetness still in his mouth, but flirts his head up and down. The bridle with its complex bit hangs from its peg. She'll leave it till last; let him move his tongue over his lips freely for as long as he can. In the gloom of the tack room, she pulls off her T-shirt and shorts, stands in her underwear, removes her bra to flatten her breasts more easily into the man's uniform, and begins to put on the stiff garments of another age. *Damn, but these clothes are hot.* She hears people arriving, the voices as they come through the gate to the courtyard, heels that click their way across cobblestones to grass. *"Bon,"* she says to the horse, "let's get moving." She crosses in front of him, holds the bridle up, and slips her thumb in between his back teeth so that he opens his mouth. She feels his hard gums, the liquid of his saliva. The bit goes in, flattening his tongue, pulling back the soft black lips so that they wrinkle. She bends his ears to the headpiece, straightens the browband, fastens the throatlatch under the big muscle of his shifting jaw, does up the tiny buckle, fixes the chain under his chin. She opens the bottom half of the door and leads him out into the cooler air.

Twenty or thirty people in evening dress stand about on the grass and on the cobbles, warned back from the gravel path that surrounds the *piscine* where the horse and she will perform. From the stone mounting block she lifts her foot to the stirrup and lowers herself into the saddle. She stands in the stirrups to test the leathers' length. High above the ground, the sky above the buildings is carved for her between the horse's ears. She touches him with her heels, moves him on. They reach the circle of gravel. On a loudspeaker a voice begins: "The horse is part of *le patrimoine de France*, and the display you are about to see is a testimony to the rapport that can exist between horse and rider: dressage, a concept that was invented here in France and perfected in the military academies at the time of Napoleon and carried from here throughout the world."

Chloé holds her lip in her teeth. She collects him at the bit, urges him on with her legs. She feels his weight shift as he moves into the controlled trot, his nose tucked in, neck arched, all the little ribbons winking red in the last rays of the sun, his hooves on the gravel clean as bells. From the trot she moves him into the canter. The voice goes on, talking about the horse as an essential part of the French military, and Chloé, her legs speaking to his sides, her hands at rest, rides him through history.

Then she sees them out of the corner of her eye: her mother wearing pink, and the tall Englishman. She can't turn her head; the horse would feel it. Her tricorn hat stays straight on her head and she looks ahead between the horse's ears. She must not let them move her in any way. The horse will know if her attention falters; he'll know as his ancestors knew if the man on their back had doubts, was a coward, or would not survive the charge.

She draws him in and he begins the extended walk, like a slow dance. His legs are not made for this; it is learned and painful as ballet. Then, the extended trot. The whole force of him is contained now, beneath her. He holds back and holds back, this horse who could break free, rear up, and gallop out of here, scattering people before him, leaving her dropped in his wake. But he draws back and in like a wave, extends one leg and drops his head over it as if bowing to the god of horses; she is pained for him, but it is nearly over. As he bends over, as he surrenders, the applause begins to spatter and fall.

Seb stands beside his hostess and watches the horse and rider circle an empty stone pool at the center of a vast courtyard. The sun slides down behind a roof, a slow red egg.

There is no sign of a concert even beginning. It probably won't begin for hours, so will end impossibly late. There probably won't be anything to eat; he feels he might simply faint from exhaustion. He should have bought something to eat on the train, even an overpriced sandwich, while he still could. What does all this have to do with the unfinished work of Henri Fournier? He thought he had ended his tryst with Fournier years ago, when the book came out, followed by an article he was asked to write for the *Times Literary Supplement*; but the man seems set to follow him through life, a presence, a voice whispering secrets into his ear, suggesting sudden journeys.

He shifts his weight beside Isabelle de Giovanni, whose dress has creased up around her behind and is stretched tight across her bust as if she has recently put on weight. His legs and shoulders ache. Sweat pools in the small of his back, under his shirt. He has hardly been out in the evenings since Annie's death. Oxford friends have invited him, usually to meet a sad woman, a recent widow, with whom he will have a lot in common. We all have death in common, he's often wanted to say—but mostly, we keep it out of sight. He's been down to London a couple of times to see his children or his publisher, but has usually fled home on a commuter train among the pale, suited young men still at work on their iPhones and laptops, as if the office were now everywhere, spreading its ganglia up into suburban and rural England, never letting anyone go. He knows that he is antisocial, but surely it is his right to be so. Perhaps one day it will be different, perhaps not. Meanwhile, he's thinking that he should have insisted on going to a hotel; it's always a strain, staying with someone you don't know.

Isabelle is telling him something.

"You see, the place was built as a staging post for the king's mail, in the eighteenth century. The country was divided into sections measured by how far you could go before changing horses. It started by being the king's mail, then others started using it. It only stopped with the arrival of the train, the Paris-Bordeaux railway. The family who own the property are descendants of the last master of the king's horses. I'll introduce you."

Now he watches the horse, because that is what people are doing. The white horse with smoky nose and balls—not castrated, he notices—and a tail like a knot in water. Why make horses do this kind of thing? Why watch this before a concert? What has it to do with music?

Isabelle at his side touches his arm, whispers, "Dressage is very French. You probably don't see it much in England."

I wouldn't know, he thinks. It seems to him mannered, even perverse. But he only nods gently, thanks her for the information. He watches the horse and rider. Surely, the rider is a woman? Unmistakable, once he noticed the curve of the waist, the tightened cloth across the breast, and the shape of the thighs that grip the saddle. He sees the young woman's skill, how she directs the horse with a pressure of thighs, a small movement of hands, a shift of weight in the saddle. Behind him, someone has begun getting champagne bottles out and lining them up on the table, as the sun goes down behind the building opposite. At least they are going to get a drink.

Outside the house, which occupies the east side of the courtyard, he sees people come out onto the vine-covered terrace. Candles have been set in brown bags all around the edges of lawns, weighted with sand. As the light drains from the sky, the pallor of stone intensifies and the roofs turn darker. He glances around. People move toward him across the gravel. A young woman and a tall, thin man, she attached to an IV drip, the sort people have in hospitals. A transparent bag floats like ectoplasm above her, attached to a pole. He sees her sink down into a wheelchair, the man leaning above her. Isabelle takes his arm. "Come on, let's get a drink. Then I'll introduce you to everyone. We've plenty of time before the concert begins."

They move toward the table with the champagne. The children of the house are handing out the glasses. He glimpses the young woman in the chair, with the drip attached to her. She wears a square-necked white dress like a smock and takes a glass of champagne. She swallows, and laughs, then drinks the champagne, as the young man with her leans closer, buries his face close to her mouse-furred head.

Through his fatigue—he has not felt so tired, surely, since the days after Annie's death—Seb hears the buzz and soar of the string quartet. His body has simply given up. He shifts about on the hard chair in the heat of the closed barn that is the concert hall. The first piece is a Bach concerto. He dozes, music coming and going, its cadences like staircases he is too tired to climb. Then, Mozart, flute and strings: a young man with a face like the god Pan purses his mouth to the flute. *Excuse me, Pan, I can't stay awake even for you.* Saint-Saëns, for violin and harp, he sees from his program. A large woman in black, with feet flexing in gold sandals, strokes a huge harp somewhere above him. Then Debussy, a solo flute. The god Pan again. He makes himself sit up. Late Schubert, now, strings. He is aware of sagging over Isabelle de Giovanni as his eyelids close for a moment. But she doesn't move away; rather she seems to position herself to support him. He is woken again by a sound that could be rain on a roof; but no, it is applause. Women in black evening dresses and men in black suits bow on the platform before him, the gleaming bodies of violins, viola, and cello held by their necks like bouquets of flowers. The big chandelier overhead strikes jewels and bow tips with the same fire. The platform empties. The air is stifling. A man goes on in inaudible French for far too long, and Seb drops again into near-sleep; but then they all get to their feet, fumble for bags and wraps, begin slow processions out into the cooler night.

Isabelle whispers to him, "You must be tired. But it was wonderful, wasn't it?"

He mumbles in agreement.

"This is Sébastien Fowler," Isabelle is saying, drawing a dark-haired woman toward him, a dress in deep sea-green shiny material, a surprising décolletée for one not young.

"Monsieur Fowlair," she explains him in French, "is here to do some research on my great-uncle. He's a writer. He wrote a famous book. Marianne is an old friend, we were at school together. She kindly invites me every year, to these wonderful concerts."

Seb hears from her tone that she feels inferior to Marianne; is it a remnant of school days, or class difference, based on Marianne's evident aristocracy, money, house, the whole setup? He feels briefly sorry that she has to sound so sycophantic.

"Do I know your work?" The woman takes his hand and keeps it, drawing him closer to her, taking him with her to the crowd by the table with the bottles. What would be a possible answer? *Probably not?* Or, *I wrote a rather scandalous book in the 1970s about my hostess's great-uncle's love life?*

"I love your house," he says, to shift her attention.

"Yes, isn't it wonderful? It's always been a magical place for me, ever since I was a child."

"So, you grew up here?"

But the woman in green is not listening. She has so many things to see to. Distracted, she gives him a wide, blank smile, squeezes his hand, and lets it go. She touches a handkerchief to the sweat on her forehead. "Forgive me. Oh, yes, wonderful that you could come. So glad Isa could bring you. Did you enjoy the concert? This is my niece, Simone. Simone, this is Monsieur Fowler? Fowler, like someone who snares birds? He is a writer. An English writer."

The girl in the wheelchair, her long white arm, her hand held out. The other is on the chair arm, close to the drip, which follows her about like a mute bodyguard. Her man, with wild hair and an engaging grin, is at her side. *"Enchantée, monsieur."* Her voice nearly a whisper. He guesses, from her extreme thinness and paleness, the short, soft fuzz of her hair, cancer. She is really the only person here he feels like talking to; the sick are more accessible, these days. But she is with the young man, who might be her husband. The young man begins feeding her foie gras on tiny pieces of toast, and she opens her mouth like a bird's beak to take it from his hand and her sleeves fall back down her arms like wings.

Seb takes a cold glass and champagne fizzes in his mouth. He bites into foie gras and it's delicious, even though the yellow fat on it will wrap your heart and kill you, if the guilt of it doesn't first. He thinks, *Here is a young woman who must be having chemotherapy for cancer; she is eating foie gras, drinking champagne, and why not? Taking the pleasures of the world into her mouth, before it is too late?*

Swallows still swoop across the courtyard; or perhaps they are bats.

"The children are all Marianne's grandchildren, or nieces and nephews," Isa is saying. "It's a big family. Oh." She pauses and looks across the courtyard. He sees her surprise, even a slight shock. "Sébastien, I must introduce you to my daughter, Chloé."

They walk toward a young woman with a sulky mouth and hair twisted up on top of her head in a knot, in a red dress that is more like a long silky undershirt skimming visible nipples. He recognizes her from a movement of her head, easing her neck—of course, the dressage queen.

"Bonsoir."

"Bonsoir."

Isabelle says, "Chloé, what are you doing here?"

"Well, Maman, I did tell you I was coming home. Don't worry, I'm not staying at the house, I'm at Martin's. I said I'd ride for him tonight, because he's sick. So this is your famous writer friend?" She puts out her hand to him.

"You were the rider tonight, weren't you?" Seb says. "I thought you were great." Chloé's hand, he sees, is still lined with grime from the horse's sweat. When he takes it, it's small, strong, and warm.

"Oh." She glances sideways at her mother. "So even my own mother didn't recognize me. You didn't know me, Maman, did you? But your English friend did. I must go and talk to Simone, she looks awful. God, what those treatments do to you. Still, at least her hair's growing back. See you later."

Long tables covered in white tablecloths have been set out on the terraces. Seb sits next to the hostess, the woman in sea-green, and just down the table is the young woman in the wheelchair, her IV drip upright at her side with its little shining bag. The children bring out big wheels of pizza, cut into slices, and then there is salad, cheese, ice cream. A children's menu, but served with good wines from the house's cellars. His neighbor, a small woman, a cousin of Marianne's, nudges him. "The children did all this. Cooked it, everything. It took them most of the day."

Late in the evening, when even the desserts had been cleared away, he hears squeals and scuffles from the bushes where all these kids, their duties done, hide and play. Nobody tells them to go to bed, though it must be well after midnight. It strikes him that he is a very long way from where he began his day—from where his real life goes on, surely, as if he has left part of himself behind.

He glances down the table at the thin girl in the wheelchair and she gives him an ironic smile. He supposes she is used to being stared at; he wants to make some amends, but there are none to be made.

"Do you know where the toilet is?"

"Go through the salon and down the corridor, there's one on the right." She waves her pale hand in the direction of the house.

"Thanks."

One of the little girls in smocked dresses follows him and points the way. "Through there, just up those steps."

He walks through a long room where a girl of about fifteen sits at a grand piano. She plays a chord, then a phrase—Mozart?—and then stops as if waiting for him to leave. Feeling like an intruder, he crosses to the steps, lets himself into the bathroom. He thinks of the moment in Fournier's novel when Meaulnes goes into a room where a young woman is playing the piano, and imagines for a moment, like a flash forward, that he is married to the beautiful stranger who plays for him.

Coming back to the table, where tiny cups of coffee are being placed, he sees the girl in the wheelchair being fed chocolate ice cream by her husband, one slow spoonful at a time.

The finger of water from the fountain rises and falls. He stares at it, to try to keep awake. Finally, Isabelle takes him by the arm. "This way, come on, I should take you home."

He walks with her to the parked car, mutters about not being good at late nights, slides beside her onto the seat. Trees open a way before them as Isa drives off the main village street and into the country that seems to swallow them and draw them into itself.

He wakes to see fields, white under the moon, and then they are back at her house, the engine cutting out, silence, the grassy smell of the summer night. He's aware, embarrassed, that he fell asleep against her shoulder as she drove. She looks at him with her small enigmatic smile. "Goodnight. I hope you sleep well." And he crosses the moonlit courtyard to go upstairs to his room.

12.

In the library at their country house at Trie, she sat down in front of a good fire with the manuscript of his book. *Le Grand Meaulnes. Not much of a title,* she thought. He'd handed it to her after dinner, without a word. As if he were handing her a part of himself.

They had hardly had time to talk, since she came back from America. Tension hung in the air between them like dust caught in light. Claude was taking up all the room there was, with his constant calls on Henri's attention, his demands on her about housekeeping arrangements, lists of guests they must invite. As if he knew something already, that even they did not. He bustled and strode through rooms, leaving doors open. He seemed to be everywhere. When she was sure that he had gone to his room for the night, she sat down, breathed out, and began.

She read all evening and into the night, sitting beside the fire that shifted and sighed, ash building up; she threw another log on, stirred it all with the poker until the fiery sparks rose upward and the wood cracked and spat—too green, this log, she must tell the gardener not to bring last year's wood in till it was quite dry—and went on reading.

A tall boy of around seventeen comes into a country schoolhouse and sits down. He is Augustin Meaulnes. His hair is cropped short as a peasant's under his cap. He's come to lodge with the narrator's family as he lives far away. Who is he? He is everything anyone ever wanted. He brings with him a whiff of adventure, as when someone bangs a door open, bringing in the sharp cold scent of the outdoors.

She read the sentence aloud to herself: "And it was then that it all began, about eight days before Christmas." *It all began*. A story cracks open.

Meaulnes asks François, the narrator, to cover for him in class, because he has to go somewhere. He doesn't explain. François sits in the classroom, waiting for his friend's return.

Augustin Meaulnes, the boy free as a young captain, strangely adult for his age, drives an old horse and cart into a wood where he finds a party is taking place in an abandoned château. It is a fête organized entirely by children. He hears that it's a wedding party for a boy called Frantz de Galais. He's welcomed in, spends the night, and wanders through the rooms until he meets a beautiful girl, Yvonne de Galais, the sister of the young bridegroom. He knows at once that he has fallen in love. The fête ends abruptly because Frantz's bride, Valentine, does not arrive. When Meaulnes gets home, and tells his story to François, the only proof he has that his adventure was not a dream is the embroidered old-fashioned waistcoat that he still wears, for the wedding that was not to be.

So, this is you, my beautiful young man, this is your essence? She stood up and walked around the chilly room, poked the fire embers into flame, wrapped herself in a warmer shawl, and went on reading. Outside the night was starless and silent. The house creaked a little around her. The book drew her in.

At the beginning of the second section, the boys François Seurel and Augustin Meaulnes fight in the snow with unknown adversaries who want to steal the map Meaulnes has made of the way to the château. They then make their pact of brotherhood with the gypsy leader, a young man with a bandaged head: when one of them whistles on a certain note, the others will always come.

Pauline got up and walked about, pulling her shawl tight around her. The story agitated her, and she did not know why. The gypsy is the boy whose wedding feast was held at the lost estate: Frantz. Now he has a bloody bandage around his head from a suicide attempt, and a map that he stole from Meaulnes during the fight. How had these schoolboys suddenly become so adult? It was as if she had always known them—and yet they couldn't have been further from her own protected childhood. Had there been a story that Papa had told her? Was this just the fantasy of the unhappy girl she'd been, left alone too long, longing to have adventures out in the world? The girl sitting in funereal black, outside a room in which her father had died. The girl whose brother was sent away to sea. She thought of the map in *Treasure Island* and the *X* that marked the spot of the buried treasure. The boy Kim astride the great gun, the Afghan horse trader, the secret in the amulet. *So you, too, knew these things? You, too, sat astride the gun Zam-Zammah and leapt ashore at Treasure Island? You, too, heard blind Pew tapping along to the Admiral Benbow to deliver the Black Spot?*

The clock chimed, after its wheezy preparations. Three o'clock. She stoked the fire with the rest of the apple wood from the tree that had fallen in the orchard, lit one of Claude's little cigars, and read on. The fire spat and sizzled. An owl called outside in the woods. This night, this fire, this book. A book is a map of life.

Augustin Meaulnes is looking for Yvonne in Paris when he meets by chance the missing bride, Valentine, who is working as a seamstress there. He takes her to the theatre and later makes love to her. Then he continues his search for Yvonne. François waits for him in the country where they were at school together. There are letters found in a trunk, a secret map; the trappings of mystery novels, yet with a strange quality of normality to them. François reads Augustin's journals and discovers what has been going on. After Augustin returned and married Yvonne, he left again. She has his child in his absence but dies in childbirth, mourned by François, who was probably in love with her all this time.

In this last section, childhood became adulthood. The young men stood at its threshold, dreaming of sworn allegiances and whistles of command from the deep woods. The real shock was the lost estate, which had seemed dreamlike, becoming an actual place, and love that had been idealized made physical. When you loved a girl, the book said, the writer said, you made love to her, married her, made her pregnant; then you left her. She was shocked at the speed of it. How could he do this? How could he tell her one thing—that childhood is innocence—and then, write quite another? Life rushed through this book, barely pausing. Everything that had been play and fantasy became direly serious. It was like reading *Peter Pan* and Thomas Hardy back to back. Yet the prose, its relaxed, almost conversational quality, undercut the occasional melodrama of the plot. The author seemed to be saying, *Come with me, trust me, and I'll make you believe all this.*

At dawn, she scribbled a note in blue pencil on a scrap of paper. *I love your book. It's phenomenal. Congratulations. P.*

She folded it and pushed it under his door and went to her room in daylight.

The story escaped its own bounds, as if the writer was running backward to hit a high ball on the baseline of the tennis court. The lost domain of childhood: *you lose it,* she thought, *through sex or death.* For herself, it had vanished at her father's death. For Henri, she guessed, it had been sex with a real woman. (Who was the woman? There was always a woman.) This was what lay behind the confusion and pain of the second half of the book. Did his heroine die because she was too real? Did his hero have to walk out into the world, leaving everything and everyone behind?

In the morning he was there at the breakfast table when she came down late. He looked up from his coffee, half stood as she came in.

"No, sit down, do. I finished your book. I couldn't stop. I read it all night."

"I found your note. I can't tell you how much it means to me."

"I've never read anything like it. Really, Henri, it is *bouleversant*."

He sat intently listening, a half-eaten brioche on his plate, a crumb on his moustache. He looked straight at her as if her judgment were the only one he ever wanted to hear.

"It reminds me of English literature, you know. Stevenson, even Defoe." She still couldn't say it: *You have written the story of my unlived life, my dreams when I was a girl. I, too, wanted to find the enchanted place, and fall in love. But as a woman, I am shocked with the brutality of your ending.*

"No girls in either of them, though, are there?"

"No, and nothing erotic either. You combine childhood innocence with a strong erotic quality. I can't imagine any of that happening to Jim Hawkins, or David Balfour, or even Kim."

As she said the word *erotic*, she saw his face change. He wiped his mouth with the napkin. *Oh, so I have touched a nerve?*

"I was going to call it *The Wedding Day* at one point. Or *The Lost Domain*. Or even, *The Country with No Name*. Then I thought it's Meaulnes's story; he should be in the title. Did you really like it? You know, you can't ever tell how it will strike someone else, and Jacques and Isabelle are too close to me."

"It's really good. I think you may be a genius."

He broke the remains of his brioche, and dunked it into coffee, making a mess on the white cloth. He grinned at her sideways. "Really? You mean it?"

"Really. It's the most original thing I've ever read."

"What did you think of the ending?"

"It scared me. It's violent. But it's beautiful."

"Jacques says a reader should discover what's happening at the same time as the character in a story. That's what the English writers do. I sent you *Kidnapped*, didn't I? I loved that, more than all his others except of course *Treasure Island*. When David Balfour was setting out to the House of Shaws, I was shaking in my shoes. And Alan Breck's such a great character, he almost takes over the book. You're right, they don't pay any attention to girls. But I've just been reading Thomas Hardy's latest, *Jude the Obscure*. It got bad reviews in England, but it's a masterpiece, and he really gets to the heart of the love question. Probably why none of the reviewers could stand it."

He talked fast. He dripped crumbs into his cup and mopped at the cloth with his napkin.

"Leave that. It doesn't matter. The place—it must be your home, where you grew up?"

"Yes, the place is where I grew up. The Sologne. The son of a country schoolmaster, like François Seurel."

"And the lost estate that Meaulnes finds? Does Les Sablonnières really exist, or did you invent it?"

"It exists. There's a real place, not far from where my parents live, called L'Abbaye de Loroy. I went there first when I was quite small, with my parents and Isabelle. But it's an imaginary place too. You know, the way children imagine things?"

It was as if they walked a tightrope toward each other, trusting their words to keep them on the wire.

She said, "It's harder for girls to have real adventures. Nobody lets us go out on our own. But we long for them just the same."

"The only girl I've really been able to ask is my sister, Isabelle. She isn't very interested in adventures. She likes staying close to home."

Pauline thought, *Maybe it depends on what is going on at home.* "My only adventures were through reading. I read to escape what was real. And it made the books seem more real than anything. I had an

English governess, and she read aloud to me. Then I began reading all her books myself."

"I imagined the book as a sort of back-and-forth between dream and reality. Don't we live somewhere in between when we are children?"

"I think so. Unless reality becomes too hard."

"I think a happy childhood is one in which you can invent yourself. Meaulnes had perhaps too happy a childhood, so François envies him, because he has that kind of freedom, you know, as if he'd been given the gift of knowing himself at an early age."

"So, do you think we can invent our lives? I have been thinking about this all my life." *All I could do,* she thought, *was ensure my own bare survival. Men, boys, do what they want to do; we girls and women act in the small spaces left for us.* "But tell me about the real place. You went there?"

His hand on the tablecloth, resting beside the plate, the fingers slightly curled. A strong right hand, the thumb bent a little way back. It was only inches away and she could reach casually, touch it, even cover it with her own. She touched his arm instead, just for a second. "Do go on."

She thought, *So, you, too, were given the gift of yourself at an early age?*

"One day, when I was about thirteen, I set out to go to the old abbey. I think it was empty, or a recluse had lived there. It wasn't as remote as it is in the book, but it felt as if it existed in another world. I crept through the undergrowth, as Meaulnes does. And I remember thinking what if there were an extraordinary fête going on here, run entirely by children—wouldn't it be astonishing? And I'd come out of the bushes and be welcomed, and I'd go to the house and meet a beautiful girl, and we would love each other."

"You were thinking about beautiful girls when you were thirteen?" The summer she was thirteen, after her father's death, she had been stuck in a park outside a casino with her maid, Dora, in some spa town—Luchon, she remembered—while her mother went to "throw down a few louis" with her awful lover, Alfred, the banker from Rouen. A bad orchestra played *Turkish March* or *Overture to Zampa*, two pieces of music she could never again hear without revulsion. At nine thirty, she had been allowed to escape to her room in the hotel. To lie in the dark and plot her escape, yes, but not know how; not until the moment when Le Bargy, the middle-aged actor-manager her mother knew, came to the house in Paris, asked her, at seventeen, to marry him, and to go on the stage.

Henri said, "Yes, I've always thought about them. I had a dream when I was very young of a girl sitting at a window, sewing, with her back to me, waiting for me to wake up. In the book, she's playing the piano, but it's the same feeling."

She thought, *In that one statement you are telling me everything.*

Then Claude came into the room, wanting breakfast, fussing over hot milk for his coffee, and the day fell apart and reassembled around them. Like the pieces inside a kaleidoscope, fractured, bright, falling into place. A broken blue vase, letters on a tray, their envelopes stained with snow: and now, the pages of a book. In it, a deserted château. A girl at a window. A boy caught in a dream for life. A tragedy, waiting to happen.

13.

He opens the shutters and the light rushes in. Yellow fields behind the house, a strip of indigo sky. It must be late. He's slept for longer than he has in months. He supposes there will be breakfast. Coffee, at least. He dreads meeting Isabelle de Giovanni this morning. (Did he snore? Did he mutter in the car?) He wonders if Chloé is here, and what the trouble is between them, why she seems so bad tempered. He stands barefoot, looking out. A line of shimmering poplars makes a frieze against the sky. He can hear a river. The Cher, or one of its tributaries? He should know which river he is near. The hum out there is perhaps bees in the hollyhocks that stand like guardians at the front of the house. Directly below the window there's a deep bank of nettles and elder, and beyond that a gravel path, and to the side of the house, a big tree, a sycamore or lime.

The moment has a peculiar familiarity to it. It's the feeling of being young, not knowing what the day will hold, waiting to have it announced. As if somebody else may have a plan for him. (When did anyone last have a plan for him?) He has a slight hangover, a feeling he has not had for years, that lurking headache and unease in the gut; too much champagne on an empty stomach. (Where was that place they went to? Was it really near, or far?) He thinks, *I must call home.* Then, *There is no point.* The knowledge is not always there when he first wakes; it arrives slowly and when it does—and is real, not a dream—he feels as if a stone drops into a well deep inside him. *She is not there. She is dead. I will never see her again.*

The antidote to such thoughts is hard to find. Perhaps it is out there, beyond his own confines, in the brilliance of the morning, the bees in the hollyhocks, the line of poplars that must line the riverbank; perhaps it is in the house with the work he has been asked to do. Going on living—really living, not just surviving—is all about finding the antidote. Sometimes it's Annie herself, urging him on. He splashes his face with cold water in the little sink, scrubs his teeth, gargles, rinses, spits, thinks about shaving and puts it off; the stubble doesn't grow quite so fast these days. He flattens his hair, in which gray is beginning to overtake brown, looks into his still-bloodshot and red-rimmed eyes, puts on dark glasses, and shambles downstairs in jeans, a short-sleeved cotton shirt, and sandals. He hopes that he will find someone who will offer him strong coffee and then say no more.

Isabelle and her car are gone. It's Chloé who sits at the kitchen table, thumbing through pages of *Libération*, a coffee bowl with its dregs at her side. Her shoulders hunched in a sleeveless T-shirt, her arms, he notices, thin, muscular, and brown. Her fingers tap on the tabletop as she reads. She looks up, raises her eyebrows, goes back to her reading, then says, "Coffee?"

"Yes, please."

"Sorry, I'm not much use in the mornings. But, did you sleep?"

"Yes. It was a long day."

"Yeah. Why Maman had to haul you all the way over to that do, I can't imagine. She feels she has to go to these things, out of obligation to Marianne de Courcy. Keeping her end up, I suppose. They're terrible snobs. It's okay if you have a horse to ride, but I wouldn't have gone otherwise."

"I enjoyed it. I didn't come here to sleep."

"Sit down, have some coffee. Do you want toast? The bread's always yesterday's here, since this isn't Paris, so we toast it."

He accepts a tepid bowl of coffee and watches the bread she has jammed in the toaster begin to smoke.

"Is your mother out?"

"She went shopping. There's a supermarket only a few miles away now, so she goes there, it saves time rather than going round all the shops in town. She's annoyed at me, simply for being here. We don't get on, these days. I was supposed to be in Spain, but I came back. Anyway, since it's my house too, I thought I should be around. You know she wants to sell it?"

"No, I didn't." He drinks the bitter coffee, spreads plum jam on charred toast. "But I'm only here to talk about Henri Fournier's manuscript, or so I thought."

"Ah, that's where it gets interesting."

"How?"

"It's all connected. She only found the new papers because she was clearing up the attic."

"She found them quite recently, she said."

"Last Easter. She came down to get rid of stuff so she could put the house on the market. She wasn't even going to tell me, at first. But I'm her heir, so I guess she had to."

"Have you seen the papers she found?"

"Nope. But they must be worth a bit. Nobody knew he'd even written another novel except a couple of Italian academics who came here years ago asking about it. The stuff Maman found this year, well, there's apparently a new version, with a new ending. Didn't she tell you?"

"I knew it existed and was unfinished, and that she's found some new parts. I haven't seen them yet."

Chloé lays her brown arms across the spread paper as if holding it in place. Her eyes are dark as the coffee, her eyebrows like black wings above them, an intense and disconcerting glance. Not beautiful, certainly not pretty, perhaps not even pleasant—but extraordinary. The hair that was pulled back and tied under the tricorn hat last night explodes into little ringlets, almost corkscrew curls, around her face. She is so unlike her mother; takes after her missing father, he guesses, who must be an Italian or Corsican with a name like that. She leans toward him across the table.

"Sorry about the toast. You don't have to eat it, you know. That toaster always burns it, I don't know why she doesn't throw it out."

"It's okay."

"Listen, I'll tell you what the scene is before she gets back. The house is hers but it belonged to my grandmother, and before that to her mother, who was Henri Fournier's sister, the other Isabelle. Got it so far?"

"I think so."

"According to French law, it will be mine when she dies. I don't have any brothers or sisters. After me, she couldn't have any more. My father left, anyway. Now. This is the point. She wants to sell the house because she's broke. She has a studio in Paris, where she shows her stuff, but it doesn't bring in much, and my father doesn't give her anything, never has. Then this new manuscript appears, and it's probably worth a fortune. At least, it will interest a lot of people. I'm still not allowed to tell anyone, or I would have found out how much it's worth. So, she should sell the manuscript, keep the house, and let me have it when she's gone. But no, she has this crazy idea—excuse me, but it is—of giving you the manuscript to work on. I know, you wrote that sexy book about Uncle Henri, didn't you? But you'd have to take it back to England, out of France. It belongs here! It's part of what they call *le patrimoine de France*. It mustn't go out of the country."

"Hey," he says, "I've no intention of taking it out of the country."

She isn't listening. "He was one of France's greatest writers, everyone knows that, it's like finding another volume of Proust."

"Were you made to read him?"

"Who, Fournier? Of course. Every kid in France is made to read him at some point or other. He's on the syllabus. But because he was my relative, I was sneakily interested in him before that. I remember reading my grandmother's copy one summer when I was here. I liked the part about the running away, and the weird party, and everything, but I couldn't see why everyone thought it was so great, or so moral. The guy in the book, Meaulnes, is a complete cop-out; he gets the girl pregnant and leaves her to die, and his friend, who thinks he's so great, is just a wimp."

"So you weren't that impressed."

"Well, no. But what I couldn't swallow was the way everyone, in this family at least, thought Uncle Henri was such a saint. He obviously wasn't—well, you know that. Anyway, he may be about to save our skins with this new stuff coming to light, so perhaps he's a saint after all. This place is where it all happened. You can't read his book and not have it happen here."

Seb does not say that for him it happened in southern England, but he knows what she means. It's personal.

"So, look, I assume you're a decent guy and won't make off with this manuscript, now that you know the score. For God's sake don't tell her I said anything. I'm out of here. You can figure it out together. I'll be back, but I have to see to some stuff today."

She pushes herself up from the table, swallows the dregs from her bowl, searches him again with those black eyes, her arms tense as she leans against the table, her body in its torn white T-shirt, a bra today, he notices, her head between her shoulders like a matador's.

"I'm not going to take the manuscript anywhere," he said. "And nobody has asked me to."

"Well." She frowns. "Okay. Good. Look, sorry to involve you in all this, but it's kind of vital for me. Oh, God, here she is."

She slides out of the door just as the Peugeot comes up past the window and Isabelle brakes in the yard.

On the side of the car, someone has written with a finger in dust, *Lave-moi!* The driver's door swings open and he goes out into the singing morning to help Isa with the groceries, string bags as well as plastic and canvas ones bulging with bottles of oil, wine, pastis, milk.

"I thought I'd better shop for the week, then we don't have to bother. I know your time is precious. Did you sleep well? Did you have coffee?"

He assures her, yes, on all points. From the back of the house, he hears the little fart of Chloé's car starting. As they enter the house, her red Renault Mégane bounces off down the driveway and disappears between the fields of sunflowers and on to the road.

"She wants to avoid me," Isa says. "Thanks. I'll just put the bottles in the fridge, and that whole bag of vegetables can just go in the larder for now. Then I'll make some more coffee if you like—that stuff looks disgusting—and we can start."

Seb sets down the bag of potatoes and packs of spaghetti and rice. Isa puts butter, cheeses, sausage, lemons, coffee in the refrigerator. Bread in the linen bag hanging behind the door. The wine, several bottles of it, he's glad to see, in a rack. They are not going to starve or run out of alcohol while he picks his way through the moral niceties of what he will be asked to do.

"You don't mind if we plunge straight in?"

"It's what I'm here for. But I'm unsure about the details, what it is exactly that you want."

"Oh, I'll fill you in. Here, do you want some more coffee? I can do better than that brew Chloé made."

He watches her tip Chloé's cooled coffee down the drain. "No, no, thanks, I'm fine."

"Okay, well, I'll show you the papers without more ado. I only found the new pages this past Easter, when I was beginning to clear things out. The part I found recently hasn't been seen by anybody."

He follows her upstairs, and stands in the doorway of her room as she climbs on a chair to lift a small case down from the top of the wardrobe.

"Give me a hand with this? I'll pass it down."

He stands behind her, receives the case from her hands. Isabelle's behind in black trousers, and her white, slim, exposed ankles appear before him as she stands on the chair.

"I found it up in the attic, but I thought it would be safe enough down here for now."

She scrambles off the chair, her hair coming down.

"It's all in here?"

"Yes, the parts some Italian academics studied years ago, when my mother was alive, and the ones I found recently. I put them all together, but in separate folders. The papers were in a family archive. I'd actually forgotten about them, but I got them out so that you can see the originals. There's the monograph that the Italians put together, and the raw material, and then the new bits, so you can make what you want of it all."

Seb stands with the case in his hand feeling like someone waiting on a station platform in another era. He watches while Henri Fournier's descendant brushes her hands against her thighs. Dust spins in the air between them.

For someone who died at twenty-seven, Fournier left quite a pile of information behind him. He thinks of that other time and place: almost forty years ago, when Pauline gave him access to the astonishing correspondence that was at the heart of the book that made his name.

She grins at him as she pushes back her dusty hair. "What's the matter? You look as if you've seen a ghost."

"Perhaps I have. It was Pauline who set me on the track of all this. I was just a kid, really, and she helped me on my way. She was amazingly kind to me. I still don't know if I let her down."

"I knew about her from my grandmother—who called her the dreaded Madame Simone. She hated her. She thought she had corrupted her brother and ruined his life. She even thought he was better off dead than with her."

"I know. I read your grandmother's book. It was hard going. Hateful, really."

"So it was Madame Simone herself who gave you the letters?"

"She let me read them. She wouldn't let me take them out of the house, of course, but I went several times to stay with her, and worked on them there."

He remembers when there was no answer to his own letters, when he'd stood in the rue du Bac and waited, until the concierge told him that she had gone. To Biarritz, to a nursing home. That she did not want to be followed and had left no address. He'd stood in the street, then, emptied of all feeling except an inexplicable shame—his own book under his arm, the one he had wanted to give her, at last. Too late to thank her properly. Too late to say goodbye.

14.

Whenever they could seize the opportunity, they talked. When did you start writing? What do you think of Claudel, of Baudelaire? What music do you like? Don't you love Debussy? Have you seen *Pelléas et Mélisande?* Didn't you think it was wonderful? In the house in Paris, at quai Debilly, they met in corridors, leaned up against walls, stood looking out of windows at the street below. If somebody came, she could always pretend to be giving him instructions about something, or he could be consulting her about some detail of Claude's work; they could move a foot apart, stop looking at each other. He could get out a notebook, be busy with a pen.

At Trie, during their country weekends, it was easier. She could suggest to him, "Let's look at the greenhouses, I want to see if there's blossom on the fruit trees," or, "Let's go and talk to the gardener about whether the potatoes are ready to dig up."

He tucked his little black leather-bound notebook into his pocket; sometimes he wrote as he walked and she wondered what he was noting down. They strolled to the edge of the lawn, their hands behind their backs, until they reached the line of hazel and chestnut trees that screened the property, then would follow the hidden footpath that led to the kitchen gardens, with their water pumps wrapped in straw and sacking along the way. Here was yew and elder and old man's beard, and the trees shaded the path. Laurent the gardener was the only person who would see them, as he passed with a wheelbarrow full of weeds he'd pulled, or new potatoes still dressed in the webby dark earth they had grown in. It was a place where gnats hung in the air, and the smells were of damp earth, mold, weed heaps, and bonfires; a place where Claude never came, just as inside the house he never went through to the scullery and kitchen, believing that the running of his estate was best left to the people he paid to do it. It was a margin, a hidden part of the garden, not for show. At the end of the path were the kitchen gardens with their brick walls and glass cucumber frames, their rows of bluish cabbages and covered strawberry plants, with borders of marigolds set to keep insects away. From here Laurent brought the dug vegetables to the back door in his wheelbarrow, to deliver them to the kitchen each day. Nobody who lived in the big house saw the vegetables—beets, carrots, cabbage, lettuce in summer, green beans, and later the big marrows and pumpkins of autumn—in their raw, unwashed state. Pauline's sudden interest in the vegetable garden did not appear to strike Claude as strange. Henri, whose own mother dug and tended her *potager*, knew each plant from its leaves and could tell her when the hidden potatoes or beets would be ready to dig, and what to do about the black fly on the beans. Laurent, the old man, turned his back to them mostly and went on with his work, only helped by a boy from the village when the summer vegetables were at their most profuse, or the hard ground needed to be dug in winter. He stooped over in his leather apron, his cracked boots in the earth, his hands large and deeply lined, marked with dirt in all their crevices. They saw him plant small plants, tamp down the earth around them, darken it with drops from the can. He opened the door to the peach house for them. "Yes, Madame, we will have a good crop of peaches this year. The white ones are coming on well, and they're always more difficult. It's possible that the nectarines will ripen first."

Henri said, "It's amazing what a difference a hothouse makes. You'll have peaches this early?"

"Yes, Monsieur, earlier even than they'll have them in the south." The old man knew that he was talking to a countryman. "When you come back, perhaps."

The hothouse air was thick and damp. Henri put out a finger to touch the hard furred nub of a peach. He was leaving soon, for his military service. He would be marching along the roads of France, bivouacking, calling out orders to his men. He would carry everything he needed on his back, and be facing into the sun, away from her.

On the way back to the house, she said, "If you leave your manuscript with me while you're away, I'll take it to Emile-Paul. Do you want me to try?" Emile-Paul was a publisher who had been a friend of her father's. He kept the bookshop she had visited on her way home from school.

"Of course. That would be marvelous. Jacques hasn't offered me book publication, only serialization in the magazine, so there shouldn't be any conflict. If he does want it, that is. I don't want to take anything for granted."

"I really think he will."

"When you've been working on something for so long, you can't really have any sense of its worth to other people. Jacques is family, after all."

"Well, I'll have confidence for you, then. Don't forget, though, that Jacques is one of the best editors in France."

"Yes, but he's seen me working on it for years. He and Isabelle know it almost as well as I do."

"Leave it with me, Henri," she said. "I'll take it out into the cold world for you. Then you can march around and drill your troops and know that it's in good hands."

The day he came back from his month of military service at Mirande, the lilac was in bloom; flower sellers laid great baskets of it out on the pavement. They had been writing to each other again, letters winging fast from Paris to the southwest and back. She had sent him a photograph of herself that had appeared in a magazine with a review of the play, and a note, *I hope you have had enough of being a soldier!* He wrote back, dazzled, ecstatic, formality left aside. A military stamp on the envelope, from Lieutenant Fournier. Inside, hardly disguised, his raw longing to see her.

She left him a message at his parents' house on rue Cassini: *I'll meet you at Emile-Paul's!*

She arrived on time at the shop on the rue du Faubourg Saint Honoré, and Henri came down the street a few minutes later, running, his hat in his hand. She saw him from a distance, dodging between the people who dawdled in front of shop windows. Always that leap inside her. *You!*

"Pauline, oh, how wonderful, look, am I late, I didn't want to be late but you know how things are, so much to see to, and I only got home last night. Is he waiting for us?"

They stood and stared at each other for a moment, as if nothing else mattered. Then, she said, "Come on! We'll talk later. He's waiting for you. It's good news, Henri, I'm sure!"

Emile-Paul took them both upstairs to his office, a small room cluttered with letters and manuscripts. They all three sat at the table, Henri turned toward the brilliant light of afternoon in the south-facing room, his skin glowing in the shaft from the narrow window. There were marks of sunburn on his forehead and nose where his military cap hadn't protected him from the sun. She saw sweat on his forehead, pearled at the roots of his hair. Had he run here all the way from the 14th arrondissement? Why did he never leave enough time to get from one place to another? He'd set his hat on his knee, like someone in a crowded train compartment. She thought, *Yesterday you were still marching around the countryside in uniform. You were Lieutenant Fournier. Now, you are about to become the talk of Paris.*

"Bonjour, Monsieur Fournier. Now, about your book. I've read it, and I admire it very much. I would certainly like to publish it." He paused. "In addition, I would like to propose it for the Prix Goncourt this year."

Henri stammered, blushed, laid his hands on the table palms down as if to control them, and the shifting world. He had dearly hoped to be published, but to be nominated for France's top literary prize was beyond his greatest dreams. "You know, Monsieur, that it's coming out as a serial in *La Nouvelle Revue*?"

"Yes, but that doesn't get in the way of us bringing it out in book form. Rivière didn't offer you book form, did he? I'll have a word with him."

"One thing: I want to have the pen name of Alain-Fournier. Then I won't get mixed up with the racing driver. He's far more well-known than I'll ever be."

"All right. Alain-Fournier. There's another Henri Fournier? I didn't know."

She sat and listened to Henri and his publisher talking, her beloved young man and the old man who had been kind to her since she was a child. The book was going to be published. Henri, if he won the Goncourt, would be famous. She saw him sit forward in his chair, all shyness gone, and begin to explain to the older man how he envisaged the book in its physical form, and what the title meant. It was like seeing him grow and become confident in front of her eyes. His hands gestured, he spoke firmly. His boyish hesitancy dropped away. No, he did not want to change a thing. The title must stay. Meaulnes was the book's hero; the book was his. Pauline thought, *He has become the man he is meant to be: the soldier, and now the writer. I love him, and I'm not going to be able to hide it much longer. But, what can we do?*

15.

She tells the boy, "For a long time, I had to refuse to give anyone any information about us, Henri and me. It was private, and it was the most important thing that had ever happened to me."

Sebastian wraps his hands around one of his jean-clad knees and leans back, taking up most of the sofa. "Were you afraid that it would just turn into gossip?"

"Well, in the theatre you get used to gossip. It was worse. It was deliberate misinformation. I couldn't answer it. I was afraid that if I talked about Henri, I'd lose him completely. In 1939, just before the Second World War, an editor at *Le Figaro Littéraire* wanted to publish a letter Henri had sent me in 1914. He wanted to mark the twenty-fifth anniversary of his death. I refused. François, my third husband, thought I should give in, because everything that had been written about Henri so far had falsified who he was, showing him as some kind of plaster saint or overgrown choirboy. Nobody had written about his immense joie de vivre, although it must have struck everyone who ever met him. François said, 'You should show him, let him be heard as if his real voice were still able to speak.' But I couldn't. I couldn't find a single letter without a detailed reference to me, to his feelings, to our lovemaking. It was too much. I had to wait forty-two years before I could even begin to sort out the letters and decide to write some of my own memories down. You know, a life is given to us to live, not to feed gossip. But at some point, I knew I would have to say, 'Look, he was not like that at all.'"

Seb listens. He hears that scores remain, even now, that have to be settled. That what he may write, eventually, could have something to do with settling them. If only he can be intelligent enough to grasp the heart of all this and take it home.

She goes on, "Jacques and Isabelle were furious about me. They accused me of taking him over for myself. But their own portraits of him were full of a kind of faded romanticism, as if he'd never changed since the age of seventeen and had gone to his death a virgin. I tell you—I can say it now—he was shy, but he was also vivacious, and proud, and capable of a nearly crazy delight in life; he could be touchy, and extremely jealous; he was full of contradictions. As we all are. They made him into a kind of Christ figure—well, I'm sure even Christ wasn't like that. Now, I'm thinking that I may leave the letters to the Bibliothèque Nationale, to be published only after my death. I can't bear to think of that happening while I'm still around. For the moment, they are all in there, under that rug."

Sebastian looks across the room to the trunk with the rug thrown over it. "You have all his letters to you there?"

"Yes, and many of mine to him. A lot of mine were lost in the war, because his sister wouldn't give them back to me. But in the end, when even she had to accept that he was dead, the family handed them over. They have been here ever since."

The boy is silent. She guesses at his longing to ask to see the letters, and admires his decision not to.

"I can't, you do understand. It's too personal."

"Yes, of course. No, I wouldn't dream . . ."

"I know you wouldn't."

"Goodnight, then." He paused. "Simone."

"Goodnight, Seb. Till tomorrow."

He takes her outstretched hand for a moment. She feels his hand's warmth—her own are never this warm, these days—then he lets go and she hears him thudding down the stairs and out into the courtyard and the night. As he goes out, across the courtyard, before he goes through her gates, he'll pause to light a cigarette. He'll go on down the street, smoking. He'll stop to look at the river, lean on a bridge. She sees him in her mind; she knows his movements by heart. Or is it Henri she sees, leaving the house on quai Debilly late in the evening, going home?

All right, she thinks, it was a test—the mention of the letters. Was it unfair? He passed honorably, as she had guessed he would. No more than a glance into the corner, and then a reassurance that he would not, of course he would not, pry into the trunk's contents. He has the finesse that she hoped for. He feels his way; he hesitates. Yes, he's young, and he hasn't done this before. He's perfect. Of course he isn't perfect. He's a young man. He's simply, beautifully, himself.

She steps back into her room, once again drained of energy. It happens all the time—the tide going out, leaving her stranded. She reaches back for the edges of her furniture to guide her back. She should not have talked so much or so long, or drunk several glasses of the excellent Bordeaux that tasted so good that it seemed to bless the tongue and throat. One should always not have done this, or that. But life is doing, talking, drinking, tasting. She stands as upright as she can, breathing for a moment, air in, air out. As long as she can go on doing that, she is still in life. She is still in charge of her story. And, she has found at last the right person to tell.

16.

He sits with Isa at the low table in front of the fireplace where last winter's fires have left a sour, smoky smell and the hearthstone black. The writing case lies between them. She's saying something. He shakes himself to be present.

"Sébastien? Are you all right?"

"Yes—excuse me. What did you say?"

He has a strange sense of remoteness about everything that has taken place between that time in Paris with Pauline and this present moment. His whole life with Annie. Years, decades, places they were in together, the birth of children. The year teaching in Grenoble. The trip to Australia. Visits to the United States to lecture, to see his mother's family. Anniversaries, parties, meals eaten, books discussed, wine drunk. Lovemaking in foreign hotels. He can remember incidents; in a sense he remembers everything about her—of course he does—but his memory of himself during all that time seems to be missing. Who has he been? What has he done? It's like having a CV but no real life, now that Annie isn't present to remind him of it. Real memory seems to go back only as far as that last Christmas, and a plastic bowl of turkey soup spreading viscous liquid across the kitchen floor. Who came for Christmas?

Were he and she alone, or did Ben and Laura come? He thinks, *I am not going mad, no, it is just another of the inexplicable aspects of grief, the ones that nobody talks about.* The wiping out of a life, his own, because hers is over.

Grateful to have a job to do in the present, he opens the leather writing case. Papers in folders and plastic sleeves lie inside: the story of an unfinished novel; the story of a swiftly ended life.

Isa says, "Good, well, there it all is. I'm counting on your discretion, not to tell anyone about these for now."

"Of course."

"Eventually, it will all be public, I suppose. But for now, I'd rather keep them between us."

"I won't tell a soul."

"I just mean, I don't want the academic world here to get wind of them yet. My mother handed over the first version to the Italians, without thinking it through. Luckily, they were honorable and didn't steal it or copy it."

"How did you only just discover the new papers? If they've been here all along?"

"Well, I just never looked. I vaguely knew about the first version of course, and those originals had been given back to my mother. I was in Paris at the time, studying. She left them in a family archive. But nobody knew about this other section. I found the case up in the attic, as I told you. Really, I hadn't been through any of the stuff here since my mother died, or maybe since Hugo left. It was all too much. You know what it's like, having to deal with a lot of objects, when you're already feeling vulnerable?"

He does.

"Well. There were suitcases full of things, and old riding boots and rusty tools and paintings nobody had looked at for decades. I suppose I could have left it all, sold the house with it all inside. But I felt I should at least have a look up there. I found this writing case, and these sheets with Henri's writing on them, tucked away under the blotter. I started reading it up there, in among the mouse droppings and dead birds, and it intrigued me. It was part of the same story, but this part, which seemed to be an ending, was about a young man and woman going off on bicycles together and making love under a hedge."

"Who were the Italians?"

"A professor from the university in Florence and her student."

"So they worked on the papers and then gave up?"

"They put together a monograph, very scholarly, but they couldn't get past his warning."

"His warning?"

"He said in no uncertain terms that none of it could be published, as it wasn't finished. You'll see."

Isa turns to him her direct blue-gray gaze: fine eyes in a pale face, freckles over creamy skin; nothing like her daughter. She pushes her hair back, refastens its knot. "So, you will make a start?"

He says, "I don't exactly know what you want me to do."

"I thought you might want to use it, perhaps for another book?"

"I hadn't thought of writing any more about him. I'm more or less retired, now." He doesn't say that the idea of writing another book is overwhelming in itself.

"Well, you'll read it, won't you? You'll have a look?"

"Of course." He has, after all, come here to do this. "It doesn't look that long, even if it looks complicated. He didn't have time to make it long, poor guy. But shouldn't you tell somebody? Isn't it part of the public domain? By the way, what is its name?"

"It's called *Colombe Blanchet*."

That name: he's heard it before. Out of the past, Pauline's voice: the novel they worked on together, the one he didn't finish. "I was—if you like—the love interest."

Seb begins to feel a wild sense of energy he has not felt for months. Fournier's lost novel. Nobody knew where it was. And all the time, it was here, in this house?

"I thought that because of this, you are the person to do it," she says, reaching under the scattered pages of yesterday's newspaper and producing a worn hardback copy of his book, *Alain-Fournier: In Love and War*.

The dust jacket has been stuck together, evidently long ago, with Scotch tape. The black-and-white photograph on the back shows a first draft of Sebastian Fowler. It's the young man he was in the late seventies, long hair and thick beard, astonished eyes and nervous smile. He remembers the photograph being taken outside the Haywood Gallery, in London, his youthful self posed still raw and full of piss and vinegar, as his mother would say, against the fashionable shuttered concrete of that wall.

"It's a wonderful book," Isa said. "I read it as soon as it came out. We all read it, of course, but in secret. It caused the most enormous stink in my family. But I was a romantic, and I was fascinated by it. Partly because the letters were so erotic—who would have imagined it—and partly because you proved my grandmother wrong, and blew up the whole family myth about Uncle Henri. She was dead by then, of course. Luckily. And luckily it was never translated into French."

"I'm glad you liked it. Isa, the title of the unfinished book, it was *Colombe Blanchet*, you're sure?"

"Well, take a look. It's on the title page. I don't know who Colombe Blanchet was, or why he called it that, but it's all yours now."

"I can't wait to read it."

"I'll have to read yours again," she says, "though my English is not what it was. You made quite a stir with it, didn't you? None of the so-called scholarly works came anywhere near what you'd found out. That's why I thought you were the right person to tell about Colombe. However confusing she turns out to be." She paused. "I'm going to have to leave you and try to find someone to put tiles on the roof for me. Buildings don't mend themselves. This house is in such a state of entropy, you wouldn't believe."

Seb turns his book over so that the photograph is not visible, so that the next person entering the room will not be caught by his youthful, dazzled stare.

His own book attracted attention back then, yes; mostly because, as Isa has said, Fournier's letters to Pauline were so passionate. He remembers feeling wildly turned on by them. Anything even slightly erotic has that power when you are twenty-five. And, the late seventies were a good time to be finding out about the sex lives of biographical subjects. But he knows, too, they affected the way he went back to Annie. They became lovers the night he returned to England, there in her rented room in Putney, where he had gone straight from the airport, straight from Pauline, straight from Henri's letter about the red nightdress, and the open-mouthed kisses he had given his Pauline as he flowed into her, there on her bed, in the last-but-one summer of his life.

His own book's sudden appearance here today and the presence of Fournier's unfinished one have made him dizzy. As if the loose ends of his life were being caught up by a strong and invisible magnet, iron filings helpless to its draw. He can't wait to open the folder Isa has given him, yet it scares him the way sudden challenges can scare you, when you have spent months avoiding them. Since Annie's death, he has become almost a recluse, yes, but also timid, in a way he had not realized. Isa has brought out the book he had written as a young man, careless of what impact it might have. He is no longer that young man, but another young man's book is in his hands asking him—what, exactly? To discover its true meaning, write the book for him, or simply to draw his conclusions, comment, and then put it away?

17.

He's been downstairs to the courtyard for a smoke and come back in smelling of Gauloises; she sniffs with pleasure. The dog growls quietly. Seb puts out a hand to him—*hello, boy*—and the Pekinese snuffles at it and puts out a curled pink tongue.

"He still can't decide whether you are friend or foe," she says. "Since you took him out, he's obliged to admit that you exist, anyway. Now, where were we?"

Seb fiddles with his little tape recorder and sets it on the coffee table between them. "We were talking about Henri."

"Of course we were. But before we go on, no, don't turn it on—let me ask you something about yourself. Have you a girlfriend? Have you been in love? Two different questions, I know, but maybe they are linked." He has asked her intimate questions about her life, pushing himself each time to do so; now, she dares to ask in turn.

She watches him blush, and his quick glance up at her. To see if she can be trusted?

Seb sighs, almost like a groan. "I had a girlfriend, but she's left me. She's going out with someone else." He can't bear to admit to her that the "someone else" is, or used to be, his best friend.

"Oh, dear. And you mind, terribly? I thought there was something. What's her name?"

"Anne. She's Annie to most people." He sighs again, his breath blowing up a lock of his hair. His despondency all comes back in a rush, now that he has said her name.

"Do you call her Annie, or Anne?"

"Annie."

"A world of difference, isn't there, between an Annie and an Anne?"

"I suppose, yes."

"And is this very painful for you? I imagine it must be."

"Quite painful, yes."

"And who is the other person in the triangle?"

"His name is Giles. He's a friend of mine. Was."

"So, it's up to Annie to decide?"

"Well, it sort of seems right. Women's liberation, you know."

"So you aren't allowed to go and sweep her off her feet. Not like in the old days?"

"No. Well, I suppose I could try, but I don't think it would work. They've been seeing each other for some time now."

She says, "I'm not trying to torment you, Sébastien, just to find out a little how things work now. So, you're lying low, not getting in the way, am I right?"

"Something like that. It's not easy, because I run into them in the street, I see them going into the pub, walking by the river, you know. We all live fairly close to each other. He used to be my best friend at college. So I've sort of lost both of them at once." Now, he thinks, *What would Augustin Meaulnes have done? He would have—did—pursue his love through hell and high water. And, when he couldn't find her, made love to someone else. What's wrong with me?*

"And you'd like her to choose you, not him."

"Yes, of course."

"But you're not allowed to influence her."

"No."

"I see. I'm just thinking she might need a little help. Women like a man who's decisive, you know, in spite of women's liberation and everything. It's not like waiting to be picked for a team. Maybe she doesn't know how you feel. Have you told her you love her?"

"Well, not in so many words. It seems kind of pointless." Again, what would Augustin Meaulnes have done? He would have declared his love. It strikes him that he has a choice, to be like Meaulnes or like François Seurel, content to be passive, to sit and wait, and pick up the crumbs of his friend's love affair, too late.

"Only three words: I love you. Try it. My advice to you. It may work wonders. Now, shall we get back to work?"

18.

May 29, 1913, Paris

He came into her dressing room that night like an urgent messenger. She was behind a screen taking off her clothes, Germaine helping her. "Henri, I'm still changing."

"I'll look the other way. Excuse me, I should have waited."

The third act had gone particularly well. The curtain call had brought sustained applause. She'd felt from her audience tonight a warmth and attention that she couldn't ever anticipate, but that when it came, reminded her why she was there. It was easy enough tonight to slip back into her real life, become Pauline again instead of Gabrielle, the woman in the play, Bernstein's much-discussed *The Secret*. Acting was like meditating: you were there, totally in the present, yourself and not yourself, able to observe and to feel and yet to be elsewhere. Some times of meditation ended more smoothly than others. Tonight, she was calm, pleased, with a sense of good work done. Other nights, she'd needed a hot bath, and wanted to scrub Gabrielle off her skin with soap. Already some critics were saying that it was a shame to show such an immoral woman on the stage. But the theatre-going crowds of Paris were not put off—rather the contrary, it seemed.

And he stood there. He stared; he fidgeted. He came to her with his announcement. What did he want to announce?

"What are you doing here?" she called to him over the top of the screen. *You, here, in my workspace?* A frisson passed through her as she felt him there, partly undressed as she was.

"I had to come. Pauline, you can't imagine."

"Where have you been?" She dropped the dress into Germaine's hands.

"I was at the Russian ballet, at the Champs-Elysées. *The Rite of Spring.* The opening night. There was a riot. It was unbelievable. People were screaming and climbing over seats. Someone even challenged someone else to a duel. But it was the music, the dancing, it was strange, barbaric, yes, but beautiful in a way. I can't explain. I don't quite know what happened. I had to come. I had to see you."

"Stravinsky had this effect on you?"

"It wasn't just the music—that was wild enough—but the way the dancers moved. People thought it was an insult, not a ballet at all, but I think it was just too new for them. The dancers jumped in the air, and when they weren't just walking about they stamped. They held their heads and arms at bizarre angles, not like ballet at all." Now, he could not stop talking; he had to tell her everything. "Something happened to the audience, as if the action had come off stage. As if there wasn't a barrier anymore. The performance made the riot happen, in a way. It provoked people. But you would have been amazed. I so wished you were there. Jacques sat taking notes. He has to write an article about it for the *Revue.* But everybody else was completely unable to sit still. Two men even got up to fight. Imagine! A woman screamed from the balcony and I thought she was going to fall off, like someone falling over a cliff. The theatre manager, what's his name, Gabriel someone, was shouting at everyone, listen first, complain afterward! But they couldn't. They couldn't stop themselves. They were not all radicals either. There were men in evening dress, top hats, women in tiaras. It was as if everyone had forgotten everything they had been taught about being in a theatre. Even Nijinsky, he was the choreographer, was standing on a chair shouting the beat to the dancers above the noise. They couldn't hear the music, even though it was a huge orchestra, at least a hundred and twenty, and the percussion section was really loud."

He shook his head as if to clear water from his ears. Pauline came out, dressed now. "Thank you, Germaine."

The dresser took the pile of clothes off the top of the painted screen. Everything was as it usually was here at the Bouffes Parisiens. Yet across town, in another theatre, the new Théâtre des Champs-Elysées, people screamed, rioted, threw things? Fought duels?

"I wish you had been there. It felt as if nothing would ever be the same again."

"Are you all right? Do you want a drink? Some cognac?"

"No, no. No, I'm fine. I'm just stunned. I mean, what will we do now? What will our theatres be like? What will we write? What do you think?"

"Come home with me, Henri. We can talk there. I'm ready. Lucky I'm good at quick changes. Germaine, can you deal with the people outside? Say I'm unwell or something?"

She put on her coat, threw her fox fur around her neck, crammed on her little hat. They left through a side door, just as people were pushing their way up the corridor to find her in her dressing room. A man carried a big bouquet of roses.

"Come on," she said to Henri, "we'll get a cab."

They walked together like conspirators. The street smelled of horse dung and car exhaust and gone-over lilac. She felt him beside her, taut as a string.

In her sitting room in the house on quai Debilly, she lifted her fox fur, its little narrow jaw and beady eyes, from her neck and laid it across the back of the chaise longue. She unbuttoned her long coat, hung it on the back of the door.

He went to close the window shutters. Out there, Paris was awake still with the long twilight, lights spilling into water, water rising in the throats of the fountains; the streets below with their dim cobbles, their gas lamps, their citizens homing in twos and threes. Trees blotting the pavements, shutters closing across the street, doors closing, lamps being lit, people going inside, talking. And somewhere just out of sight, a riot.

"Where is Claude? I thought he was here."

"He won't be back tonight. Or at least, not till very late."

"Ah."

"Ah!" Then, "You'll have some supper with me?"

There was cold chicken and mayonnaise sauce in a silver jug, a plate of cheeses, and a chilled bottle of Sancerre.

"Well, tell me more. Drink. You look like someone who has seen a ghost."

She led him out onto the balcony. He pointed up at the tipped stars of the summer sky, Orion, and look, the Milky Way. The constellation he called *la Grande Ourse*. Mars, warm and pinkish, close to Venus; his head tipped back to show her. "And, do you see Sirius, the small bright one, just there?"

The night air, the near dark filled with the smells of earth and grass that rose from the Trocadéro gardens, the locked parks and lawns; the shining streak of the river between banks of darkness. The two of them alone: this night in May. She needed to step away from him for a moment; she was almost scared of what he might say or do next. He came close, leaning on the railing where she leaned, so that their arms touched and she breathed the grassy scent of his hair.

"Pauline, all the time you were in America, did you feel it too? Do you feel what I feel? Were our letters about the same thing? I need to know." It was as if the Russian ballet had blown him toward her on a sudden violent gust of wind—one that had blown all obstacles out of his way.

"Yes, Henri."

So, tonight changes everything? Whatever happens next, we have stood here and admitted it. We have arrived. And oh, God who does not exist, what we shall do about it I really can't imagine. It's quite impossible, of course. But you, my darling, who have just blown in here picked up on the wild, scouring wind of the ballet called The Rite of Spring, *you know now, as surely as if I had married you. Two words I can't take back now. Yes, Henri. Yes, it is the same for me.*

"I should go. I should go home."

"It will soon be dawn. Look, the sky's getting lighter. There's nothing more lovely."

They stood together on the balcony, leaned together, arms touching, bodies close. Neither spoke as they watched the gray light begin to lift over the city. If they had kissed, he would not have left, she knew it. They had talked, at last, the way new lovers talk, urgently admitting everything, telling the stories, going over what they had written to each other while she had been away. They had almost forgotten to eat, and then she'd remembered she was hungry; she'd picked up chicken bones to gnaw as if they were on a picnic, and they had finished the bottle of wine. But he left without touching her. Claude could be back at any moment; he rarely spent a whole night with his mistress. It had to be, but it hurt her to let him go.

"Go, my darling," she said to him, and looked down a minute later from her bedroom window to see him come out through the double doors of the house and onto the street. She watched him stride away from her toward the river, the top of his bare head, his hat in his hand, Paris just stirring in the early morning around him, a cat on the street, a drunk at the corner, a coal barge with its lamps lit plying the Seine at the street's end as he started his long walk home.

19.

Claude was away for a few days in Brest, seeing to his shipping interests; something about material coming in from America. It was a gift of a day and night, perhaps more. They had dinner alone together at Trie. Passed salt and wine, ate little, glanced at each other. She thanked Marthe, the young woman who served them, and said she could go. They sat at the table among Claude's shining silver and porcelain, a bowl of roses from the garden set between them. He leaned forward, moved the bowl, pulled out one pale rose, and handed it to her without speaking. She saw his hand shake on the stem where thorns had been cut away. She liked that he was nervous too.

Henri put down his napkin and left the room after dinner, saying, "Come when you're ready? I'll wait for you in my room."

She went to her own room, stood looking out at the garden in the late twilight. These evenings were luminous till late; the color faded so slowly you could hardly see it happen. She looked in the mirror and saw her own pointed face, long nose, wide eyes—the face that her own mother had once described as that of a poor little drowned cat. Too late to change anything about herself now.

She left the room after a glance around as if she might never come back. Henri's room was along the corridor and up a short flight of stairs; it faced out to the kitchen gardens and the greenhouses. It had been a servant's room. She tapped at the door, opened it as she heard his voice, and went in to find him standing at the window looking out just as she had, to the garden. Strange, this was her own house and she had never been in this room before. This is where he had been all this time, where he had made himself at home, reading, sleeping, shaving, writing, thinking his thoughts. Books lay open on the table in front of the window, his pen and inkwell to one side. The jacket he'd worn today, a creased cream linen, was hooked on the back of the chair. In here, in this narrow space, he lived like a servant; she was embarrassed to realize it. Coming in here for the first time, she had abandoned her advantages, as mistress of the house, as if she had left her status at the door, and she was glad of it, as if undressed already.

In one stride he came across the room and pushed the door shut behind her. He moved his hands across her face, feeling his way. His lips stung hers with the sharp taste of tobacco. A small bunch of mint from the garden lay on the dresser; she tasted it on his breath, as if he'd been chewing it.

He stepped back, looked down at her. "Pauline." His earlier nervousness was gone. He knew what to do—she thought, *He knows, and I, the older woman, mistress of the house, twice married, know nothing at all.* He had stepped clean out of his shyness, he was in charge here, in this miserable little room they had given him; he was a free man, among his own things and occupations.

"Let's sit down. You're so tall!"

"I love you." Henri said it seriously, as if he understood her hesitation. "As I have loved no other person." He took her in his arms, held her hard to him for a moment. "Pauline, at last."

Her face, kissed all over, dried in the evening air as if he had sealed it. He took her hand and led her to his narrow bed, and together they sat down on it. He began to undo the buttons of her blouse, tiny mother-of-pearl ones, each in its sewn buttonhole.

"Do you want me to do it?" she asked as his big hands worked over the fastenings.

"No, let me, I like it. I like women's clothes." One by one, the little buttons slipped from their moorings. He opened her blouse and his fingers went in to stroke her neck, her collarbone. He kissed her ear, her shoulder, her breast. And all the time she shook, and couldn't move, and felt heat spread through her, and couldn't bear it. He would take his time with her, and this was what terrified her. She wanted to be entirely present, and her body was already in retreat. She was eighteen years old again, spread out on the bed in the red room at the Ritz, as le Bargy, her legal husband, roughly had his way with her, taking no notice of her astonished protest. She was watching Claude come out of the bathroom in a hotel in London, undoing his cuff links, in his shirt and socks, making his casual way over to her. But no, this was her young man, her beloved, her Henri. Leave the past behind, shut the door on it. From now on, let everything be different.

"Let me, Pauline. Trust me, darling."

So she lay, still shaking, while he slowly undressed her. He removed her clothes as if the material itself entranced him; he smoothed out her skirt, stroked her petticoat, gazed down at her as she lay there in her silk knickers, her stockings rolled down to her knees. His hands going in among her clothes, taking their slow time. He opened the strings of her underwear and slid his hand inside.

"I want to kiss you here. You don't mind?"

She moved her head just a little, side to side. Felt him study her, breathe on her, where nobody ever had.

"You are so beautiful."

Nobody had ever said this to her. ("A little drowned cat," "Your nose is too long," "Pity she's so short.")

She felt cool air, where she was wet, and then the warmth of his mouth, his tongue. A long moment of pure astonishment. He pulled off his own clothes and threw them all to the floor in a heap like a boy going in to swim; it made her laugh, and the laugh released her. She laid a hand upon his chest: warm, hard, nearly hairless, a young chest still, and his heart thumping under her hand, as he pressed his own over hers. "Feel it? My heart is yours." He came down over her where she lay, perhaps to say one last thing, but it was never said, and the gradual pleasure she felt came as if from far away, and after his slow care with her, he wouldn't, didn't stop. When he fell across her with a cry, she felt him soaked all over like a runner. She was there with him, holding him, tears beginning under her eyelids and then trickling down sideways into her ears. It was true, it was real, it was possible. She had not run away.

After a few minutes, "I'm not too heavy for you?"

"No, no."

"You're crying?"

"I can't help it. I'm happy, Henri."

He went up on his braced arms and looked down at her and said her name twice. Her real name. Pauline. Pauline. She thought, *He has been with other women.* Then, *It's good, it doesn't matter, it's the way things are. Everything is finally all right, just the way it is.*

The curtains and shutters were left open on a square of sky. Before dawn, the first birds called to one another across the gardens. She was surprised to have slept, and that he was there.

She sat up. He was beside her in the narrow bed, naked and warm, his long legs stretched out, his hip bone against hers. "I must go back to my room. Marthe will be bringing up breakfast."

"Have breakfast with me."

"Tomorrow. I'll tell her I want to get up in the morning. Then we can really start the day together."

"She'll wonder what has happened to you! But, servants always know. They just don't tell."

123

"She'll know?"

"Of course she will. But I know, you can count on her discretion."

"I want to spend the whole day with you, whoever sees, whoever knows."

"The day," he said, "and our whole life, from now on."

A week of light nights and clear mornings, of wet grass and thick, dark leaves against the sky. Claude sent a telegram. He was still busy; he would return to Paris at the end of the week and join Pauline at Trie on Saturday. Meanwhile Henri was to go on working on the accounts. Pauline said, "He'll go and see Fernande before he comes here."

"Well, aren't you glad?"

They leaned on the sill of Henri's bedroom window at night, looking out to the kitchen gardens with their moonlit cabbages, their flowering pagodas of beans. A chuckling sound came from beyond the greenhouses, where young sycamores and elder grew thick. Then, a long, clear note.

"Listen," he said. "It's like at home in the Sologne. We hear them often in May and June."

"Is it a nightingale?"

"Of course! You've never heard it before?"

"I grew up in Paris," she said. "I don't remember hearing it here before, no."

"Then the first time you've heard nightingales is with me."

"Do they really sing all night?"

"Yes. They're probably mating too. Can you imagine, being a bird in love with another bird, and you have to sing your heart out to make her pay attention? People say it's territorial, but I don't believe it. It's love."

She had to leave at the end of June, to go to London to play her old role in Bernstein's hit play, *The Secret*. The letters came across the Channel twice a day. The intimacy of *tu* instead of *vous*, his real voice drawing her close.

We played tennis till the light was gone, and then Claude sent me a note inviting me to dinner. We went to a little local restaurant to eat pâté and drink white wine. I hope you don't mind too much! He told me he's leaving again tomorrow, or Wednesday at the latest. Then I came home and found your letter. My darling, I'm telling you about a thousand things, and I'm thinking only of one thing, all the caresses, all the words of love, there in your marvelous letter, that I'm holding to my heart. I love you. I love you. Give me your mouth, kiss me, my love, my love. HAF

She wrote her replies in the spaces between performances and dinners out. He tried to find an excuse to go to London, but there wasn't one that would satisfy Claude. She wrote briefly, *I'm exhausted. I'm off to do the play again. We've been a great success. I love you, I'm yours to my very depths. Your P.* She had never missed France so; never so longed to go home. She imagined him, gave herself the caresses he would have given her, slept late, and woke in tears.

She wrote at night, *My love, it's late, it's nearly 2 o'clock. I came in and began rereading your letters. I think of you and love you to distraction. This afternoon I lunched in my room and some guards marched past my window playing Scottish music on the fife and drum, and how I longed to be hearing this fresh, sharp music with you, and to find your mouth, and lie in your arms. I sat in my charming room where I've been alone for four days while you're suffering in Paris and I'm lonely here. In the end I told Gaston I wasn't going to do the second week, and asked him to speak to Bernstein. I'm not going to the party on Sunday, I'm coming back to Paris that same day, and Monday I'll come and join you. Is that what you'd like, my love? In five days I'll be in your arms!*

And he wrote, *I can't wait to hear you speaking love to me in English and calling me* dearest. *Longing for Monday!*

Rosalind Brackenbury

From the Savoy Hotel, London, the night before she left: *My love, till tomorrow, come to the station so that at least I see you as soon as I get back! I'm just off to try to find you a picture of Emily Brontë, since you were talking about her book when we first started speaking of our love. Till tomorrow, till tomorrow my lover, my beloved. I love you. P.*

He wrote, *It's time to leave you and have dinner. I came back a while ago to the empty house to write to you in peace, just as I came back three weeks ago to await my terrifying, suffocating happiness. Darling love, my love, my beloved, what can I give you in exchange for everything you give me? Here, my darling, is my love, and my heart, and my body, which are all yours—HAF.*

20.

You can't talk to someone young about sex, she knows this, any more than you should ever talk to them about illness. The secrets of the body must be kept, once it is old. You can talk about love, though. Feelings of the heart do not degrade you. The truth about the body must remain veiled. She must spare Sebastian any mention of the secret place in which she and Henri Fournier met. Nobody can imagine their own parents making love, let alone their grandparents, and she is older even than a grandparent, older and stranger. She draws back, sees that he has noticed her agitation, the way her hand plucks in spite of herself at the tablecloth, guesses that maybe he understands, from her glance when she speaks of Henri. But, no. Probably not; he's too young. If you have never known a great sexual passion, you can't imagine it, she thinks. Any more than you can imagine a country you have never visited. Or the moon, if you have never landed there, as astonishingly men did just a few years ago. You can't see the back of the moon, or how this world looks from space. (Oh, how Henri would have loved it, that men walked on the moon!)

When you are old, sex is a story about the past. It's too far away to feel. Perhaps it's like that for those astronauts. They know they have been there, but they can no longer feel that beautiful distance, looking back to the blue of Earth.

She hasn't been able to reread his letters, or to give them away, although libraries have begged for them. How do you give away something that has been such an intimate part of you? After the Great War, she finally retrieved the ones that Isabelle, his sister, had kept. She wrapped and tied them all and put them at the bottom of a trunk. Letters were like the leaves of trees; they dried and turned brown and you couldn't put the green back in them, any more than you could feel the fire of sex in an old body.

She gets a ribbon-tied packet out from the trunk under the Egyptian rug in the salon, glances at the addresses—hers, his—the old ink, the youthful energy of the handwriting. She thinks, *I should not have lived so long. I should not be sitting here with these remnants of a distant time, trying to remember, trying to make sense of my life. Stirring the ashes of old fires. Because a boy wants to write a book about him. Because soon, in the way of things, I will die, and these will lie here. Until they are seen by people who will not understand what it was like to be in love in that year, 1913, before the whole world caught fire and we became debris, remnants, ash.*

She won't look at them again. She shouldn't even have touched them, the strangely small envelopes with the archaic stamps and the looped brown handwriting, the simple addresses—quai Debilly, rue Cassini—and the names of foreign hotels, and the marks left by post offices and customs men, all the hands that had touched them between the writing of them and the arrival. In his handwriting: *My love, my life, my lover. I can't breathe without you. Take me in your arms against your heart, tell me again and again, I love you and I lose myself in you.*

What life gives, and takes back.

At last she puts the packet of them back in the trunk, and replaces the rug, bought when she was playing Pirandello in Cairo in the twenties and she and François took that trip up the Nile. The boy will be back soon. She goes to her front window and looks down into the street, where a van is trying to turn and blocking the traffic, and somebody has already started to shout and wave his arms. It's autumn and the leaves are beginning to crinkle and turn, because it's been a hot, dry summer, this summer of her ninety-ninth year. She feels exhausted. Her rhythms of life have been confused, these last few days. She has her habits: solitude, television, a glass of whisky at six. It's a taste she picked up in England—the old person's drink, keeps your extremities warm. She usually eats a light, late supper, watches a little television, Bernard Pivot on *Apostrophes*, or an old film, lets the dog, Québéfi, out into the courtyard for a last time, goes to bed after midnight. Her sleeping habits are still those of a lifetime in the theatre. The dog sleeps on her feet, his black Pekinese face buried in his tail, curled like an ammonite. Her last dog. She shouldn't have got a male. They are more temperamental; this one is horribly jealous. When Sebastian comes back, she'll shut him in the bedroom again.

Time has been kind to her. Her relationship to it is unlike other people's, because here she is, nearly a hundred years old, shrunken, tiny, still fairly healthy in spite of all the aches and pains and sudden outgoings of the tide; still alive, still incomprehensibly alive after nearly a whole century, in a world in which everything has changed. She is a dinosaur, a fossil. And she was the lover of Henri Fournier, whom nobody has been able to forget.

His book: Was it a great book? She has no means of knowing. It was for so long a sort of palimpsest, a magical object for her after his death, its pages fingered soft, their edges blurred, one episode flowing into another, the dream of it and the reality, the story and what she had filled in herself. These days, do people read it? The boy said there was interest in it in England. French schoolchildren have had to read it for decades. There have been films, a television version. But the essence of it seems to escape, again and again; nobody seems able to pin it down.

A tall boy walks into a country schoolroom and everything changes. Life, and the story, begins.

The truth is, she thinks, that when somebody walks into a room who will change your life, everything is transformed. And, when that person is gone, nothing will go back to how it was. The devastation is total.

Sebastian Fowler has walked into her room, and will soon leave it, a young man she has only known for a few days. What if she were to give young Seb the opportunity he needs? What if the letters are only of marginal interest to the public, but more importantly, matter to this young man and herself, today, here, in the present, a link between them so powerful that it will never be forgotten? An old feeling of excitement begins to build in her; when you are very old, you don't feel excited, because excitement is about a future, and you don't have one, just a succession of days, then a sudden stop. But the feeling of pleasure and yes, excitement, is back, like warmth and movement coming back to a cold limb.

III.

21.

Seb has been deeply involved in reading for two days. He puts down the last page of Fournier's last manuscript. Then he turns back to confront the first page. *THIS IS NOT TO BE PUBLISHED* is written there like a "Keep Out" sign. What does it mean? He didn't want it published as it was, because it wasn't finished, because he wasn't able to make his mind up about an ending, because he didn't have time? Or, because he didn't want his family to take control of this book if he was killed? Because he knew he might die, but still hoped that he would come home to finish the novel?

Seb sighs out loud. The book itself isn't yet a book; it has no form and no evident structure. Perhaps it was simply Fournier's pride as a writer that made him want it to remain unpublished: he knew it was, in its present state, no good. Whatever the reason, it can't be published. The best he can do for it is to find an archive that will pay Isa some money for it. Would the Bibliothèque Nationale take it? Probably. He feels tired and discouraged, just having to think about it. *Henri,* mon vieux, *you made a mess of this. Isn't it nearly time for lunch?*

Yet—he turns back to it for a moment—there's the page where Fournier describes the dark girl with the gleaming teeth and a voluptuous way of standing with one hip cocked and one foot before the other that brings her vividly to life. He studies the scrawl in the margin: *I seem to have arrived in the deep country of a live soul.* The girl, whose name changes from Laurence to Emilie and then back again, is the one live thing in this confusing jumble of text. The young man and she make love, and listen to a nightingale from his bedroom window. She knows about birds, he doesn't; she's a country girl, he a soldier. He looks from his window across to where a scrap of red curtain hides the window of the gypsy caravan where she lives. Whatever the narrator is feeling, it was the writer, Fournier himself, who was evidently in love.

Seb thinks, *I'm onto something here. But, what?* He looks up, and out, from where he sits, hunched at the little table. Swallows flit across the window, diving between the roofs. Or are they swifts? Or even house martins? He wants to ask Annie, who knew about birds, and walked about when on holiday with a bird book and binoculars, exclaiming. But, she isn't going to tell him even this simple fact. The processes of grief, he thinks, must be different for everyone who mourns, simply because every missing person, every lost love is unique. Some know birds and yoga and how to tell the worth of various weights of Kashmiri silk. Everyone lives differently in the world. Everyone who is left grieves differently. There can be no one way to do this. He stares out of the window and the diving birds like dark shards in the light soar close to the windows and eaves. Swallows, yes, are the ones who make nests in eaves. So do house martins. Swifts do not. The process will take its own time. It moves through him like a waking dream, taking him to places in his mind that it seems he has never before visited.

"Sébastien!" A voice from downstairs that is not Isa's. "Do you want to eat?"

Chloé. He sticks his head out. Ah, the relief of it. "In a minute, thanks!"

The two women are taking turns to feed him. He guesses that Chloé is creating those buttery smells in the kitchen to woo him to her side of the argument about the house. Feed the man, and he'll do what you ask of him. She's apparently decided to make up for the tepid coffee and burnt toast. He goes sloppily downstairs in his sandals. These days, these days since last winter, his moods change abruptly, in ways he's never felt before. He's exhausted, then alert; angry, then sad; forgetful of things he knows perfectly well; with other people he hears himself being abrupt, even rude. The rudeness comes from fatigue, from the effort that sociability costs. But with Chloé, rudeness is hardly an issue, she's so good at it herself.

She's in blue-jean cutoffs that show her muscular legs. She wields a heavy iron pan to slide an omelette out onto his plate, a perfect folded semicircle of deep yellow, with parsley flecks. "Start. I'm just going to do mine. Help yourself to wine."

He does. He has not been so well fed for months. In fact, apart from the few dinners provided for him by well-meaning friends, he has almost forgotten about food. It was too hard to make himself cook in a kitchen where Annie and he had shared chores side by side, to sit down at a table alone, without her presence opposite. He's eaten, when he's had to, furtively. Standing up, even. Fast food that had never existed in their house before, while vegetables rotted in the fridge. Cereal, in the middle of the night. Coffee, and yes, the lure of alcohol. Too many late-night trips to the practically named Grog Shop at the end of his street.

Now, he is offered eggs from the local farm, salad from the garden, green beans, apricots, bread, a jug of wine, little round sooty cheeses that look as if they have been dipped in ash. Last night, with Isa, there was *civet de lapin*. He begins to eat, happy to be entertained by whatever Chloé comes up with, because it will not be about himself or his altered life.

Her agenda comes with the cheese, and a refilled glass of wine. "Maman's off seeing the real estate guy. That's why I'm here. I told you what she's planning, didn't I?"

"To sell the house, you said."

"Well, it's out of the question. She's mad. Can you imagine wanting to sell this place?"

"Well, no. Not unless she badly needs the money."

"Well, the money is under her nose."

"You mean, the manuscript?"

"Of course. It must be worth a stack. You could tell her. She won't listen to me."

"Most academic institutions don't have much money."

"But it could be auctioned! Someone's bound to want the second novel, aren't they? The one nobody knew even existed? I'm seriously tempted to get in touch with the Hôtel Drouet and find out how much it might fetch at auction."

She cuts a piece of cheese, carves more bread, the knife slicing inward to her chest as she holds the big loaf to her; the archaic gesture of mothers of large families. She brushes crumbs from her moss-green T-shirt. Again, her breasts. He looks away.

"More bread? We've some apple tart, if you'd like. Sorry, I didn't want to drag you into all this, but there's nobody I can talk to here. People are so weird about money. You can have absolutely none and still hang on to your crumbling inherited house and keep your self-respect, but talk about selling out for money and you've had it. Though of course people are doing it all the time. The whole area is being bought up by foreigners. Russians, mostly, though the English still seem to be here in force as well."

"What would you do, if it were yours?"

"Well, it is mine. In French law—you know, the Napoleonic Code—the inheritance is from parent to child; so in a sense it's mine already. I want to live here. Keep horses. You know I'm staying over at Martin the groom's place? He's always been a friend. It's better than being here, the way things are. But yes, I'd teach riding. Maybe have kids like the ones from the school I teach in, to stay here, get to know horses. I'll quit my job. I'll leave Paris. I hate living in a tiny apartment and having to spend hours in the metro each day and work in a school that's little more than a prison to keep kids off the streets. I'll do something good with it. But she can't see it. She doesn't trust me. She mixes me up with my father. She just can't get it, that I sometimes have good ideas. Sorry, I get upset about it."

He sees her sniff back tears. She scrubs her face with her napkin. "It's just so—unbelievable. Selling this place, which we'd never, ever get back. It would be gone forever. You might as well sell your body, in my view. You know, Sébastien? It's not your fault, it's not fair to involve you. You're only the hired gun."

"Well, I guess hired guns are hired to do something, fire the thing at some point?"

"Yeah, look, for God's sake don't tell her I talked to you, eh?"

"Okay. I'm still reading the manuscript."

"What's it like? Is it any good?"

"It's good in the way he couldn't help being good. In the descriptions and the insights that were part of him, that he let out almost in spite of himself. A lot of it's quite ordinary, then there's a flash of genius. He was on a search for purity. He was looking for a woman like that. But really, he's drawn to something and someone quite different."

"Huh. I'm not much of a reader, really. But I think men have the weirdest ideas about women, and such a lot of the stuff they write is kind of obsessed with that. I mean, who the hell is pure? After about three years old, I mean. And God, what a bore a totally pure person would be."

"You could look at it another way—purity like a good wine is pure, you know, not adulterated, not mixed with anything else. Or like this bread."

"Organic, you mean?"

"Sort of. There's another word."

"*Bio? Trafiqué. Non-trafiqué.* A person who's just themselves. I see what you mean, yeah. A sort of *appellation d'origine contrôlée* person, like wine?" She laughs. The end of the table where they sit opposite each other is dotted with crumbs, smeared with cheese, stained by a few drops of wine spilled where hundreds of thousands of meals have been eaten; knives left their marks in the wood; people who are now dead sat arguing, talking, silent. Light from the yard comes in through the deep window, falls across the table and the floor in a long stripe. This particular moment: the end of lunch, a shared joke, the afternoon yawning around them already, these stone walls holding in cool air, the heat outside making the countryside flat, nearly shadowless.

"Well. I should get back to work."

"Coffee? I'm making some. And a piece of chocolate?"

"Great."

She gets up, scraping her chair on the flagged floor. Carries plates to the sink, runs in hot water. Begins the preparations for making coffee, a small Italian pot this time, just enough for two espressos. She glances at him over her shoulder. "Don't worry about it. I just had to get it off my chest."

"Okay." But something has shifted in her; she no longer sounds angry.

"Well," he says, sensing the rashness as he speaks, "I'll do what I can, though it may not be much. I do see why you don't want to lose it. Thanks for telling me."

"You're welcome." The ironic grin is back, the little shrug. "Warn me when the gun's going to go off, won't you?"

"Chloé, do you know if there are nightingales around here still?"

"Nightingales? Of course. But only in May or June, you probably won't hear them now. And only in the evening or at night. Why?"

"Something in Fournier's book."

"Ah. Romantic, eh."

When he looks back at her before leaving the room, he sees what she reminds him of: she has flung herself down on the old couch and lounges there on her left side, her left elbow propping her slant and her head raised to look at him, in the exact pose of an Etruscan sculpture on a funeral urn. Her nose and lips, the faint smile that isn't quite a smile, and now the pose shows it to him. Her father must have come from that part of Italy, his ancestors those specialists in dissecting entrails and predicting futures, skilled horsemen whose civilization the Romans had conquered city by city without remorse.

Seb thinks, *Careful, you are a widower, not in your right mind, not a young man either, and she's doing it deliberately. Watch your step.*

In the late afternoon, he goes downstairs for a breath of air after his hours indoors. Swallows—yes, these are swallows, blue-black, arrowy—skim the walls and grass of the courtyard. The walls breathe out heat. The sky is still a hard near-white. Only the tips of the branches of the lime tree move. Chloé's car is still here. She's in the yard, apparently packing stuff into it. She stands close to him, opens her hand, palm up, as if to a horse. "Wild strawberries. Want some?"

"I thought you'd gone."

"Making the most of her not being here. There's some stuff I need."

He stands close to her. In her brown hand, the little grains of dark red, specked with white.

"They grow all around here, look. Under the bench even."

He sees where they hide among their leaves between the stalks of the grasses. He takes one from her palm, tastes it, a small sharpness on the tongue.

"They're so good, and so small. Like essence of strawberry, wouldn't you say?"

He bends and picks a few, then holds them out on his palm to her.

She smiles and takes one. The orchestra of cicadas seems to be inside his head. The dry grass of the yard smells peppery, where it has been cut: a hay smell mixed with nettles and sage.

"I have to go." She waves a hand at her car. *"A bientôt."*

He walks across the yard once she has gone, smells the dry vegetable scent of the air, hears the distant gurgle of the river, sees the shapes of the cut white stone against the dark red of the roofs, and the way pale walls curve into the distance, trees growing against them dropping their pools of shade. He can see why she so wants to keep the place. Perhaps her flirtatiousness is simply to keep him on her side. He stands still to watch a bee creep into the flower of a hollyhock, between yellow fronds. Place is not a part of people these days, or people are not connected to place. They fly over the earth, rush from one place to another. Nobody stops to watch bees. You can't see this bee on Google Earth, or from a plane, any more than you can hear the close rustle of the pale stalks of standing corn when a breeze moves through them toward sunset. Or the birds that call from the dense woods.

The cicada sounds, the deep heat, the stillness of the afternoon. Chloé, her grimy hands, her intensity. That flicker of physical interest that he thought he would never experience again. He feels at once young—the young man he was—and incredibly ancient, as if he has lived through all of history and seen it fail.

22.

Their journeys this year were across the shrinking map of France: Paris to Cambo, Mirande to Paris, the Sologne to Mirande. Trains and paved roads made the journeys shorter; he marched with his men in formation, bivouacked, shouldered arms, preparing for a conflict that never came; she followed Claude to Cambo, came back from England to Trie and to Paris, played in theatres in the provinces, Reims, Lyon, Bordeaux, Marseille. A time of telephones and telegrams and communication, of love, of business, of changing plans. Where horses had galloped long distance, where carriages had foundered in the mud of country roads, there was now the railway, linking places and people, making the remote accessible, and at last, uniting lovers with ease.

The train that had crossed most of France was bringing him back to her. It was a late train from Paris, arriving in Bayonne at nine thirty on this August night. She so longed to see him that she'd left the house far too early, and rather than wait in a smoky station waiting room, she'd asked the driver to stop the car in Biarritz.

Pauline walked the empty beach still marked by all the little hollows and hills made by families camping out there in the sand, places where people had walked, sat, picnicked. She imagined children with buckets and spades, old men in deck chairs, donkey rides, the whole traffic of the day. She walked along the sea's edge and sat down on cool sand. She watched the full moon rise, balancing the round yellow face of the casino clock at the end of the pier. Sand trickled between her fingers, an impersonal hourglass; the moon began pink, like a balloon, and then hardened and darkened as it rose over the water. The gold path of the moon on water and the prosaic white path toward the casino clock. The hands of the clock moved on toward the time when she would be in his arms; it also moved toward death. But here was the moon, bigger than the clock face, as she sat with her knees up on the cooled sand to watch it rise. Perhaps it was all worth it, perhaps life was such that happiness was greater than death and could outrun all physical limits and teach a lunar immortality?

Claude's chauffeur, Pierre Albert, waited for her with the car, smoking as he walked up and down on the promenade, his hat tipped back, one hand at his back as if to ease stiffness, a man with an unexpected moment of liberty. She walked up the beach, climbed back into the car, sand in her shoes, the moon behind her and in her mind, a lantern over the sea. They reached the station at Bayonne in time. He must know, Pierre Albert, exactly what was going on. She thought, *We live our lives under the eyes of people who are paid to be discreet. People who drive us, cook for us, keep houses open and clean for us, bring us breakfast in bed. Who have aches and pains and worries they never talk about. What do these people think?*

The long train came in, and there he was, her tall young man, leaping down onto the platform. She walked to meet him while the chauffeur waited and the porters moved to carry the luggage and wheel it on carts. He seemed to have so little luggage, just a bag he carried. She saw him move toward her on a long stride, leaning forward as if into a wind. They looked at each other unable to say a word. You. Oh, God who does not exist! He was serious, intent, showing no signs of joy; they walked together toward the waiting car. Only later he whispered to her, their hands knotted together in the backseat as they were driven back to Cambo, "I was too terrified. I've been shaking all day. I thought you might not be there."

"Of course I would be there."

"No, no, Pauline, there's no 'of course' about it. Don't let's ever take this for granted."

It was the first time that they had been alone together since June, and the first time at Cambo. She had told him when Claude would be away, in London. He said to her, "I want all the time there is with you."

The bedroom windows swung inward and the shutters, painted green, pushed outward to fasten back against the pitted ochre wall of the house. The window framed the foothills of the Pyrenees. The August sky came down blue and hard at midday, retreated into rose and gold at sunset, then turned greenish, cooler, as they waited for the first stars. She was his wife. He said so. He rolled her between coarse linen sheets. Their bodies were brown and white, piebald with sun. She could not get enough of him, his skin, the grassy smell of his hair, the sweat after he'd been running, the salt of him on her body; all the precipitations, the juices, the alchemy they made. Salt, sun, hot water pouring into the claw-foot tub, the rough rub of towels, their skins a little raw against the scratch of sun-dried sheets.

They drove to San Sebastián for the bullfight, and she hated the cruelty of it, yet enjoyed his excitement at the blood in the sand, the yelling crowd. He adored the bullfighters, the matadors: Borubita, Machaquito, El Gallito. On the way home, that first time, he said, "It's terrible, but you have to see it, don't you agree?" Why, when there was always too much blood spilled in the world? It was something he had to face, that left him nearly speechless, aroused in a way she could not share. It was like his passion for sports of all kinds, and aviation. Bugatti, Panhard, Blériot, his gods. The lyricism of speed and flight. Yet it was more. This was blood, and murder. It was, she would think later, closer to war; but a war that was ancient, not modern, a war of single combat, honor, duels to the death.

"Pauline, I'm not sure that any woman can really understand it. But you can see, can't you, how beautiful it is, even while being terrible?"

"No, Henri, it's a contradiction I don't think I'll ever understand."

Claude would not be back till mid-September. From London, he was going on to Berlin. She never asked him what all these trips were for, but Henri thought he was trying to borrow money.

He drove Claude's big open Delaunay. She was in the front seat beside him, a scarf tying her hat on, its ends whipping in the wind. The trees at the side of the road passed in a fast flicker of shade. The white roads of France, dusty and narrow, leading into the interior. He was taking her home, to the Sologne, to visit his family.

They stopped to spend a night in Tours in an old coaching inn, L'Auberge de la Poste. There was vegetable soup and then a ragout, with red wine. He dipped his bread like a peasant, explaining, "This is how we do it at home." He mopped his mouth with his napkin and grinned at her. Up a winding staircase, there was a wide room with a bumpy floor, low ceiling beams, and a big sagging bed with a goose-feather quilt. Like falling into a well, he said, a well of tenderness. They were adrift in the middle of France with only the ringing of the cathedral bells in the morning to wake them. She turned in his arms, finding him again. It was the longest sleep they had ever had together. Their faces close on the stuffed bolster, the coarse linen of the sheet tenting them, she saw his happiness and dared to recognize her own.

At the house at La Chapelle in the Sologne, Henri's mother and grand-mother were waiting. Maman Barthe as he called her, seventy-three years old in her widow's black dress and bonnet, stretched out her arms to him. "Henri, my dear boy, how wonderful. And this must be the famous Madame Simone?"

"Just Simone, please, Madame. My real name is Pauline." She took the cool hand, curtsied slightly.

"I'm delighted to meet you, Madame."

Henri said, "Maman's worried that all this isn't going to be grand enough for you."

Marie-Albanie Fournier smiled. "Well, to tell you the truth, I was a little worried. Henri, you didn't even wipe your feet. Look, you're bringing mud in everywhere." She leaned to kiss Pauline on both cheeks. They had met at the theatre in Paris, when Henri had bought tickets for his parents to see *The Secret*, but it was different meeting here. What had Henri told her? What did she know? If she wondered where Pauline's husband was, she did not say.

Henri simply laughed, as if this were all easy, and pushed everybody in front of him out into the garden. "So we can all be in the mud, and it won't be a problem. Sorry, Maman. And as for being grand, she isn't at all grand, you'll see. Come on, let's go down to the river before the light goes."

He led the way through the gate and across the grass, down to the riverbank. Linked arm in arm, Pauline in the middle, Henri's mother striding and girlish beside her, the three of them walked down to the river and watched ducks upending, dragonflies flitting across the surface, a heron standing on the far bank. The river water was brown, curling back white where it moved over stones. Weeds streamed flat at its center.

So this is where your book takes place, this is your home, your country, the place to which you will always return?

The long day was ending. Bats flew in the twilight. Lights flickered in the windows of small houses in the village. A dog barked and rattled its chain and then was suddenly silent, as if someone had thrown food

145

to it. They walked in single file now, Henri in front, up a path fringed by long grasses. He snipped the heads off the grasses with his fingers and sent the seed heads spinning into the air. Behind Pauline, his mother called out, laughing, "Wait for me! I can't see where I'm going!"

A first star came out. "Look!" he called back to her. "It's showing us the way!" Back at the grandmother's house, they all sat down at the table under the grandmother's eye as she served the soup. Pauline thought, *I have arrived here at last, in the childhood, the family I never had.* She drank her soup in the silence in which the family ate, wine poured into small, thick glasses, a careful handing of bread and salt.

"I'm surprised Isabelle isn't here," Henri said, "and Jacques. I thought they would come to meet us."

"Jacques had to be in Paris," his mother said, "and Isabelle thought it better not to come without him. I'm sure you'll all meet up again quite soon."

Pauline thought, *They did not want to see us. Or rather, they did not want to see Henri with me.* She glanced across at Henri, but he hadn't reacted to what his mother said.

"Why is Bébelle not here?" the grandmother asked, cupping her ear to hear.

"Her husband is busy, Maman. She has to stay with him."

"Jacques does nothing but work," Henri said. "Paris in August? What is he thinking of?"

"And you, Madame Simone," the grandmother asked. "You have quite a grand house, I suppose?"

At that moment, she disliked her grand house and everything about it. She wanted to be like them, to be one of them: to be accepted simply here as Henri's wife. The trouble was, she was not Henri's wife, and at present there was no way she could be. She lowered her face over her soup bowl. "Well, it's large, but actually I prefer smaller houses. They are more comfortable."

Henri said, "It's pretty grand, *grand-mère*, but it isn't half as nice as here."

The grandmother looked satisfied. "He's a good boy," she said to no one in particular.

She slept in a small bedroom under the eaves, and he on the sofa in the salon, his feet sticking out over its end. The next day he took her to the schoolhouse at Épineuil, where his parents had run the village school. It was here that Seurel and Meaulnes had first appeared in the world. Up in the attic he had first read *Robinson Crusoe* and his characters had found the leftover fireworks. "Do you want to go up? It might be rather dusty." She followed him up narrow, steep stairs and he brushed cobwebs from her hair.

Life and fiction were joined here; she was in it with him, watching the snow fall, waiting to discover what Meaulnes's secret was, listening for the whistle from the forest; and she was with her lover, the actual man who sucked a cut finger he had sliced with a piece of sharp grass pulled to make a whistle in his cupped hands.

"I was always late for school, because all I had to do was come downstairs! So I read, up to the last possible minute. Here, do you know how to do this? It's how boys make whistles. I'll show you."

They walked close, blowing at blades of grass held vertically between their thumbs.

"This is a place I wanted to show you." He led her to the edge of the forest, where they walked on sandy soil leaving footprints, and he pushed low fir branches and brambles aside to let her pass. There was a clearing, and several slanting stones set in coarse grass. The place was so wild and abandoned that she didn't see at once that it was a little cemetery.

"Here's where we'll lie together," Henri said, "side by side, in our last sleep. Like that night in Tours, only forever. Close as we were then."

Rosalind Brackenbury

She thought then, *Do you really equate death with a sound sleep after making love to me?* She followed him through the long grass. They stood together, looking down. The letters on the stones were blurred with moss and lichen.

"Believe me, it's as easy to get across the divide between life and death as it is to push open this gate."

Pauline said nothing in reply. How could he speak so lightly? Fear lay hidden here, a scythe in the grass. She just let him push open the sagging gate for her and walked through. He clicked the wooden latch on the gate shut, once they were both through; she heard it close.

23.

Outside the house, fields deprived of their ancient hedges stretch into vast blond waves, the faces of sunflowers like people peering to see over each other's heads in a crowd. The bed of the river, water rippling a shallow passage over boulders, its waterfalls, its places where black sticks turn on the current and small animals scuttle in mud. The owl at night. The heron flying upstream. The shivering leaves of poplars. The sheen of heat. *La canicule*, heat every day for two, three weeks. Cracked earth, in spite of the rainy spring. Harvests, hurried in. A country that holds them lightly, and will let them all go, because for centuries people have come and gone, been born and died, farmed this land, fished these rivers; troops have marched across it, both French and German; children born here have gone to the cities and come back. For centuries, there has been this afternoon summer silence. Decisions made, not made. Slight movements. Small changes. Sleep, after eating. A single person standing in the yard, calculating the time from the angle of the sun. It could be anyone, at any time in history.

From the window, he sees that it's Chloé. The lime tree, the angle of the roof, the slant of the light, five o'clock already. The red car, its doors open to let air in. She gives him a small wave. He goes down, quiet past sleeping Isa, her head tipped back on the couch, her mouth slightly open. Out into the hammer of heat in the yard, heat that radiates from the stone walls and will go on doing so long after the sun has moved off them. He gets in beside her and watches Chloé's firm brown hands with their dirty nails on wheel and gears, her feet in short leather riding boots on the controls, as she twists her head to back out of the yard and turn the car in the space between the low wall and the tree. She smiles at him. "Had a good siesta? Maman's still out for the count, as you saw." It was slightly too conspiratorial to tiptoe past sleeping Isa, and he laughs with the tension.

She accelerates, and the car bounces between walnut and plum trees, yellow fruit squashed on the ground. He smiles back. She reaches across and pats his knee, just before the car leaps forward onto the main road. He decides to ignore the brown hand's pat, and the sensation that goes with it.

She stops the car beside a Romanesque church on a small hill just outside a village, ten or so kilometers on. "There are some wall paintings you ought to see."

They go into speckled gloom, once she has pushed the inner door with its felted swish. The place smells of earth and incense. At first he can't see a thing. But she takes his arm, leads him toward the altar: the paintings are all on the walls of the narthex. "Look, it's the Last Judgment. See, all the people having a merry old time over here, and on the other side, the judgment."

The medieval perspectives, or lack of them: Legs of people and of horses drawn like concertinas, piled upon each other. A couple embracing. An advance, as far as he can see, into battle. Then a feast, with goblets. A man with an incredibly long trumpet, another strumming a sort of banjo. The faces are all identical, as if the artist had drawn, over and over again, his own face, finding none other to copy. The men wear little short skirts, droopy hose, and pointed shoes. The warriors have brisk haircuts, pointed helmets.

"But, look," Chloé says, "look at the Judgment, you see, there isn't any hell?"

He goes closer to the opposite wall, to look. The colors are the same: dusky pinks and reds, with worn midnight blues here and there like the cracked bowls in Isa's kitchen. All the people seem to be ascending; there is no downward topple, no demonic clutching at legs and other body parts. The painter has simply not depicted the descent into hell.

The church is the church of St. Martin of Tours, who gave half his cloak to a beggar, thinking that he might be Jesus in disguise. St. Martin is on the south wall on his horse, the beggar in his skimpy loincloth on the ground in front of him. One man reaches down, the other up, and the piece of cloth changes hands.

"Why half his cloak?" Seb asks. "Surely he should have given him the whole thing?"

A deep crack runs across the wall, dividing the saint from the beggar. Some of the painted plaster has flaked off. But the handing over of the half cloak, its folds ruched like a ballet skirt, is clear.

"Apparently it would have been dishonorable for him as a soldier to have ridden away without a cloak at all. Also, quite sensible, wouldn't you say, to give half, if you weren't entirely sure that the beggar was Jesus? Hedging his bets. Half for himself, half for Jesus. Maybe that was how the painter saw it, the man who couldn't bring himself to depict people going to hell."

She stands with her head thrown back, looking up. The pure line of her throat, the black curls at her neck. He smells her fresh sweat. They wait together in front of a mystery, that of the unknown medieval artist. Here, in this grainy dark, she has brought him to see something that she wants him to share; perhaps this is all she wants.

"There are churches of St. Martin all over, here. He was a very popular saint, as well as a local one."

"Why do you think there isn't any hell?"

"I don't know. I guess the painter didn't believe in it. It's quite a relief, don't you think? I always feel uncomfortable looking at those flames and little pitchforks. I think they might well be there for me."

"Were you brought up Catholic?"

"Oh, sure. School was all about that. Hellfire was a reality. I worried about it all the time. You know, being a sinner." She laughs. "Well, just being a woman was bad enough. They taught us that. But at least my parents weren't religious. My father was an atheist, so at least I didn't get any lectures from him. He was a major sinner, my papa."

"Do you see him, ever?"

She takes a step back, looks at him with narrowed eyes. "Yes, but you mustn't say anything to my mother. I think she'll hate him forever for leaving her for a rather stupid, much younger blonde."

"I won't. It's your business, anyway. What's he think about the house, her selling it, all that?"

"He doesn't have any say in it. He never did. It isn't his. Come on, let's go, if you've had enough of St. Martin."

The saint leans from his saddle; the beggar reaches up. Luckily, coincidentally, the soldier saint happens to have guessed that the naked man on the floor is actually Jesus; but he's realistic enough only to give away half his cloak.

"Why did you want me to see this?"

"Thought you'd be interested. You strike me as the kind of guy who'd do the same thing. You know, give half of something. Not go the whole hog."

"Well," Seb says, "whatever you think of him, he did become a saint."

She closes the door behind them. Sun strikes them with its fierce heat as they step out of the shadow. Plane trails slice through the sky. Swallows dip around them, aiming for the church doors. "You have to shut the doors properly, or the swallows come inside. Where to now? You want to go for a drink or something?"

"No, really, I've work to do," he says, and regrets it at once as she shrugs and turns toward the car.

"You're married, aren't you?" She turns the key in the ignition.

A sharp pinging pain begins in his ear—or is it the scream of crickets? "My wife died. Not long ago."

"I'm sorry. You do seem kind of sad."

"I am sad," he says. "Sometimes incredibly sad. But I'm less sad here than I was at home. Too many memories, you know?"

"Yeah, I can sort of imagine. What was she like?"

"A beautiful person. It wasn't just me who thought so. She was very full of life, always. The last person you could imagine dying that young."

"Was it sudden?"

"Very sudden. We had no idea. She'd had headaches, that was all."

Chloé turns the car and a cloud of dust flies up. "So, it's better being here?"

"Yes, because there's nothing of hers. I don't open a book and see her name in it, or a letter with her handwriting on it falling out of somewhere. I don't have to be on my guard."

"Hmm. I see." She seems to have slotted the information away, and remains unperturbed.

She turns the car onto the main road. "D'you know, Maman really hasn't had anybody in her life seriously since my father left her all those years ago? Don't you think that's sad? It's better to have had someone who loved you and died, than to have had someone who simply walked away."

Seb remains silent on whether abandonment is worse or better than sudden death. "Yes, I think I've been lucky. It's hard when that person dies, but you know you've lived a life of love, and that's what counts, in the end."

"So, do you think you could ever love somebody again?"

"I hope I do," he says, as firmly as he can. "You get into a habit of loving. It's a hard one to stop."

Rosalind Brackenbury

She says no more, but moves her hands to the top of the wheel, the thumbs sticking up, her expression intent. She seems to be thinking about something other than the way back to Les Martinières; but he sits back, feeling suddenly tired, as if he has delivered himself of more than he wanted to. *St. Martin, saint of half-hearted men,* he thinks. The sort of guy, she said, who wouldn't go the whole hog. She sees him, Seb, that way. But who and what else can he be, now? And, what is the challenge she's given him? He closes his eyes for a moment as the car bounces down over the ruts between the walnut trees and then jolts to a stop in the yard.

24.

September 1975, Paris

In Paris, the Indian summer goes on. Morning sun turns the side of the building opposite golden; she has opened the shutters in the salon to look out. She watches the light move down the walls, spread like spilled paint toward the ground. The world lit one more time, and she here for one more day to see it. She loves the light of September, the glow of the city in autumn, even if by the end of October the leaves will be wet in the gutter and the trees nearly bare. A clock strikes; then the bells of the church across the street begin to ring. Markets will be set up already in the streets, people already choosing and weighing and carrying home their vegetables, cheeses, loaves of bread. The mornings of Paris. She knows them by heart. *As you age,* she thinks, *you take more and more of the world inside you, you swallow and digest it, it becomes part of you; so not being able to move around it easily matters less.* She sits down to await the footsteps across the courtyard, on the stairs, the tap at her door: someone coming. Today, it isn't just someone; it's Sebastian. Last week, he wasn't in her life; now, he fills it. In a few days, he will be gone again. Is there always something more to lose?

Normally she gets up at noon, as she has all her life, but it wouldn't do for the boy to arrive and find her still in bed. She wakes from a doze in her chair to the barking of the dog. She goes to let the boy in, hoping she looks all right. The breakfast tray, with her coffee half-drunk and the crusts of bread and honey, gives her away. Did she really fall asleep again in the middle of her breakfast? She covers it over with a white napkin. She fluffs her hair. She opens the door to him and the cool air of morning.

"Sorry about the dog. He's extremely jealous of all other males. Did you have a good evening? Did you walk? Did you get to the Tuileries? The Palais-Royal?"

"Oh, yes, great. I walked miles. Aren't these dogs supposed to live in emperors' sleeves?"

"Well, being Chinese isn't quite what it was. So they have become quite uppity. Social dislocation, you know. Ignore him. I'll shut him in the bedroom if he's a nuisance. Québéfi, lie down! Perhaps before we shut him in, you would take him out for me for a minute; he might want to do his business. Downstairs, go through the courtyard, and at the back, there's an iron gate and a few trees, and a wall with ivy. Notice the stone lions while you're down there. They're smiling."

"Fine. Come on, what's your name, Chinese boy, time for a men's excursion."

He goes down, the dog reluctant at his heels. He crosses the court-yard to the overgrown wall at its back, where there are, yes, two smiling stone lions. He lights a Gauloise and smokes half of it, grinds the rest out on the gravel. He can tell she's imagining him down here, even if she can't see him. This morning he's a little edgy, feels the need to escape her attention. The Pekinese lifts a furry leg to pee, looking up at him with his squashed face and staring eyes. Seb comes back up the wide stairs, the dog clattering his claws as he scrambles ahead of him.

She lets him in. "Sit down, Seb. We've got time." Two days ago, she had wanted him to leave as soon as possible. Now, she dreads to see him go.

"I was worried I was late. I overslept. I couldn't tell what the time was. The clock in my room was wrong I think." He's feeling muddled this morning, as if an unremembered dream still has a hold on his waking life.

"Well, I even fell asleep over my breakfast!"

"Anyway, sorry if I'm late."

"Henri always used to arrive late for things, and he never knew what the time was either." She aims to console him, to calm him down, but mustn't, she thinks, overdo her likening him to Henri.

"Really?"

"Jacques Rivière told him he was going to be late for the war. That was a bad joke."

"Ouch. Yes." He accepts the coffee she has made.

Silence, while they muse together. She sits in her armchair; he's thrown himself down on her sofa. He asks her, "Did he talk to you about it?"

"The war?"

"I meant the book. But, yes, the war too."

"He'd nearly finished the book when we met. I was the first person to read it in its entirety. I sat by a fire and read it all night. I'll talk about the war later, if I can bear it."

"So you were his first reader? How amazing."

"And then we talked about it in the morning. I told him he was a genius. He laughed."

"How extraordinary to think of him not knowing."

"Actually, I think he knew. He was in his own way very sure of himself. For me, the sticking point was of course Yvonne de Galais. Or her real counterpart."

"I can imagine. Did you ever meet her?"

"Oh, dear me, no. The nearest I got to her was a letter she sent him on perfumed pink paper when he sent her a copy of the book. The real woman was called Yvonne de Quièvrecourt. She was there between us, at the beginning, a sort of perfect ghost, like someone who had died young. In reality, she was married with two children by the time the book came out. She haunted me to begin with, almost as much as she did him. This perfect blonde all in white. Imagine."

He says, "She wore a brown cloak in the book."

"Oh, yes, so she did. But I always imagined her in white, as he first saw her, the real Yvonne in Paris, when he was eighteen. I once did an interview with someone who asked me if I was the model for Yvonne de Galais. I said no, absolutely not."

"How bizarre that someone should think so, after all this time."

"The real damage, for me, was after his death, when the book became famous. Jacques and Isabelle insisted he'd always been in love with her, and that he was a kind of angelic creature who never knew physical love. They brought out a book called *Miracles*, a collection of very early things he'd written, with an introduction by Jacques. It's ancient history, but it did blight my life at the time. Not only had I lost him, but I'd lost any claim to his love, his serious intention to marry me, our plans for a future that never happened. It was like being wiped out. I couldn't even defend myself. I was too proud even to try."

"But now you can?"

"Well, now I think, truth will win. As it always will, in the end. I've no interest in trying to prove anything. Everyone would understand now that Yvonne was his muse, not his actual lover. He only ever saw her about three times, and they had the briefest of conversations, and then she married quite young, a naval officer. Anyway, I've outlived all of them, and now, nobody really cares."

"Oh," he says, "they do. People want truth. They want reality. They want to hear about a great love affair."

"Well, it was that, certainly. Even if a very short one. It has, however, filled my life."

"But you married, afterward."

"When I say it filled my life, I don't mean that I sat piously mourning him and refusing all happiness. No, that would have been an insult to him, almost as bad as Isabelle's version. He wanted me to be happy with François. I knew it, and I was. I had nearly thirty years of a very good marriage."

At this point in her life, the long years with François count more in a way than the brief flame of Henri. No, not more: it's simply that the calm companionship of those years has made her who she is now. Marriage is a container, when it works. Her affair with Henri was never that.

"No, it filled my life for that brief time, right up to the brim and overflowing, and when that has happened to you, you are not the same afterward."

"Is it rare," Seb asks, "that it happens? That kind of love?" He thinks, *How incredible to be able to talk of thirty years of this, thirty years of that.* Life, for some people, goes on so unbelievably long. And love. He wants to know, to be given a clue.

"I've no way of knowing. It happened to me."

"Everyone wants to believe in it."

"Yes, but in an easy, pain-free Technicolor version. Life is pain as well as happiness; that kind of love is—well, indescribable. Though I think it was Colette, always such a realist, who said that as a writer you should never say anything is indescribable because a writer's job is to describe it."

"Would it have been the same if he hadn't been a great writer?"

"I can't tell you. Writing was so much a part of him. He wrote all the time, letters, journals, postcards, jottings. It was like being with someone who was running after something he'd only just got in his sights. Like a hunter. Like going through a forest, holding your breath, to see what he saw, to listen for the slightest sounds, to smell something on the wind. The way a tree fell sideways. A pattern of light in a clearing. A scrap of red silk blowing against a window. You know? It was exciting, being with him. It was, as I say, like a sort of treasure hunt. Then you saw the scrap of red, the pattern of light, the leaning tree showing up in his writing, and it was like being in it with him, at the heart of the myth. But I make it sound all rather ethereal. He was also a very good lover."

Sebastian blushes, as Henri would have blushed, to hear it.

Watching him, hoping he isn't noticing, she thinks about male beauty. The line of cheek and chin, a sharpness to the set of the shoulders, muscle that swells like an apple under a shirt. Henri was such a sportsman— all those tennis games and rugby matches, as if like a young horse he could not stop himself from running about. Five-a-side in the gardens at Bagatelle on Sunday mornings, scrums in the Parc Montsouris. Tennis singles until he dropped, or his opponent did. A handball game called pelota that he and his friends borrowed from the Basques in Spain. His excitement over cars, airplanes, his passion for speed and flight. Even his passion for the bullfight. She thinks, *It was his beauty in motion that I loved; inside and outside, both.* The blood up just below the surface of his skin, after running; the way he flung himself down on the grass, legs spread, head tipped back to stare at the sky. What would he have been like as an old man, a very old man nearly as ancient as she is herself? She wonders at what might have been. Death changes all the tenses. But now, here it is again, that heedless energy: a beautiful young man flung down on her couch, unaware of himself, fine-tuned as a thoroughbred horse. And she is a very old woman, right at the end of her life, and she can look, and appreciate, and be grateful that he is here. He looks up at her and grins. "Lucky you, then."

A child with Henri's face.

"Yes, indeed. Lucky me."

25.

At her suggestion, Henri rented a small apartment with two rooms on the ground floor of a building on boulevard Arago. A *garçonnière*, as they were called: a bachelor apartment. He'd seen the "For Rent" sign as he was walking from rue Cassini toward the avenue des Gobelins to visit a bookshop one day. It was furnished with ugly furniture, but they didn't care. The bed creaked and the headboard banged against the wall, and when one of them arrived there alone to wait for the other, it felt cold and bleak till the fire was lit. When he waited for her, he would pull out his little black notebook and write, filling the page to its edges by writing sideways in the margins. She imagined him turning the little book sideways, looking up, smiling, scribbling again. When she waited for him, she felt the old chill of uncertainty creep over her: waiting on a bench, waiting in a room, waiting for adults to decide what to do with her; waiting for her life to begin. She could not help it: at last, she would poke the fire alight that he had laid the day before, blow on it, watch the small flame take and grow and hear the kindling begin to crackle. And then she'd hear his step outside, and his key in the lock, and he'd open the door and once again she would be in his arms.

"You!"

"Who else did you think it would be?"

Then, one late afternoon in October, he came in with a slim packet in his hand. The first copy of his novel. He handed it to her, watched while she unwrapped it. "Pauline, it's for you. My first reader. I'm so happy to be able to give it to you, my love." She took it, opened it—the book cracked a little as she flattened the pages, read his inscription. "Henri, this is wonderful, congratulations." Then, "Shall we read some to each other?" But he bent to kiss her, his face cold from the outside chill, his lips warm, and even the book was put aside.

Sometimes they missed each other. Each of them had a key. He wrote a note to her, *I knew you'd been here; the armchair was pulled up close to the fire, the ash was still warm, and there was a hairpin on the floor.* Like a detective, picking up clues.

When she went to meet him there, usually between five and seven in the late afternoon, she asked the chauffeur to drop her off on the avenue des Gobelins, and walked up Arago to the plain, anonymous little front door. When she left, she hailed a cab to go home. "Boulevard Arago" became their shorthand for lovemaking. Boulevard Arago made everything possible. They only had to write *B.A.* to know exactly what the other meant. Now, they no longer had to rely on Claude being out for the evening, or risk discovery.

Henri leaned back, put his feet up on the wall beside the fireplace, his long legs crossed. "This is the first place that I've ever had that's really mine. My home with you. Isn't it ironic that it's just a little rented nowhere of a place?"

She said, "I feel that too. All the houses I've lived in, and only here can I really feel at home."

She thought of her parents' house, with its chilly corridors, and Charles le Bargy's house on rue du Cirque, where she had lived in her own room like a small animal in a nest, eating patisserie in bed while her husband spent her money redecorating the whole place in oriental style, and then of Claude's houses, both here and at Trie, in which she lived apart from him, politely meeting him at mealtimes, watching him come and go. Houses for her had been traps of class and lovelessness, from which she had only wanted to escape. This little place in a poor neighborhood was only temporary, yet it was hers and Henri's, their own.

"Let's get rid of the furniture and rent it unfurnished," she said. "Then we can make it really like home."

"Yes, why not? Let's."

They asked the landlord to take the furniture out, and chose new things together; she let him pay, since his book was already beginning to make some money, and he was embarrassed at being paid by Claude while making love to her.

The trees on boulevard Arago grew darker with autumn rain. The leaves turned brown, fell into the gutters, and were trodden underfoot. Henri brought chestnuts in his pockets, from the garden at rue Cassini. Pauline bought dahlias and Michaelmas daisies from a woman at a street corner. In the little apartment, he knelt to light the fire while she drew new curtains across the shuttered windows. The chestnuts roasted and exploded in the grate, and they picked them red-hot from the coals and tossed them from hand to hand until they were cool enough to peel and eat. Their blackened fingers left smudged prints upon each other's skin.

The Prix Goncourt was to be decided in November. Léon Werth, Valéry Larbaud, and Alain-Fournier were the favorites. Henri—the youngest, the least known—was thought to have the best chance.

"The only problem is, the Goncourt judges will never choose a story written by a peasant that takes place deep in an unknown province of France."

"Henri, you aren't a peasant."

"Yes, I am, and that's what you like about me. My peasant hands, look. But they won't, not that lot, I can tell you. They don't know a hawk from a handsaw."

The day of the announcement, they were all having lunch at quai Debilly. A friend was to telephone Claude as soon as the news came through; Claude was listening for the telephone to ring in the library.

"If I get it, I'll give the money to my mother; she terribly wants to buy the little house next door to hers at La Chapelle. Five thousand would do that. She's so excited, already. But I shouldn't count on it, should I?" Henri chattered on, as he did when he was nervous.

"You will get it. Yours is the best book."

It was two o'clock already, when the telephone rang. None of them had touched their lunch. The door to the library opened, and Claude came out with a tightly rolled newspaper clenched in one hand and the other held in front of his face, moving his index finger from left to right as if cautioning a child. Pauline stared. What did he mean? Henri was white. Claude said, "It's all decided. There's no more hope. It's gone to a man called Marc Elder."

"No," she said.

"They make some bizarre choices, that's certain. A couple of years ago they could have had Apollinaire or Colette, and some outsider got it instead."

Pauline straightened her back and immediately set about the process of acceptance. The old habit, learned after Papa's death: after every loss, every failure, you accept, you move on, because you have to. Henri would go on to write yet more great books, he would be doing it all his life, the prizes would come, he would get his recognition. This book was just the beginning.

He said simply, "Maman will be disappointed."

It was not only Marc Elder who changed the mood of that winter. Claude sank deeper into bankruptcy and depression, and in spite of

Henri's efforts at bookkeeping—never his strong point—he could do nothing to save him. Henri added up the figures in Claude's bank account and tried to make them come out differently.

"Pauline, you'll have to grasp the nettle. This can't go on. You must ask him for a divorce. We're all on a knife edge." Henri was unusually brusque. She thought, *He's been shaken by the Goncourt going to somebody else, when his book is being talked about and written about all over Paris. He doesn't realize what goes into these prizes, the politics, the tit-for-tat. Who is Marc Elder, after all?*

"I'll do what I can. But it will finish him." *You mean,* she thought, *I have to do it now? Open this whole thing up to the world, lay us both bare to divorce, scandal, everything that will inevitably follow?*

"He knows now all he's ever going to know, I'm sure. And he has what's-her-name to go to."

"Fernande. But she'll drop him like a hot potato when she knows he's run out of money."

"But you can't go on protecting him."

She knew that she was also protecting herself—and Henri. But the cover was wearing thin. "I know. I'll try to find the right time."

Then they changed positions, and it was she who accused him of protecting Claude. "You can't go on working for him, Henri; he won't be able to pay you. It doesn't make sense."

"Pauline, divorce him. You have ample grounds. Then we can be married."

"But I don't want your family to be dragged into this. It would be awful for them."

"But if you divorce him for adultery, they won't have to. I'd be named only if he divorces you."

"All right, I'll think about it. Really, I will."

"I want to marry you. I want us to live together, and have children. I want nobody else in the way."

"I know, I know, my darling, I want that too."

He had told her of his dream: to live peacefully together in a cottage in the country and have children. But what of her life in the theatre? "It exhausts you," he had said, "it wears you thin. You could go on acting, of course, but do less." She thought then, *From a cottage in the country? With a string of children?* And knew then that the flaw was in their different visions of how their life together might be. Boulevard Arago was a better solution. Yet, she could not come out and say this. *I can't be your wife, Henri, not like that.* She did not want to say it. She did not want it even to be true.

One day in December, they found themselves alone at the house on quai Debilly. Claude had gone to Brest to try to sell some of his shipping interests.

"Henri, what about going to spend the weekend in Trie? I'm dying for some country air."

"What if Claude comes back?"

"He won't. Not till Monday. Anyway, if he does, he probably won't care."

So they went to Trie for the weekend, both exhausted with lack of sleep. It was surprisingly warm. The sun was the pale sun of December and the days were short, but the air was pure and clear. In silence, they walked together round the great lawn, as they had done so often before becoming lovers. His arm was around her waist. They breathed together and walked in step. Up and down in the vegetable garden and along the muddy banks of the stream. Nobody was there, not even the old gardener. He'd left small dead animals pinned out on a fence, she saw, like pieces of leather dried in differing degrees by the wind. Moles, weasels, a tiny shrew. What were they for?

"To warn the others," Henri said. "That's what they do in the country. It's like a sort of charm."

The small dried bodies hung out on the fence looked barbaric to her. "So much goes on that we don't know about."

Henri said, "Yes, the countryside is full of its own laws and habits. Scarecrows, boggarts, even witches and goblins." He sounded quite unconcerned. "Look." The scarecrow in the vegetable patch was wearing old clothes of Claude's, with a white scarf both stained and jaunty around its neck. A twig stuck out through the hat that Claude must have once, long ago, worn in summers on the coast. "The old gardener got him in to do his work for him, it seems."

To see a parody of Claude standing there staring at them with onion eyes was unnerving. "Let's go back."

"You don't like meeting Claude's double in the vegetable patch?"

"Well, do you? It feels as if he's spying on us even though he's in Brest."

"Ah, maybe that's the real Claude, and the double is in Brest. But this one can't budge out of the mud, look. He has to watch us enjoying ourselves but he can't move a whisker to follow us."

"Henri. Don't."

"Sorry. You're very sensitive today. We'll go back, make a good fire, draw the blinds and the curtains, and he won't be able to see a thing, poor scarecrow."

They were about to go into the house when Henri noticed a garden seat set out on the terrace, put there to protect it from autumn rain, and they sat down on it together.

"There. No more scarecrows or dead weasels. Isn't that a better view?" He laid his hand over hers and held it hard.

"Did I tell you, that when you first came here, I looked out of the window one morning and saw you sitting on the ground over there, leaning against that oak tree?"

"No. I don't remember."

"You didn't see me."

Late afternoon and already dusk was coming in. The bare branches of the oak and the chestnut and plane trees were black. Light drained from everything as she looked at it. The temperature dropped but neither of them wanted to move yet. There was a shift of air as the sun went down, red behind the black trees. She felt the pressure of his hand on hers. She'd been ridiculous about the scarecrow. It was all right. All the worries of their situation fell away as they sat on, not speaking. She couldn't think of Claude, or debts, or divorce. He sat with his face turned up to watch one last rook make for the woods. Pauline thought, *We can make our life in the interstices of real life. It's like what goes on just offstage, in the wings, before you go on and have to say your lines and be the person in the play. Life, real life, is in the wings. It's that moment of breathlessness and tension and then the breathing out, knowing that you can do anything, stepping out into the lights.*

He drove her back to Paris that Sunday evening, holding the big car's wheel between his hands on the empty roads. She sat beside him in the early dusk, trees going past like exhalations, occasional figures at the roadside stopping to see them pass. Difficult moments would come, but they could live through them as long as they were together. He was stronger than she was, because of his country upbringing; nothing seemed to alarm him. Neither of them, during the whole weekend, had mentioned the divorce. There was a breathing space to be had, perhaps. Pauline thought, *Something will happen, something we have not yet thought of. It always does.*

26.

Isa parks up under the plane trees at the far end of town and walks back because there is never a parking place on the main street. The real estate office is on the market square where the stalls are still up and a few people wait for vegetables, fish, and bread, though it's nearly midday. The supermarket outside the town has lured people away from the street market, but the wine man still does well, and the cheese woman too, and there are new stalls—a young Englishwoman has begun selling scones and biscuits and English tea, a Welshman has laid out royal jelly and jars of pollen, pots of clear honey ranging from pale to dark. These are the new people who are buying up houses around here because they can, and because they are permanently in love with what they think of as the French way of life, even as they cling to their English one.

The English will be her target, because not only will they be grateful and enthusiastic and have the money, they will love her house, and nurse it into its extreme old age after all these decades of neglect. They will make a swimming pool, plant roses where the tangles of grass and nettles are, sit down to their nice English tea and scones under the big lime tree, have friends to stay who will exclaim and admire and love it too, and probably want the next one that comes up for sale down the road. So much for Chloé and her theories about *le patrimoine de France*. They are all Europeans now; people can live where they like, as long as they have the money to do it, and the English, selfishly and yet with admirable cunning, have not given in to the euro and so still have some of their weighty pounds to spare.

"Madame de Giovanni." The man across the desk half stands, shakes her hand, indicates the studded fake-leather chair where she should sit. Isa sits, crosses her legs. Light filters between drawn Venetian blinds. A fan turns on the desk. It's already mid-July, and everyone will be on holiday for the whole of August, and she wants to get things moving before that long empty month begins. Perhaps she should have contacted one of the new English real estate agents who are buzzing around the area these days hunting for houses, barns, even ruins for their English clients, chatting up mayors, buying bottles of wine to soften deals, puzzling local builders with their bad French and frivolous ways. But this man has known the area all his life, as she has, and if he is self-seeking and bored with his life, as she suspects, he is not as greedy as she has heard these English agents are.

"Yes, well. Monsieur Destry. I contacted you some weeks ago about my house. Les Martinières? I've made up my mind. I'd like to get in on the market this month, before the holidays, and be sure it gets some publicity while the foreign tourists are here. Time goes so fast."

"Indeed it does. Well, Madame, we do have some people who are looking for just that sort of house, as it turns out. I could bring them over, if it suits you. When would be convenient?"

"As soon as possible, really. I'm still going through some of the things. A friend is here to help me, but we will be done in no more than a week, so any time you like to suggest."

She feels her hands rough and grimed with gardening, the nails ragged. A blister on one palm from the handle of the mowing machine. Somebody has to cut the grass, and it always seems to be herself. She tucks them out of sight. She tries not to feel that she is doing something shameful.

"Would next Tuesday do? I have to be in the area that day. A house not far from yours has sold, very well, really, to some very nice people. Swedes, or Norwegians, I forget which. But nice, and very impressed with what they saw."

"That would be fine. I'll expect you at—what, ten, eleven?"

"Eleven, probably."

Next Tuesday, fine. She will have to make sure that Chloé is not there. She shakes hands with Monsieur Destry, who is probably thinking, *So easy to please, these people desperate to sell, who can't afford their ancestors' lifestyle anymore.* The place in Paris, the place in the country, the long summers doing nothing but picking fruit and reading books, the grandchildren coming, the whole lazy enviable inherited French way. And how lucky for him, who has to handle all these suddenly unwanted properties, that things are going just the way they are. Thinking of a good lunch and the percentage he'll make from the sale, no doubt, he opens the door for her as if she were still his superior, and sees her out. Isa hopes that nobody has seen her coming out of his office, but the street is empty.

It's done. Now, it's only a matter of time. Isa walks back across the little square under the plane trees, past the fountain. She feels both the relief and the shock of it.

All those years in the house: herself, the cousins, living the long summer holidays without rules except to wash your hands before dinner and to kiss *grand-mère* goodnight. The adults sitting about, sipping coffee, handing little cakes on plates, talking about politics and the weather; really, their lives must have bored them to death. Now, she is the only adult, as she can't count Chloé. There will be no more children to run through those rooms and out into the blinding sun, the shade of the big old lime tree, the alleyways of freckled light that lead down to the river. Isa thinks, *I will not tell Seb about this visit.* Curiously, she wants him to see her as someone honorable, and this encounter with Monsieur Destry hasn't felt quite that way, however reasonable her decision.

She walks the other way up the main street from where she parked, to see if Chantal can fit her in for a cut and color. She has not had her hair properly cut in years. Chantal, in the only hairdressers' shop left in town, looks up from her magazine and cup of coffee, yawns, excuses herself, and says that yes, she can take Madame right away. Isa sits, her shoulders wrapped first in the black gown, then in the plastic shawl, looks at herself in the mirror, and says, "I'd like it cut to here." Her hands at chin level, drawing a straight bob.

"Really, Madame? As much as that?"

"Yes. I've been thinking about it for some time. And, color."

"All right. Fine. Here is the color chart. Would you like some magazines? Coffee?"

She chooses a coppery swatch like a miniature paintbrush, looks at pictures of women far younger than herself, and reads about them worrying over what to do with their lives: how to juggle work, children, a husband, how to find sexual satisfaction in marriage, how to feel less tired, lose weight, conceal from their husbands that they have lovers. Isa feels remote from these women. *At nearly sixty, these are not your concerns, not anymore; once you have sold your inherited house, alienated your only daughter, freed yourself from debt, what is there left to worry about? Only, if you are any good as a painter, and if you have enough time and money left to find out.* None of the women in the magazines ever think about such things; she closes the heavy glossy one on her knee, leans back with her head in a basin, gives herself up to Chantal's energetic fingers massaging her scalp in warm water, and thinks that she should have done this long ago. Her wet hair is sleek about her face, after the color has taken effect. Pale face and reddened, darkened hair. Chantal's scissors, slicing about her face, then thinning, making downward cuts; small tufts of hair are held up sideways, snipped, leveled. She watches a woman with short red shining hair appear, a woman with round surprised eyes and good bone structure and a jawline that is not exactly firm, but not weak either when she holds her chin up. Why did she keep all that gray hair in its messy chignon that used once to be considered artistic, but had become simply unkempt? This is what happens when you make a change: you can't imagine why you have not done it before.

The dryer puffs around her, blowing up fine red strands, a wild halo that is at once smoothed around Chantal's brush. At her jaw, the hair curves. At the crown, it lies flat. It shines under the lights. Inside her two black gowns, she is sweating, with the heat of the day and the hot air blown around her.

"Thank you," she says. "Thank you so much." She feels the moving air, all the little hairs blown away from her face, then her cheeks and nose are brushed with a soft brush as if she were an animal.

"There," says Chantal, daughter of the man who still keeps the fish stall on the market, girlfriend of a man who plays tenor sax in a local band. "You look wonderful. Very beautiful, very, very beautiful." Chantal, who when younger was a dropout and a worry to her parents—when the band had been wilder and younger and possibly involved with drugs—is now looking earnestly at her in the mirror and telling her what she wants to hear.

She hears it, and believes it. How long is it since someone told her she was beautiful? Whether it's true or not hardly matters: it's the words, *très belle, très très belle*, that count. She pays, tips Chantal twenty euros, and steps out into the burning afternoon to walk to her car.

When she comes back into her house, she sees in the spotted hall mirror a woman who looks, with her straight fringe and bell of red hair, more than a little like the filmmaker Agnès Varda.

The combines are all out now; they crawl across the fields and block the narrow country roads. The air is full of dust and chaff. The fields are being cut this week, after this extraordinarily dry summer. This heat wave has made harvesting a simple enough task for once. The strong stalks stand, grown shorter than they used to be for easy harvesting. They are cut down in their yellow ranks, to lie sliced and even upon the ground. They are then converted into the immense round bales that lie waiting to be collected, each one with its dense blot of shadow under the midday sun. The sunflower heads grow heavier, darker with their weight of seed, and they all turn together toward the sun; they will not be harvested yet. The trees in the orchard droop with the weight of plums, apples, pears. The dryness has turned their leaves leathery.

After two weeks in this country, Seb begins to notice seasonal change. The seeds falling from the lime tree. The dew early in the morning, in the shadow of the wall. Sunset earlier, the sky redder, the dawn slower to break in. The moon on the wane again. After mid-August—*le quinze août*, that milestone—summer will be essentially over. Then, there will be only two weeks left till the *rentrée*, when the whole country will get up and move back to the cities, the year having turned. He will have to go back to England. He will have to decide what to do with his house, his things, the rest of his life. It's so unwelcome, this thought, that he stands at the window of his room and stares miserably out, as if for a last time, at the scene outside; as if he were about to be exiled from it. Then he sees Isa's car come bumping down the unmade road, dust flying up from its wheels, and feels immediately lighter, happier. It's not yet, after all. There's still time. He opens the window, waves down to her as she drives and parks with her usual jolt beside the woodpile. There are days and days, in which to feel what he feels now, at ease, at home, looking forward to dinner and to telling her what he has discovered.

They sit, each of them with a glass of wine left from dinner, rabbit cooked in white wine and mustard. How, he wonders once again, does she manage to produce such good meals so quickly? She sits in the armchair, old cracked leather nailed with brass, he on the couch. A low table between them, with old copies of *Le Monde*, a pile of classically creamcovered books in French that nobody is reading, and the wine bottle nearly empty. The shutters are open, the night sky still pale to the west.

Isa looks across at him, the tip of her head, the shine of her new hair, a reddish bell. Who was that French filmmaker with red hair cut that way? *It suits her,* he thinks. How suddenly women can change themselves; it's a sort of magic that no man can achieve.

"It looks good," he says. "Your hair. Really nice." Of course, he should have said something earlier.

She inclines her head—thanks. "So," she says, and turns toward him fully, her hands around her skirted knees. "Tell me. What's new with Uncle Henri?"

"Well, I want to tell you what I've found. What I think may have happened." All day, while she was out, he's been longing to tell her. "The pages you found in the writing case are clearly Fournier's own final ending, as you thought, and they are about his real-life lover, Pauline, the dark girl who is called Emilie in the book. They are the two people making love under a hedge, out in the country, after a bicycle ride together. He changed the ending. He left Colombe Blanchet out, and ended the book with Emilie. He did it just before war broke out. Literally days before."

"But why were those pages hidden, or at least in a separate place?"

"I think your grandmother found them and hid them, so that the manuscript ends with Colombe, his virginal blonde Yvonne lookalike—the one who takes to a convent because he, the hero, isn't pure, as she'd once imagined. He wrote his new ending urgently—you can see from the fast handwriting, almost a scrawl, just before he went off to war. She must have read it and hidden it. At least she didn't destroy it, but she did what she could to falsify his last intentions."

Isa looks at him steadily. Her eyes are made up tonight, the rims penciled with black: a style of makeup that reminds him of the 1970s. Cleopatra eyes. "Well, I wouldn't put it past her. But if that's the case, then, you should write about it. I think he'd want the truth to be known, even if he never finished it. After all, if he'd lived, he would have used that ending, isn't that what you're saying?"

"I do think so, yes. Did you see what he wrote in the margin?"

"No?"

"'I seem to have arrived in the deep country of a live soul.'"

She looks back at him for a moment. Silenced, both of them, by Henri Fournier's words.

Then she says, "That's beautiful."

He says, "I think that's where all writers want to arrive. And it rarely happens."

"Well, then." She raises her half-empty glass, pulls herself back from some edge, perhaps, stops herself from gazing at him. "To the new version. To Uncle Henri. To—what was her name? In the book?"

"Emilie."

"She's your responsibility now."

"Okay." Seb feels the need to be brisk, now, too. "I'll do what I can. It may not be much. He said it couldn't be published, we can't ignore that. But maybe, an article, at least. I might try the *London Review of Books*. Next year will be the hundredth anniversary of his death, so there might be some interest."

"You think my grandmother hid it, because it was obviously about Pauline?"

"Well, yes. And, it was so overtly sexy. What do you think?"

"I think it's more than likely. She must have been afraid of the scandal if people ever connected it to Henri's real life. She was terribly puritanical. She used to punish us for swearing, I remember, we had to wash our mouths out with soap. And, as for sex, well, it didn't exist. I had to sleep with my hands tied to the bedpost more than once."

"She sounds alarming." He has a quick thought of Isa, young, in a brass bed, wanting to touch herself.

"She was. We were all scared of her. But she could also be very loving at times, when she chose to be. I think she probably never got over Henri's death."

"But her husband died too, surely?"

"Yes, but my mother always thought she loved Henri more than Jacques. I don't mean that it was incestuous, or at least in those days one couldn't say so." She paused. "But I wonder why she didn't simply destroy the new ending?"

"She loved Henri and so couldn't bring herself to? She hoped he would come back from the war, of course. But what if he came back and found what she had done?"

"Of course."

"Well, goodnight. I'm going up." He hesitates a moment. "Between us, it looks like we've solved at least part of the mystery."

"Bravo, for finding it out!"

She stands, and he gets up too, comes round the low table between them, and leans to kiss her on both cheeks, feeling the warm pressure of her face to his, held there for just seconds more than necessary, and the silky swing of her hair at the sides of her head; noticing the smell of hairdressers' salons that reminds him of Annie after she had the blonde highlights returned to her own fine brown hair. Women change their hair for a reason, he knows, that has often less to do with attracting some man than with an inner shift, a certain resolution. Their hair is in advance of the rest of them, perhaps, like a flag at the front of a procession.

"Goodnight, Isa. Thanks for a lovely dinner." He stands, inhaling her, caught uncomfortably between the memory of Annie and the vivid presence of Isa: sadness and desire, neither of them welcome. The deep country of a live soul. Where they nearly foundered, nearly stumbled, and only caught themselves just in time.

27.

Pauline went alone that cold spring day to the eighteenth-century building on rue de Seine where Madame Sarah Bernhardt's doctor had his rooms. A blank-faced concierge let her in—*You would need a blank face for this job,* she thought—and motioned her to a staircase to the left of the courtyard. She walked up the stairs, and knocked at a door. A woman let her in—the doctor's wife? "He will see you in a moment, Madame." Her name was not used. Neither was the doctor's.

He came in, drying his hands on a towel, and stood aside to let her go into the inner room. She looked around her: medicine cabinets, a desk, two chairs, and in the corner, a high bed. It was a room that must once have been a drawing room, with fine wide-planked oak floors and a carved fireplace.

She passed him the envelope from Sarah Bernhardt. "Madame X. A very great lady. I am glad to meet a friend of hers. Now, Madame, I believe you have a little problem with your menstrual cycle?"

She was shaking as she walked across the creaky wide oak boards to undress behind a screen that he put up for her. She lay down on the bed, looked up at the ceiling, lifted her knees to spread her legs apart when he told her to. *Oh, God who does not exist, make this easy.* But it would not be easy; how could it be?

"It's better that I don't give you ether, as it slows the body down. This will hurt just for a moment. Later, you will feel pains, a kind of birth."

The pain was sharp and clear and shocking, in spite of the drug he gave her to drink, which she thought must be laudanum.

She'd begun to feel queasy at the beginning of February, but had gone on working, playing at the Ambigu in the evenings and rehearsing in the afternoons at the Gymnase. By the middle of the month, she was sure. She'd woken in the mornings to get up and vomit as quietly as she could in the little bathroom beside the room where she slept alone, down the corridor from Claude. Then, looking at herself in the bathroom mirror, she saw how yellow her skin was, as if jaundiced, and how it stretched tight over her cheekbones. Gradually, morning after morning, feeling her belly with her own hands, she knew there was no doubt. As her waist thickened and her breasts grew sore, the rest of her seemed to shrink and tighten. Her face with its cheekbones and nose was her father's; her body, shamefully her mother's. She and Claude had not slept together for over a year: there could be no doubt whose child this was.

She'd thought of telling Claude, of begging him to say he was the father. She'd thought of running away with Henri to a place where nobody would guess that they were not man and wife. She'd thought that without Claude's patronage, Henri would have no job; without her earnings in the theatre, she would have no money; and that Claude, independently of both of them, was losing his money fast. She could think of nobody to consult except for Madame Bernhardt, who had been kind to her when she was young; so one afternoon she took a cab to visit her at home. Sarah Bernhardt saw at once. She took Pauline's hands in her small swollen white ones. "My dear, you have a great career before you. Do not let this get in the way."

"I don't know what to do."

"Yes, you do. What we all have to do, if this happens at the wrong time. I will give you an address. He's a good man, and very clean. It's important to go to a real doctor, as the women they call the angel-makers are regularly raided by the police."

She took the paper with the address on it and a note scrawled from Madame Bernhardt.

"Nobody must know."

"But of course! Who do you take me for? Now, do it soon, and eat something. You look half-starved, and audiences notice, you know."

Afterward, the doctor said, "It is best you wait here, Madame. It is safer. If you were to hemorrhage, I will be here. We can deal with everything in the house, so to speak."

She thought, *Women are perforated, they become infected, they die. They fall down bleeding in the streets. They are found and thrown into jail. People who do what this doctor has done are sent to the guillotine if they are caught.* She nodded, unable to speak.

"Don't be afraid. The worst is over. Please wait next door. You may lie on the sofa if you like. My wife will bring you tea." He was a kind man. He gave her arm a pat that was almost a caress.

Hours passed, and pain ran through her; she contracted and condensed into a hard knot. She thought she groaned. The woman, who was indeed the doctor's wife and who was, she imagined, the one person he could trust, brought her a tisane and wiped her face with a wet cloth. She thought that there was someone sitting in a corner of the room, in the winter dusk as it came in. "Who is there?"

"Nobody, Madame. There is nobody else here."

She thought of the small squat figure she had seen on the street all those years ago, when she ran home from school the day her father died. Who had that been? His or her hand had been stretched out to her, she thought to grab her, but more probably to ask for money. It had seemed like an omen, at the time.

"You are sure there is nobody here?"

"Don't worry, Madame, it will be all right."

"Are you sure? Is this normal? Is this what always happens?"

"Always, Madame."

At last, the scrap of flesh swam out of her. She felt it pass down the channel of blood she had become. The woman brought a basin.

"Can I see?"

"Best not to see, Madame."

"No, I want to."

It was very small, curled like a shrimp, but recognizably human. She had not known it would look like that. So, there was someone to say goodbye to. She wept, then. The woman took the basin away. She padded her open vagina with cloths, brought more water, padded again. "The bleeding will stop over the next day or so. There is nothing to worry about, Madame. It all went very well. He is a good doctor."

"Your husband?"

"Yes."

"Can I ask, why do you risk so much to help women with this?"

"Ah, we know that someone must do it, and if it is not a real doctor, but someone just doing it for money, the women risk far more. We see many women in your profession, Madame. He has a good reputation. But it is better that you don't know his real name."

"Just as you don't know mine."

"Exactly, Madame."

So, it is like being onstage? We are all three of us playing roles, each of us pushing to play this scene as best we can with the text we have been given?

"May I go home now?"

"I will order you a cab. You will be picked up at the corner of the street."

The folded notes had already been passed over; the play was in its third act, about to finish. She would go out through a dark door onto a street where a cab awaited her, the way she sometimes did from her dressing room when she did not want to meet the public. She was alone, as she was alone coming offstage. She was emptied out. *So,* she thought, *this is what it is like. This emptiness is mourning, just as it was at that open graveside, all those years ago. A life goes and a gap is left: they cover it over with earth, or put a cloth over the basin, and you can't see it, but it will always be there. They cover the mirrors, and the basins, with cloths.*

When she went out into the street to find the waiting cab at the corner, she was bent over like an old woman, holding her coat close. She glanced up and down the street to make sure she was not seen. Did someone short scurry around the corner, going back toward the river, out of sight? She thought so. It was dark now, and she could not be sure.

Henri came to see her that evening at home, where she lay in bed. Claude had simply told him that she wasn't at all well. The two of them passed each other at her bedroom door, and Claude bowed his head as he let Henri in to stand in the doorway. She lay there and thought, *This can't go on, can it? None of us able to speak an honest word?* She was still bleeding quite heavily, had told Claude that it was the time of the month, but thought he must have guessed.

"Thank you for coming to see me," she said politely to her lover. Claude left them alone. On his face, now that Claude was gone, she saw all Henri's raw hurt at not being able to act or speak the truth, let alone prevent what had happened without him.

What would a child of theirs have been like? Too late to ask. In the novel, there had been that wild shout of laughter that linked Meaulnes with his little daughter, that complicity between man and baby. The solid little girl clutching the backs of chairs as she pushed them along, trying to walk. He had ended his book, memorably, with fatherhood.

Perhaps one day a long time from now, she might be able to speak of how she'd lifted and opened her knees in a chilly, high-ceilinged room in exactly the same physical position that she had opened them for Henri. Letting love in, letting love out. The inbreathe and the out-breathe. The passing, whatever anyone thought of it, whatever anyone believed, of a human life.

She sat beside him, days later, on the bench in the far garden at Trie. He'd found two benches and nicknamed them, the Happiness Bench and the Misery Bench. He said, "We're never going to sit on the Misery Bench again." They sat upright beside each other on the Happiness Bench, not yet happy, she thought, but trying for it.

It was still a cold spring, and the ground was hard, the trees bare. There had been so much hurt, in so short a time. He had been angry with her, that she had not told him, and then sad, to think of her going through it alone. Would they survive this? He put out a hand to her, and she took it in her gloved fingers.

She thought, *There will still be, won't there, that gap, that blank? The child we made who never had a life. It will always be something that happened to me that did not happen to you. I, who chose to look into the bloody basin and see what lay in it.*

They sat on in silence. She thought, *If we can survive this, we can survive anything.*

He said, "You have to ask Claude for a divorce. I don't understand why you won't do it. We have to take the risk of him accusing me. I don't care. I just want us to be married."

"I will ask him. He's just so—destroyed at the moment, with everything that is going wrong."

"And I'm not?"

"Henri, you'll never be depressed the way he is."

"Well, even if you do divorce him, he'll probably show up on your doorstep every other day looking for sympathy. But it's gone on too long. Look what it has made you do."

"I'll tell him," she said. "Then we can live in peace." She pulled off her glove, to entwine her cold fingers with his. He stared ahead, not looking at her. Perhaps she had demanded of him a maturity that was not yet his to give; perhaps she had shocked him beyond repair.

He said at last, "When we're married, we'll have our children. Lots of them." She didn't, couldn't, reply.

IV.

28.

The Villa Souberbielle was a spacious house with a big wild garden and white roses growing round the door. They were back in Cambo-les-Bains for another summer and she had found this slightly decrepit house to rent. Claude had gone to Vittel, to find the woman who needed his presence only slightly less than she did his money, Pauline thought, and who must be feeling the lack of both. Henri and she traveled together on July 14, leaving Paris to its Bastille Day fireworks and dancing.

He sat beside her in the garden, covering pages. He was writing his new novel, *Colombe Blanchet*. She had wanted him to write something for the theatre, and they had sketched out a play together about a couple living deep in a forest, but since his publisher wanted *Colombe* as soon as possible, he had switched back to the novel.

Pauline closed her eyes against the sun and heard bees buzz in the lavender. Time passed easily in the movement of shadow across her closed lids, the scratch of his pen, the slight alterations of his breath at her side. *When you are happy,* she thought, *time neither speeds nor slows around you: you are simply in it.* Henri hummed when he was pleased with what he was writing. He tipped his straw hat to shade his page, and she heard the paper turn, and his satisfaction in the quiet hum, almost like the bees, almost like the hum of summer heat.

They had begun working together on *Colombe Blanchet*; he asked her every day what she thought of a new part, whether she liked the direction it was taking. She was trying to help him pull from his tangled notes a story that still eluded him. There seemed to her to be too many people in it: three different potential heroines, for a start. And what was the point of the bet among the young men, that the first one to have a woman in his rooms would buy all the others champagne? It showed the worst aspects of men, she said.

But the very worst thing about it was the ending. "Henri, I simply don't believe that anyone would kill herself when she found out that her lover wasn't as pure as she'd thought." Now, she need not hold back on her criticism of the ending, as she had with his earlier book. Here, the suicide was even more violent to her than Yvonne de Galais's death in childbirth.

"Well, perhaps I could have her go to a convent?"

"No, I don't believe that either. If she cares so much that he's had other women, it falsifies the whole book. It makes her rather ridiculous."

"Ridiculous? But Pauline, she's an idealist."

"But I don't think she's the real heroine. Look, you have him making love to Laurence, the dark girl, and there's that moment when they hear the nightingale together. That's real. Then your ending seems to deny everything your hero has felt so far."

"Hmm. I see what you mean. But Colombe has been the heroine all along."

"But she isn't, not really. Don't you see? The writing comes to life in the scene with the dark girl; it's so obvious. Then he turns his back on her."

"Well, perhaps I need the dark girl to merge with the intellectual one, Emilie."

"I don't see why you need so many potential heroines. Leave Colombe in her convent, merge Emilie with Laurence, and have him end up with her, why not?"

"I don't know if I'll ever be able to finish this," he said. "It's ironic. I have a publisher and no novel this time, just all these bits and pieces."

"It just needs patience," she said. "Patience and time. And for you to be clear about the ending, and who the real heroine is. You have the whole summer, don't worry."

"All right. I'll have a go at another ending."

"And don't kill anybody off, this time!"

They had just one week. On July 23 they heard that Austria had given an ultimatum to Serbia, after the murder by an unknown Serbian assassin of an Austrian archduke. That morning she held *Le Figaro* out to him. "It's going to be war."

Oh, so this was what was happening while they made love, listened to the bees, while they slept, while they made up stories?

"Serbia will give in, surely. It's only an empty gesture from Austria." She heard the uncertainty in his voice. He was shaken to the core by what was going on. They had not been paying attention. Like millions of others, all over France and elsewhere, in Austria and Serbia no doubt too, they had been focusing on their own lives, their pleasures, their problems, their pains and joys. What else was human life for?

A few more hours only—of walks, writing, smelling the roses. She held his arm as they walked together, felt the bone and muscle inside the flesh beneath his sleeve, tried not to let in her fear. Then Russia declared war. Time was no longer theirs; it had been snatched from them. Passionately, she resented it, and yet, what could they do? All over the country, couples like themselves were having their time, their choices, removed from them. Henri sent a telegram to ask his mother to send on his military uniform and belongings, as he would not have time to go back to rue Cassini. "I'll have to go straight to Mirande. Can you come with me? Can we take the car, darling?"

On July 30 a message from the Ministry of War came for Lieutenant Fournier, offering him the option of acting as an English interpreter for the duration of hostilities. "You'd be perfect for it, with your good English. Do take it, Henri. You'd be so much safer. It's a really good offer."

Suddenly everything was on the outside. It was all arrangements, decisions, departures. They'd lost their private life in one moment, while they were looking away. People said, "It won't last." They heard it everywhere—"Oh, it won't last. They'll be beaten back to Berlin by Christmas." Were they trying to cheer themselves up, denying the seriousness of there being a war in Europe?

Henri sat on the edge of a chair, bent over, lacing his boots. She would see him like this in her mind's eye for weeks, months, his slow pulling of the laces from one brass eyelet to another. He was trying them on, as he hadn't worn them since the spring of 1913, and they had to be comfortable. At last he straightened and looked at her. "No, I don't think so. I wouldn't feel at ease with it. If war does break out, I want to be with my comrades."

It was Franz in the forest, calling out his band of brothers. It was Meaulnes obeying the call. There was nothing more to say. *You mean,* she thought, *you will just get up and go, because you have been called? You mean, this is what men do? They whistle to each other and go off to war?*

"I think I'd better get some new ones, just to be sure. An army marches on its stomach, I know that, but its feet are just as important."

The next day, a notice marked with two little flags neatly crossed appeared in the mail. He couldn't put off his departure any longer. They drove together to Bayonne to buy the necessary supplies. All along the roadside, peasants and farmers waited in little groups. The harvest had been abandoned; corn stood ripe in the fields. The heavy green trees of August seemed incredibly still. In town, she sat on a chair in the Galeries Parisiennes while he tried on a tough pair of boots with thick soles. The bells began to ring while they were in the shop. First distant, then closer; then as if the clanging filled the little space they were in, and even moved inside their own bodies.

"That's it, then," the saleswoman said.

Henri looked up. She saw in that instant a wild distress in his eyes, as if he saw something beyond her, beyond this place.

She couldn't speak. She just nodded. *This is all we can do, now?*

"Will Monsieur take the boots?"

"Yes, please. I'll wear them, to break them in a bit."

Outside in the baked streets, they glanced at each other and, without speaking, walked fast toward the cathedral. It was completely empty. The lamp burned in the tabernacle, the doors stood open, deep coolness rose from the stone floor. They knelt down, hands joined, at the altar steps, like a couple about to be married before a priest. There was no other refuge but the watery cool of this cathedral and its ancient promise of salvation. *If I pray to your God,* she thought, *then will He save you?*

She said, "We'll marry, won't we, as soon as you get back? I'll ask Claude for a divorce immediately."

His turn now to nod, unable to say a word.

29.

"Did you have a sense that war was coming, then?" Sebastian asks, a lifetime later.

"Me personally, no, not at all. I was completely immersed in my own life. As one usually is. Although I am sure that there were people who did. People who were paying attention. You know, there was more than a hint of what was coming in 1912, when the Serbians, Bulgarians, and Greeks attacked the Ottoman Empire. I remember that Henri thought that our sending a warlike ambassador to St. Petersburg made it all the more dangerous. Henri had been training as a soldier for years, and so had thousands of other young men. But we didn't ask why. Or I didn't. We accepted things as they came."

"But everything changed as a result."

"Everything. We were a generation whose lives were ripped apart."

"It's hard to imagine."

"It's impossible to imagine unless it happens to you."

"Simone, do you have any regrets?"

"Yes, I have one, and it's private. But a regret is not the same thing as remorse. You can live with regret, but remorse kills you."

"I'm sorry, I shouldn't have asked."

"I said that you could ask me anything, and I could refuse. Now, shall we have our coffee?" She poured the brown stream into white porcelain. "We had no idea at all what was coming in the sense of what it would mean. It was like being in a different world, all of a sudden. The old world disappeared. France disappeared. Our life together disappeared. And this happened to millions of people. All for no good reason that I could see."

"Did there seem to be a reason at the time?"

"Henri thought so. It was everywhere, the propaganda—nowadays, we would call it propaganda—about fighting for one's country, doing one's duty, God being on one's side. I couldn't see it. We had to go to war because some old archduke had been shot? What had that to do with us? Of course, it was all to do with agreements and alliances, and power, and as always, money. There were huge fortunes to be made out of armaments. Behind all that sacrifice, a sordid manipulation of young men by the old and venal. I'm even less patriotic now than I was then. And then, I didn't let Henri know what I thought."

"He was all for it?"

"Young men were, at the time. They called it glorious, when it was anything but. But it can't have been glorious for any of them after the first five minutes of marching to a band. I hated it then. I hate it more now. But the rest of our story, if you can bear it, is all about that war."

"If you don't mind telling me. It's what I'm here for."

"How long do we have? You're leaving when?"

"On Thursday."

"Another day and a half. That should do it. Bring a new tape with you tomorrow, we're going to need it. And I'll try to get a good night's sleep and be up bright and early. Do you know the Georges Brassens song about the 1914–18 war?"

"No, I don't think so."

"It says there were lots of other good wars, great massacres and all wonderfully bloody, but the best one, the one he really likes most of all—the song's a send-up of course—is 1914–18. The bloodiest and most pointless of them all." She sings a few bars in her old, cracked, but still tuneful voice for him. He's looking at her as if she's endlessly surprising. "So, get some dinner and make it an early night, if you can do such a thing in Paris, and come back around ten, I should be ready. Then we can do the bloody war justice. *D'accord?*"

"*D'accord. Bonsoir.*"

"*Bonsoir,* Seb."

He leans forward and kisses her firmly, one on each cheek, in the French fashion, but with a little smack of the lips, the way a child might say goodbye. Then he looks embarrassed. The English, she realizes, don't do this. For him, it's a further mark of trust. She nods her appreciation to him, and smiles, and watches him as he hurtles down the stairs.

When he's gone, she pours herself a mouthful of whisky, because the desolation has got to her, because remembering all this only tells her how far she is from its reality. Another century, nearly, another era. Her own era, dead and buried and gone as surely as the men who fell in that war. Everything going down into the pit of forgetfulness. Then, with the whisky burning her gut, she pulls the blinds tight and turns back to the room. Her room. Her last days, maybe even hours. Her remaining slice of life. Her choice, still: how to live it.

30.

Isa talks in snatches to him as she draws. Her gaze flickers across him, remote, professional. He feels sweat in the creases of his knees and an itch at the back of his neck. She uses charcoal, draws, rips off a page, begins again. Her hand moves fast; she stops, stares, goes on. He hears the soft occasional squeak of the charcoal on paper. She talks euros, rents, studios, paintings, doing what she must, and then falls silent.

He doesn't speak, wanting to stay still for her. It's like being at the dentist, a one-sided conversation with grunts from the motionless patient. Then she stops drawing, stares at him, and says, "That'll do for now."

Released, he shifts gingerly, feels the stiffness in his back and neck. "Have you any recent paintings of yours here? I glanced at the ones in my room, but I assumed they were old work."

"All my new ones are in Paris. While I'm here, I never seem to have time. It's actually good to do some drawing here."

"Has your style changed much?"

"I went through a whole long period of doing abstracts, but not anymore. It got too hard to stick with portraits. Too unfashionable. Everyone was doing abstract painting or worse, installations. I started because I wanted to do portraits. I was inspired by Lucien Freud. I saw an exhibition of his work when I was in London, years ago, when I was quite young."

"Portraits must be the hardest thing, I've always thought."

"Self-portraits are the hardest. But for a while recently I've been doing wrapped heads. Heads with the faces invisible."

"Really? Why wrapped? You mean, as if bandaged?"

"Yes. But not wounded, necessarily. Just with the features invisible."

"Why? It sounds rather—well, alarming." He wants to say *spooky* but doesn't know the word.

"It was a stage. Maybe to rid myself of influences. Who knows? Then I began to do self-portraits, and I've done a lot of them. It's what you always have with you, your own face, and you are what you know least." She stands back for a minute, looking at him as if she has never seen him before.

"Hmm, I suppose so."

"I know, it may sound egotistical. But it's not about that."

"No," he says.

She stands looking at her drawing.

"Any good?"

"Not bad. It's a start. You won't recognize it, so I won't show you yet. Anyway, it's not about pleasing the subject. But you've a good face."

"Well, thanks."

"But that isn't the point, really, either. Bone structure helps. But it's the surface of something, a face. I began because I didn't want to hire models. It's expensive, and also people always have a vested interest in looking nice. Then I saw it differently. A face, a body, is simply a map of experience. You wrap it, you unwrap it. You see it fresh. If you can see it that way, you never come to an end."

"Isa, it's not my business. But couldn't you paint here? Then you wouldn't have to sell the house. It seems a shame, to let it go."

"I've made up my mind," she says. "It took a long time, but I have. You've been talking to Chloé. Chloé blows in the wind. She has one scheme after another. I'm amazed that she's stuck with her teaching job as long as she has, that she even passed her qualifying exam in the first place. It's quite a tough one, the CAPES, to work in the public sector. Chloé is like her father, a fantasist."

"But she isn't a child."

"No, but she behaves like one. I'm sorry, I know you mean well, but this is nothing to do with you. It's ancient history. The only way I'm going to manage is to sell this place, invest the money, and live in Paris. It's just a fact of life."

Silence. He backs off, then. A foreigner, a man, a fox in the hen coop. He must keep to his side of the bargain, which is to read Fournier, eat meals, sit for his portrait, say nothing controversial.

But she goes on, "She's like Hugo. Very impulsive and wrongheaded and utterly stubborn. I see him in her. It makes it hard for us to get on."

"Tell me about Hugo?"

"Very much the love of my life, very attractive, Italian but grew up mostly in France. A good lover, a hopeless husband. I met him when I was very young, at art school. He was part of the whole '68 thing—anarchism, occupying buildings, stirring up revolution—so of course I was impressed. He made me read Marx and Gramsci and Fanon. He taught them. I expect he still does."

"Do you ever see him?" He thinks, *I wonder how I would be described as a husband? Boring, probably. Faithful, sure. Do most people end up more like brother and sister, after forty years?*

"No. I don't want to. He lives in Toulouse still, I think. He is someone who was hard to forget, but I had to, to stay sane. He left nearly twenty years ago, when Chloé was six." She stands back and looks with narrowed eyes at her drawing. He sees a steely determination in her that he hasn't noticed before. She has made herself forget. Has she also denied herself any other lovers? Chloé's remark in the car suggested it.

"Now, do you want something to eat, before we go on? Have a plum. These are going soft, I'll have to make compote. Oh, and there are some apricots, just a few. I'll make coffee."

"You want to go on?"

"Oh, yes, if you can spare the time. I'd like to try another angle."

He doesn't say that his time is hers, that he even likes sitting there under her assessing eye. He chooses an apricot, yolk-yellow speckled with red. When he splits it open, there is a narrow gap between the stone and the flesh.

He sips from the green porcelain cup she sets before him. "Great coffee. This must be pure arabica?"

She stirs hers, looks at him. "Of course. So, if you don't mind, back to the original pose. I'll move over. Your hand was—like this."

She picks up his hand, rearranges it as if it were an object unconnected to a body. He grimaces, then sets his face into what seems to be a neutral expression. Sitting for her is strangely restful; no need to make any effort, except to sit still. He tries to empty his mind. The faint sound of her charcoal touching the paper, the small buzz of a fly around the fruit plate, the distant sound of a machine in a far field. A point of stillness, to which he travels: breath, blood, bone. His face, stripped, visible, grows on the paper between them with her short strokes, then longer, gentler ones. As if she is remaking him to her own design. His mind twitches and moves off like an animal grazing at random.

Your face, your skull, holds the secret of who you are. Portraiture as mind theft; Isa as mind reader; her charcoal as scalpel. What can she see of him? What does anybody see? He, and every man alive, holds his secrets. He and Annie said no secrets, all those years ago. Yet of course there were the things he did not say. In a long life together, how could you say everything? You spared each other. You did not lie, but you left things out: out of tact, out of kindness. You left fears unvoiced, hopes dormant. You had to. There were the silences, the courtesies, as he saw them, of marriage. You didn't blurt out your feelings. You did not apply scalpels.

He sits and lets Isa draw him. Is this extreme passivity happiness? It's certainly relaxing. You sit still, and let someone examine you, draw you on paper, and you are absolved. Someone—was it Genet?—said that to sit for a portrait is to be restored to your own solitude.

Isa lays down her charcoal stick. "Chloé told me about your wife. I'm so sorry. You didn't say. No reason you should have, of course, but I wondered, since you never talked about going home."

"I don't know if I even have a home. I have a house full of things, mostly hers, that I can't face looking at. Chloé asked me if I was married, so I told her. I don't think I was trying to hide anything, just to give myself a chance not to talk about it. But I'm glad you know."

It's different talking about it in French, as he himself is a slightly different person here. In another language, his story has a different slant. Neither Chloé nor Isa sounds shocked, inquisitive, or sanctimonious about it; perhaps this is what allows him to feel more at ease. Almost the worst thing about being in mourning is other people's responses: you are either a pariah, or someone to be ceaselessly questioned, patted, offered food. He's crossed streets to avoid people who might be about to say that Annie is now in a better place.

"It must be hard. It was good of you to come here," she says, her hand moving over her paper again, not looking at him now.

"It's good to be here. It was very timely, your invitation. Nothing reminds me of her here. It's a relief. I think of it as emotional ambush. Do you know what I mean—the sudden appearance of something of hers? I have to protect myself against it, for now."

"One day, you will come to an end of it, though. And those things that lie in ambush will have no more power, and it will be both sad and a relief."

"I suppose, yes. It's not her I don't want to talk about. It's just what happened."

She sprays her paper with fixative, then looks at it hard again, her lips pressed together, a small frown between her brows. "I understand. You're really asymmetrical, did you know that?"

He smiles. "Isn't everyone?"

She raises a hand to push a strand of hair back, and leaves a long charcoal streak on her temple.

He says, "You've got charcoal on your face."

"Oh, it gets everywhere." She rubs her cheek. The smear that results makes her look like a street person. He wants to reach forward and rub it away for her, carefully, but resists the urge.

Yes, she's thinking, has been thinking for some time, *it's a good face still,* and he hasn't changed much from the way he was in that youthful photograph except in the interesting way that faces change as they age, with more surface marks and more bone evident. Less hair, of course. And that sadness that he wears. She's been looking at him as an object, as far as she can, for the past hour, hour and a half, and as her charcoal has moved across the paper, she's been remembering the Bernsteins, and that London visit, and the book that Phyllis Bernstein had given her to carry back to France. The photograph of Seb Fowler on the back cover, and all that exciting information—she'd been eighteen, very intrigued by it—that had come her way.

In the late 1970s, she had been on an exchange visit to stay with an English girl, Harriet Bernstein, and her family in London. London was fun, then, in a way that Paris simply wasn't. The two of them, still only just escaped from being schoolgirls, had swung down the King's Road together in their long skirts, their high boots, their faces covered in pale makeup with soot-black raccoon eyes. Fashion in Paris was still serious; in London, that year, it was like playing. They went to coffee bars and smoky pubs, played jukeboxes, stayed out late in a way her own mother would never have allowed. Harriet told her about boys. Boys,

English boys, hung waiting for them outside the pubs and coffee bars where milky coffee that you would give to babies gushed from steaming machines. They all smoked, and blew smoke rings, and stamped on their half-finished cigarettes.

"I thought French girls were allowed to do anything," Harriet had said.

"No, no, not at all. You'll see. Wait till you have to come and stay with me."

Harriet's parents had lived in Hampstead, on the edge of the heath. Her father was a psychiatrist, her mother a painter. It was here that Isa, who had always loved drawing and painting, had first realized that she must go to art school. Harriet's mother, distracted at the end of the day after hours spent in her studio, flopped down on a sofa, poured vermouth and lemonade drinks for both girls, and whisky for herself. She painted. A woman could paint. A woman could be out all day in her studio and not know what was for dinner, because they would go to a restaurant or order in. A woman could have children—Harriet, and her brother, Nathan—and not think about them all day. Isa had loved Harriet's mother for not being like her own. When she and Harriet stamped around the heath, walking the family dog, Isa tried out her announcement that she was going to try for the École des Beaux-Arts in Paris. There were moments in life when you moved on in one single stride—this one came in borrowed Wellington boots in the puddles of Hampstead Heath under the gray skies over London.

Harriet's mother, Phyllis, gave Isa sketchbooks with thick pages of creamy paper to draw on, and suggested pastels. "There are so many wonderful art materials shops in Paris, darling. Look, let me give you some addresses." She admired the portrait Isa had tried, in charcoal, of Harriet herself.

"Izzy, you are really, really good!" Harriet said. "Look, Ma, she's got me down just amazingly. There's no way they're not going to let you go.

You'll get in easily! And if you don't, well, you could live with us and go to art college here in London, couldn't she?"

"Yes, well, of course," Harriet's mother said in her vague way, as if she hardly knew or cared who lived in all the rooms of her large Victorian house at the edge of the heath.

The book had appeared on the Swedish coffee table just a day or so before Phyllis Bernstein said—so casually, so certainly—that Isa was definitely destined to be an artist too. Phyllis, with her short dark hair cut in a fringe, her slight body in its elegant clothes, her hands that were blunt and useful, rough and marked with paint. The two things were linked, then: the book about her great-uncle's love life, and Isa's new certainty about herself. The book was about love, yes, but strangely, what it told her was about painting. Or, about herself, and who she might become.

She wanted to ask Phyllis about it, but didn't know how to begin. One evening when Phyllis came in to pour her evening whisky, she was alone with her. Cut-glass decanter, tumbler on a tray, the sour, peaty malt whisky smell. Isa thought that her own mother would never drink whisky on her own at five thirty in the afternoon. Wine with dinner, and only if other people were there.

"I see you're still deep in that young man's book? How are you liking it? It's all about your family, I know."

"I like it." She couldn't, for the moment, say any more.

"No problem with the language?"

"No, it's as if it—how can I say? As if it speaks directly to me. You know—how can I say it—in families, we tell lies about each other. I never knew the truth, till now."

"They say he's been mentioned for a prize. It's his first book, and look how young he is! Fanciable, too, wouldn't you say?"

"Fanciable?"

"Attractive. *Séduisant.*"

"Oh. Oh, yes. But there is something—well, it seems I know the story already—as if it is about me. Of course, I knew about my great-uncle, but only what my family told me. Not this." She had had this elated feeling before, with sunsets, certain patterns of light and shade, intense color, deep-green trees splintered by sunlight, blue dizziness of sky. Almost anxiety, but closer to excitement. And, when a painting or a drawing really worked.

"What is the feeling of 'this' exactly?"

Since her young guest did not answer, Phyllis Bernstein said no more. Knowing Isa wanted to paint, she passed her a card with a painting of a naked young man, very pale, with limbs like cuts from a butcher's shop and a very pink penis. She asked if she would like to go with her tomorrow to a gallery opening for an artist who was married to a friend of hers, a man called Lucien Freud.

Isa thinks, *How strange it is that life has great loops in it like this. Or do we make them happen?* Is it really not surprising that Sebastian Fowler is here with her, and she drawing him? *Do we simply follow the tracks that have been laid down for us, so that what we decide has little weight, in the end?* Was she always going to be a portrait artist, with or without Lucien Freud (who had come to dinner, she remembers, with his equally terrifying wife)? Was Sebastian Fowler also always going to be widowed, and come here to her house? And was it all perhaps Henri Fournier's fault, for writing so clearly and passionately about his love that in the end, nobody would be able to lie about him anymore, because the evidence was there, in a hundred or more letters, in the story in her grandmother's attic? Was it inevitable that after all this time, in another century, Sebastian Fowler and she were here together, to pore over the past and discover, piece by piece, minute by minute, what it would mean to them?

31.

The young chauffeur, Jossien, had already been called up, and Pierre
Albert was too sick to drive. But the garage man in Cambo was still
there. She found him and begged him to drive them to Mirande. They
left the next day after lunch in the same car in which they had driven
to the coast less than two weeks earlier. Henri was wearing his black
tunic with the number of his regiment on the collar: 288, embroidered
in gold thread. He was upright beside her, no longer the carefree young
man who had lounged in light flannels on their last seaside trip to
Biarritz.

She thought, *Tomorrow I will come back up this same road, alone. He
will have gone.* It was as if he had already begun to leave.

She summoned the stoicism she had learned young. She chattered;
she could hear herself making light of this dire journey. She talked about
the theatre; about the time she'd been dressed as a pheasant, in feathers,
in Rostand's play *Chantecler*; about the time her cousin Julien left his
hat on a bench in the Jardin du Luxembourg and someone recognized
it and brought it back to him; about her brothers and how they had
soaked horse chestnuts in vinegar and had battles with them, swinging them from strings to crack each other. She told him about Katy

Brassington, and how they had walked about Paris together when they were young. She told him how her mother had ordered a piano to be delivered, and how they had rushed outside to watch it being hauled in through a high window. He listened, his arm tight around her now, and whenever she stopped, asked her like his little niece Jacqueline when anyone told her a story, "Go on! Go on!"

The web she wove and unpicked and rewove lasted them all the way to Mirande. There, he went to the depot, while she paced in the little room that was to be his for the moment. There was a cradle next to the bed. He came back and saw it as a symbol of hope. To Pauline, it was a shocking reminder of the baby that was not to be.

"I've chosen my orderly. He's called Jacquot. A solid type, he'll know how to manage things."

They had their roles. Yes, she knew how to do this. She could simply leave out everything that was not in the role, put up her chin and forge ahead.

Early the next morning they woke to hear a newspaper seller shouting in the street. The English had declared war. She would have to leave Mirande that same day. She gave him the letter she had written the evening of his mobilization. In it, she'd given him what he had always wanted: she'd promised to be baptized when they married, to obey the commandments implied in baptism, to practice the Catholic faith. What could hurt about borrowing his religion, if it would make life easier for him?

Neither wanted to say goodbye. It was better to pretend that they would see each other again soon; that this was no more of a separation than all the ones they had been through already, with herself abroad or him on military maneuvers. She saw him look at her hard, as if to memorize everything about her.

She got back into the car, and the driver accelerated away. Her last sight in the mirror: a young man in a black tunic and red trousers— but was it Henri, or someone else? Men had become indistinguishable overnight. Perhaps women had too. In Tarbes, she asked the driver to stop; she rushed into the Galeries, bought a warm scarf, some sweaters, gloves, and socks.

He was still there when she got back; he had not vanished into the crowd of men. Her officer. Her lieutenant. He still walked the same earth. They had not parted for good. He was scarlet with happiness and surprise to see her again. She pushed the packets into his hands. How could she have let him go without all the things that he would need? In among the clothes she'd placed a copy of Stendhal's *Le Rouge et le Noir*. She'd rolled his thickest sweater around it. They stammered a second goodbye, in front of the others. She tried to put hope into her eyes, into her smile. *You. You, forever.* Then she turned and left.

Back at Cambo, she walked into a silent house. All the things they had loved, the garden chairs, the white roses, the curtains that lifted and floated in the breeze, were just scenery. She walked about flailing at the air with her arms like a drowning swimmer.

Then a letter came from him, two days later. They were not leaving immediately for the front; possibly she could return. Already, letters were different; they were from soldiers to civilians, from active men to passive women. What chance did love have here? And then, perhaps it was time now to be active, to make love work. She thought, *We are turning into new people overnight. Nothing is as it was. What is being asked of us is beyond anything we could have imagined.*

The next day, she found another driver who worked in the garage for the owner, who had already been enlisted. The young man had a disability: a twisted foot. She went in among the old cars with their lifted hoods and flat tires, the wheelbarrows full of tools, the cartwheels and pony carriages tipped on their shafts. "Can you drive?"

"Yes, Madame."

"Can you drive me to Mirande?"

"To Mirande? Where the garrison is? If Madame can pay for the petrol, I can drive anywhere."

For a third time, she was driven down that same road. She did not care if it would embarrass him, or be a mistake, or make her feel worse. She had to see him one more time, her hunger for his face was so great.

He was dressed as a plain soldier, in a blue cloak. His head was shaved, so she could see the bones and planes she had so often felt with her fingers in the dark.

She watched the line of marching men as they drilled, heard the song shouted by hundreds of male voices rise and then fade as if they disappeared already toward a place at the edge of the great confused darkness that was the war.

The departure of the regiment would be from the railway station at the nearby town of Auch. She followed, in the car, with her disabled driver, and moved into a room in the town. How many times would they have to say goodbye? She felt strung out with the tension; but there was no way she could not be here, as long as he was too.

They would have only six days together before the regiment left for the front. Henri was drunk with exhaustion already. The church clock in Auch struck the quarter hours, carving their time together into sections of fifteen minutes. It was hot. Night fell. The little room was airless and men shouted under the window, late into the night. She didn't care. If they ate, if they slept, if they sweated in the heat, she didn't care, as long as she was still with him. They did not speak much, made silent love deep in the night with a sharp intensity; it was as if this last goodbye would be the final one. He held her to him hard, touched her face as if memorizing her. It was almost more painful to be drawing out his departure this way; surely there was something she must say, or do—yet to try for either seemed pointless.

He was gone in the mornings when she woke, and she only saw him at the end of a hard day of drilling his men. He began to look worn, like a stranger. Yet it mattered, just to be there, with him, in what had become his daily life.

On the third day she found a bathhouse. She walked to it, as she had been directed by their landlady, down an avenue of plane trees, their peeling, patched trunks reminding her of home. Sun pierced the shade to fall on the ground like pieces of gold. Pauline could hardly see to walk; tears blurred everything, light and shade. The last days at the Villa Souberbielle in Cambo played over and over in her mind: Henri writing, she dozing at his side, the quiet buzz of bees, the old roses, the luxury of arguing about the plot of a book. That would never—whatever happened—come again. Even if the war ended, as people said it would, in a few weeks, there could never again be such innocence. The lesson she had learned at the death of her father—and had forgotten too soon—was that everything can change in a minute. This was the truth underlying all of life.

In the bathhouse she smelled strong carbolic soap. The woman who welcomed her was tall, dark, her still-beautiful face marked with sorrow, or perhaps just sleeplessness. She showed Pauline to a cabin and began to run hot water into a huge bathtub, and then mix in the cold.

"Do you have a towel, Madame?"

"I have nothing. Can you lend me one?"

She handed her a scratchy square of cloth. "Is your husband with the 11th Chasseurs?"

"No, with the 288th Infantry."

"Ah. My boy's a brigadier in the 11th Chasseurs. They're saying that the regiment won't go to the front till November, because our deputy here has a brother in it, and his second son."

"I'm happy for you."

"You haven't heard anything in town, have you, about the next departure?"

"No, nothing."

"Ah!" It was nearly a groan.

Pauline undressed, listening to water shoot noisily into a neighboring bathtub for another client, and the woman asking the same anxious questions of the invisible woman bathing next door.

She sat up to her breasts in hot water and scrubbed herself with the carbolic soap. The plumbing ticked and roared and she lay back with her head only just above the water. As long as she could stay submerged, she might not have to feel anything. On and on went the questions behind the partitions. "Have you heard anything? My boy is with the 11th Chasseurs. They're saying that they won't leave till November. Have you heard anything in town?"

"No, nothing."

Over the partitions that went only halfway up the wall, in the steam, in the breath of women, in the hopes and fears of them all. She asked the same questions of every new arrival, who could say only, "No, nothing." Nobody knew.

On the morning of the last day, the general in command reviewed the 288th. It was more like a simple goodbye: from the town to the soldiers, from the soldiers to the town. Company after company, the regiment stretched and formed across worn, dried grass. Henri's mother had arrived the day before, determined to say goodbye to him. Pauline hung on Madame Fournier's arm—like herself, his mother simply wanted to be here with him as long as she could—and watched him in his blue cape, with two thin gold stripes on his sleeve. He stood immobile at the head of his section. She saw from his expression that he had seen them in the crowd. His right hand in its suede glove hitched its thumb to the bandolier across his chest, to touch his heart.

"How handsome he looks," his mother said. Pauline thought, *She has not let herself imagine even for a moment that he could die.*

In the evening Pauline, Henri, and his mother made their way to the station. Henri found a reserved carriage, and his comrades. His mother hung back, allowing Pauline and Henri some time alone. He held her to him hard, her face against the harsh cloth of his uniformed chest, and then let her go. "My love." She couldn't speak. They walked together down the platform.

"Everyone says the war will be over in three weeks," he said to them both from the train window, where he leaned out, among the other leaning men; it was all he could find to comfort them, though none of them believed it.

His face was so pale. She saw him as if from a distance, through the blur and fog of evening, the steam from the engine, under the station roof. A clock struck eight. From a corner of the station, trumpets and drums struck up, as if the musicians were announcing the beginning of a country dance.

Everyone was saying, out of pity for each other and themselves, "*A bientôt.* See you soon!" The doors clanged shut. He still leaned out of the open window, holding her hand. His face closed against the moment, even as he held her hand firmly in his. Madame Fournier had embraced him again before he got on the train, but Pauline did not dare. This firm hand would be all she had of him, until their fingers parted. His eyes held hers, steady under frowning brows and the edge of his cap. There were to be no more goodbyes. *La Marseillaise* struck up its first notes. And the train began slowly to move, really slowly, so that all the women holding their men's hands could go on doing so for a long, impossible moment until they had to run, galloping down the platform to its end, until they had to let go, stopping, gasping, feet on the beaten-down earth, watching a simple red light disappear into the tunnel of the dark.

32.

Chloé begins to lay out photographs from a sagging cardboard box in a pattern on the cleared table, the way people lay out tarot cards. Herself as a baby, her mother and herself as a small child, herself on a swing, an unknown couple, the house, an old portrait in sepia—a grandmother?—a wheelbarrow with a baby in it from at least a century ago, a wedding group, a young man with cropped hair and a cigarette, herself again on a donkey, a 1950s car with a man like a brigand at the wheel, and again, the house, this time photographed from the back. A portrait in faded color of herself with her hair pulled into tight braids, in what looks like a school blouse, staring with that shut expression he has already seen when she has to listen to her mother speak. She is absorbed, as in a game of patience.

Chloé; who is Chloé? She has been flirting with him, playing with him; what is she showing him now?

He glances over her shoulder, sees her brief return glance up at him—black eyes, pursed lips—but she is absorbed in what she is doing. Her hands begin moving the photographs about, slapping them down like cards, shuffling and laying them out again.

He sees a photograph of a pale boy with freckles with a bandage across his head, aged not more than twenty. Chloé slides it under some others but not before he has seen the intensity of his eyes, like a cat's in the dark.

"Who was that?"

"He was my husband. For a very short time."

"Why the bandage?"

"He tried to kill himself. He succeeded, later."

"Oh, God, how awful for you." He hears himself, his appalled spontaneous remark; now he is the one responding to a death. Yes, it's hard not to get it wrong, whatever one feels.

"Yes, it was. It was a long time ago. I was really young."

"What was his name?"

"Luc."

"Can I look at it?"

"Why do you want to?"

"Because. I suppose because you nearly showed it to me already."

She slides the photograph out again. A thin-faced young man with those cat's eyes, the bandage slanted across his forehead.

"I didn't know you'd been married."

"There's a lot we don't know about each other, wouldn't you say? Now this one, this guy in the car is my papa. Luckily he's got rid of that moustache."

The brigand is indeed Hugo. He sits at the wheel of an old Citroën 2CV with the roof down.

"Doesn't it all look old-fashioned? Another era. Who'd have thought?"

Seb thinks, *She wanted to show me; she wants me to know her.* "And this is you, at school."

"Yes, what a little tyke, wasn't I? And this is Maman and Hugo getting married, all in white, what a joke. Look at those flares."

The past, the gone century, the missing people, the dead young husband: she is showing him her life. She is, though mocking and flippant still, inviting him in. Telling him, *I have been there too; I understand.*

She shuffles the photographs together again. "Isn't it funny how we remember the things we have photos of? It's almost like remembering a false reality. A memory of a photo of an event, or a person. I often think, the people we really are never get seen. Do you ever think that?"

She has a way of asking him questions, quite intimate ones, and then not waiting for an answer. She is familiar with him now, as is Isa. Chloé with her offhand intimacies, drawing him in and then cutting him loose, Isa with her slightly fey look and absentmindedness, then her sudden, fierce focus. It occurs to him that he hasn't really known any other women apart from Annie, for years. When you are married, one woman stands in for all the others. But here he is, alone with two women who have over the last weeks somehow become intimates, who show him their acceptance in practical ways, including him, asking him questions, not waiting for answers, walking through rooms without addressing him, passing him dishes at table, as if he has always been here. He is neither husband nor father, nor lover, nor exactly friend. But he is being allowed to be himself, and it feels like an extraordinary gift.

He watches her shuffle her photographs like cards, like a practiced gambler. Then she grins at him, pats him on the shoulder in passing, and leaves the room, leaving them on the table. Isa passes the window, peers in, and waves, and goes on down toward the vegetable garden. It all feels both ordinary and pleasant. He thinks that he will miss them, when he leaves, which he will presumably have to do soon. He wonders whether they will miss him. Or will his presence here be immediately erased, submerged in their everyday, and will they only refer to him occasionally, that English guy, the one who came that summer, the sad one whose wife died—remember?

Seb feels bereft at the thought. He picks out some of the photographs: Isa, young and long-haired, with a cat, laughing with the black-eyed Hugo, beside a river. Chloé as a baby in the sort of backpack in which he once carried his own children. The boy with the strange eyes and the bandage. Chloé in a bathing suit. Chloé under plane trees, with both of her parents, he in flares, she in a sun frock, while acrobats hang from the branches above them. Chloé on her knees with a goat. Lifetimes in which he had no place, that went on without him and will go on without him, in which his brief presence here will appear as fragile and forgettable as a dream. He looks up just as Isa comes into the room, sees her glance at him, her basket under her arm with vegetables for dinner tonight, her red hair like a helmet. He thinks, *I don't want to be forgotten, to be absent. I want to be in this life, I want it more than I want anything, but it's irrational, it's crazy, they don't want me, I'm not a part of it all. Or, am I?*

Isa says, "Chloé left all her photos out? You know, she hasn't looked at any of these for years, as far as I know. She completely blocked out what happened." She picks up the picture of Luc. "It was all such a tragedy, from start to finish. Poor Chloé."

"Did she miss her father a lot, when he left?" He in turn picks up the photo of the man under the trees, pointing upward to the acrobats, his daughter close at his knees.

"Yes. It was traumatic for her. I think it was why she fell for Luc so hard—he was someone she could hold on to, because she could help him."

"I see." Seb thinks, *It explains something, perhaps: she has to flirt with an older man, because it's the only power she has to make him stay.* He breathes out, relieved. No damage has been done. He has played his part as well as he could. Now, he knows. He puts out a hand to take the photograph from Isa and lays it down with the rest. She takes his hand, squeezes it briefly and hard, then says, "I must get the dinner on, or we'll not eat till midnight. Will you wash the salad?" It's the most intimate thing he has been asked in months; he goes happily to run water into the sink and watch unbelievable amounts of earth turn to mud among the leaves of lettuce.

33.

She went back to Cambo, taking his mother with her. Letters from Henri came every two or three days: from Bourges, then from a camp at Châlons, then from an unmarked destination. The 288th had started fighting at Étain. She couldn't stop the thought that recurred all day: *Is this the moment that someone's firing on him? Is this the moment a bullet is entering his head, his arm, his chest?* She felt the places on her own body: head, chest, arm, as if checking through her own flesh that his was still whole.

From Mons, from Charleroi, from the retreat before enemy soldiers, they learned only what the official communiqués deigned to tell. *So, this is what the world we knew has turned into?* And, *how on earth do we do this? Where, oh, God who does not exist, is the way through?*

She wrote to him almost daily; sometimes their letters crossed. He was well, he was busy, he was where he was supposed to be. His postcards, with their official stamp, seemed impersonal, designed to distance him from her—and any soldier from his beloved. But in his letters, written late at night and by lamplight, he let her see the face of his misery and loss. Once he had reached Étain, there were few letters, only official postcards. He was hers, she knew it—but oh, the tenuousness of the thread that linked them.

At the end of August she went back to Paris by train only to discover that the Germans were at its gates. (How had she become this person who could just get up and go to Paris when the Germans were at its gates?) The man who was in charge of the city had, she heard, been given instructions to burn all the bridges across the Seine if the Germans should enter. At the last minute, these orders were rescinded. But there were barricades set up in all the streets, in some places made only out of heaps of furniture that had been thrown from windows and built into pyramids like bonfires about to be lit. Pauline walked fast past rubble and broken furniture. She tried to get through to her own house, and found it impossible. As for finding the minister who had offered Henri a job as an interpreter—there was no way to discover where he was. She couldn't even get across the river. The bridges were closed. "Go back, Madame. Can't you see? It's not safe. If you've anywhere else to go, leave at once. They are said to be about thirty kilometers from here."

She traveled straight back to Cambo by slow train, terrified by what she had seen of Paris. If she was being forced into change, so was her beloved city. The transformation of the whole of life—landmarks razed, bridges closed, communications impossible—had happened in just a few weeks. How could they, simple humans, keep up? The government had, she heard, removed itself entirely and installed itself at Bordeaux.

"I'm going to Bordeaux to look for the minister of the interior," she told Henri's mother, who was waiting for her. "He'll be able to change Henri's occupation to something safer. I only hope he will accept." It was a slight hope; in her heart, she knew he would insist again on remaining with his men.

"I'll come with you," Madame Fournier said, seizing her hands. Pauline thought, *We have to become soldiers ourselves, give up the luxury of feeling. We must harden our women's hearts.*

She found Monsieur Briand at the Hôtel de Bayonne.

"He's having dinner, Madame. Who shall I say wants to see him?"

"I am the wife of Lieutenant Fournier of the 288th. He was offered a post as a translator, an interpreter. I need to see Monsieur Briand without delay."

"Well, I'll ask if he will see you."

She crossed the dining room to where the minister of the interior was eating soup democratically enough, a napkin tucked under his chin.

"I've come to request a transfer for my husband, Lieutenant Fournier. He was offered a post as an interpreter."

"You came all this way to see me?"

"Yes, Monsieur. I tried to see you in Paris, but I had to leave. The Germans seemed about to invade the city. They were searching everyone."

"Well, I'm going back to Paris tomorrow, if I can get through. I'll do what I can. I'll see the fellow who can arrange for him to be transferred, and I'll send you a telegram right away so that you know what's happening."

Pauline went to find Henri's mother, who was waiting outside. "Let's stay the night. He's going to help us. He said so. He'll arrange for Henri to be transferred. It seems they still need an English interpreter, even more so now that the English are so involved in the war. Let's stay at the Chapeau Rouge?"

Their usual hotel was full to overflowing. Everyone was in Bordeaux now that the government had moved there. They found a room on the third floor of a modest building, with one table, one chair, and two little iron beds. Madame Fournier looked around her. "Not exactly the Ritz, I'm afraid." Pauline never told her what memories the mention of the Ritz brought up, or how much she preferred being here in this miserable little room. She pulled back one of the thin bedspreads, and there they were, the bedbugs that awaited them, advancing in a military-looking column.

"I suppose we can sit up all night?"

"I think we'll have to."

"Briand did promise. I know he'll tell us if he gets any news." She wanted to sound as optimistic as she could.

The two of them sat up all night, taking it in turns to sit on the single chair, while the bugs filed across the beds and up the walls. Now Pauline was the one wanting to be told stories, so Henri's mother told her about him at all his different ages and stages: child, schoolboy, adventurer, finally the young man who had written her into his novel.

"He left home to go to Paris to boarding school when he was twelve. Both our children went away to school, as where we lived, there was no secondary education. Henri was always very independent, anyway, though he loved his home."

"Go on," Pauline said. "Tell me everything. Please."

"Well, he was at Lakanal, the school in Sceaux, just outside Paris. He was still quite young when he went to London to study English. He worked for a wallpaper firm called Sanderson's, and stayed with a family called Nightingale, I remember. He wrote us such long screeds in a mixture of French and English, we wondered if he ever had time to do anything else. I worried about him. He was always writing home for more money, to pay his laundry bills, he said, because he had no idea how much it would cost to send out laundry. Several times he asked me to send French bread because the English bread was so tasteless. He seemed to be always hungry. Later, when he failed his exams for the École Normale Supérieure, he decided to join the army rather than teach, because he thought it would give him more freedom to write."

"Tell me about Henri and Isabelle, when they were young."

"Ah, they were marvelous together. He virtually brought her up. They both used to read all the time. We got a case full of new books at the end of every school year for prizes for the following year. Every July, always at the same time. Henri and Isabelle waited for it to arrive. They were beautiful books, bound in red and gold, with lovely paper. They even smelled new, they seemed to smell of printing, of fresh ink, glue, varnish, whatever they use, they even cracked a little when you opened them. They had pictures, with thin paper over them. Henri said that when you read them, they left little gold flecks on your fingers."

Outside, somebody yelled in the street. Dawn was beginning to bleach the sky, coming in through the cracks in the shutters.

"Go on." She wanted his childhood, every detail of it. If his mother went on talking about him, he would be all right.

"He and Isabelle used to fall on them and devour book after book. They had to leave them looking unread, I told them, or we couldn't give them as prizes, so they sat there with their books only half opened not to crack the spines, peering in at what was inside, one on each side of the table. I can't remember what they all were. Books that were popular at the time, Gérard de Nerval, Laforgue, Jules Girardin, the sort of thing nobody reads now. They both liked adventures, children who ran away with gypsies, stories about clowns and street performers."

"Tell me more. Tell me anything. Anything you can remember."

"Well. Another major event of course was always the gypsies and performers coming to the village, every year. The traveling fairs too. They'd come and put their tents up in the square in front of the church. There was a young man with a trained goat that stood poised with its little hooves on upturned glasses, which he removed one at a time till the goat was perched on the last one. And tightrope walkers, walking between trees. Acrobats. There were musicians, fiddlers, so we could dance."

Pauline said, "I can imagine it. You dancing. The goat." The goat kept the night, and the war, away. Henri's mother's voice, the tightrope walkers, Henri's safe childhood. She hugged her knees, shifted her back against the chair.

"Very little happened in our village. Both children were wild to know about the outside world. Later, Henri would send Isabelle all the books and notes he'd used at school, so she could read them too. He told her which poets to read, and which philosophers. He was very influenced by Claudel, so she was too. Their letters to each other were sometimes far above my head." Then, "Don't worry about Isabelle, Pauline. She's got a sharp tongue, as you know, and she's a jealous person. But anybody who loves Henri will always be her friend."

Footsteps, sharp on the cobbles of the street. Every now and then one of them would try to squash a bug with a bar of soap, without much success. The church bell tolled the quarters, as the clock had at Auch. Time was measured meanly; hours dragged. War was dirt, and uncertainty, and sleepless nights. In the morning, as the sun came up and palely lit the squalid little room, they woke and realized they had been briefly asleep, she on the chair with her head sideways against the wall, Henri's mother wrapped in her shawl on the floor. The story had stopped, without either of them realizing. Shocked, they saw each other's faces, lined and grimy, as if they were strangers.

34.

The summer days are shorter, the air blues and chills, and fruit hangs on the trees, plums, damsons, early apples. The date on which he was to leave has come and gone. You can change your ticket on French railways quite easily, he's discovered. He asks Isa, "If you don't mind, I'd love to stay on another week or two? Would that work for you?"

"Of course."

"You're sure? I'm not really doing anything, now I've finished sorting Henri's manuscript, as far as I can."

"There's fruit to be picked. You could help with that. And, if you don't mind going up ladders, I could do with having the gutters cleaned."

He likes the simplicity of it: tasks to do, small achievements and visible outcomes.

The idea for a possible future comes to him one early morning. He throws back his single sheet and stands at the window, looking out at the stripped fields where corn once stood. The whole cycle of the harvest has followed his time here: corn to bales, the roar of the harvester to the dusty after-silence of its passing, and now the vanished cylindrical bundles of straw, the fields swept and empty, everything beginning again. He thinks of the small animals that live in the margins of these fields, and how they will creep out now, and begin once again to inhabit them. He is a small animal at the edge of something bigger than himself: tentative, alarmed. The blades have come very close. He thinks of going back to England, to Oxford, to his former occupations, to his house, to those painful dinner parties and hushed conversations in shops, and knows he can't do it. It would shrink him, where he needs to expand. Retirement, and dinners for one at the dining table, and evening television and early bed with a pill. Nobody to talk to—about portraiture, about a manuscript, about bottling fruit. There has to be another way. He is not ready to be old and lonely and give up on happiness—but whoever is?

Annie, he says to her that morning in his room looking out over fields whose shapes have become familiar over these last weeks. *Darling, what should I do?* He imagines her, but he can't imagine her answer. She is not here. He is in a place, a situation, a life in which she has no part. That is the point of it; it has always been the point. She can no longer suggest to him what he might do; all he can conjure back is the conversation, long ago on that English beach, when, digging her long fingers through sand, she told him that if by any chance she died first— unlikely thought—he must live on and be happy with someone else.

Someone else. For so long, the words have struck him as meaningless. Who else could there be? There was a brief moment in the early eighties when they talked about the possibility of "other people." He'd known at once that the discussion wasn't just theoretical, how could it be, and the thought that Annie might have "someone else" was so intensely painful, bringing up all his ancient fury about Giles, now a neighbor and his son's godfather, that he had to say to her, "Please, tell me if you love someone else, tell me if it ever happens." *And I'll do what? Shoot myself? Kill the bastard? Murder you?* Annie had smiled, perhaps a little sadly. They had been talking about a couple they knew, who had split up because one of them had "someone else." Was it sheer sexual jealousy he felt at the very thought, or a childish desire to possess? He didn't know. Yes, there had been a woman in Oxford on a Fulbright, a young visiting American writing about Emily Dickinson; he and she had shared a drink and a rueful chat about anti-Americanism in England, and he had admired her sleek fall of black hair, her lifted eyebrows, the way her lips puckered around a straw as she sucked up—what, Coca-Cola? But the stride from that conversation to any idea of taking her to bed was only in his imagination. He had too much to lose. He had Annie.

And what did Annie say in reply? How one forgot things: one of the most important conversations of his life, probably, and he can't even remember what she said. "I wasn't thinking about us, stupid." Or, "No, there could never be anyone else." Or, "There's this bloke I fancy, but of course I wouldn't do anything." Or, "Well, I've been meaning to tell you . . ." Something interrupted them. The conversation was never concluded, as so many in a long life together were not. A phone rang, a baby cried, something began to burn on the stove. And now, he can't even remember what she might have said. Something else happened, and they went on loving each other, with whatever it might have been left either unsaid or unheard.

He hears a call from below: "Sébastien? Coffee!"

He goes downstairs, relieved, and finds Isa in the kitchen at her espresso machine shooting dark coffee into two small green cups, one for each of them. The light comes in sideways, so that she is lit like a woman in a Vermeer painting, busy and ordinary and yet somehow eternal. The things of life, the simple objects that come alive when someone uses them, handles them; that only become dead matter when that person is gone. He stands in the doorway, just looking.

"What's up?" she asks, half turning toward him.

"Nothing. You just remind me of a painting."

"Anyone I know?"

"Vermeer, actually."

"Ah, the eternal woman in her room, with the world outside."

"Something like that, yes." He takes the cup she hands him and sniffs it. "Thanks. When I look back on being here, I'll remember the coffee. Oh, and all the food, of course."

"But not us?"

"Well, you, of course."

"So, you're looking back already?"

"And forward. We're always stuck between the two, aren't we?" He wants to pretend still that there is something to go back to in Oxford, yes, and wants her to think him more independent than he is. Yet he suspects she has seen through him. Then, "Isa, tell me more about Chloé? She showed me the photo of Luc and told me that he'd killed himself, and then clammed up."

Isa sits down at the table and motions to him to sit. He pulls up a kitchen chair. "I thought she'd made a terrible mistake, and that's partly why she doesn't trust me. She met him in a prison, where she was teaching prisoners art. He did try to kill himself, very dramatically, with a gun to the head, but he only succeeded in grazing himself. He was a drug addict, though she says he was clean after they married. He died by crashing his motorbike, in the end. Not immediately. He was in hospital, in a coma. They had been married a year."

"God, how awful." *You think you have tragedy in your life,* he thinks, *and then you hear something like this.*

"After he was killed she came down here and slept every night in the stables, over at Martin's place—you know, the groom? She found comfort with the horses. I couldn't do anything to help. She hasn't slept in this house ever since."

"Poor Chloé."

"I know. She still can't forgive me. I suppose she guessed that in a way I was relieved. He was dragging her down. She'd never have gone on teaching if he'd lived. She'd have been tied to him—I know, one shouldn't judge, but I am her mother, I know what a bad marriage does to you—and he would have used her to the bitter end."

"Well, thanks for telling me. I had wondered, you know."

"Why she's so angry? Well, that's it. And being around me. She worships her father, and that's the way it's always been, and Luc's death put me permanently in the wrong."

"She does think about you, though."

"You think so?"

"She said the other day that you haven't had any love in your life since her father left."

"Well," Isa says, "that's not her business, true or false. Or yours."

"I'm sorry," he says. "You're right. It isn't." He finishes his coffee, and leaves the room, angered by having been put so easily in the wrong. Of course, he should not have mentioned what Chloé told him. He goes to pull a ladder out of the barn and sets it against the side of the house, where grass sprouts from long-untended gutters. Standing on a high rung with a small trowel he's found, he scrapes and cleans. Earth and grass roots, and the dark brown scum they have grown in, and twigs and seeds fallen from the overhanging lime tree. Whatever lack Isa has or has not in her life, there has evidently not been anyone to clean out these gutters in a decade. It's probably why the house feels damp, in spite of the long hot spell of this summer.

When she passes him on her way to the vegetable garden, she just gives him a glance upward, with a faint eye-roll, but says nothing. He feels chastised, and still irritated, and more than ever sorry for Chloé. Chloé, who slept in stables with horses to find her comfort. Well, it's not his business. He scrapes and pokes till the sun is high at midday, then comes down and drinks a long glass of water in the kitchen, followed by a glass from an open bottle of sauvignon blanc in the refrigerator. So, Isa wants to transform him into a handyman, now that he is done with being the resident scholar? He will show her what he can do.

35.

Her cousin Julien came to see them every day in Bordeaux to bring the latest news of the war. *It was not today, then,* she thought. One more day, and as far as she knew nothing bad had happened.

"Pauline, you must try to relax. You can't go on like this, you'll make yourself ill," Julien said.

"But we haven't heard anything for weeks."

"Listen, there's every possibility that he's alive. Men in battle don't have time to write letters. That's all."

"I've heard from Claude, only a week ago." Claude, who had joined up only a month after Henri, who had sent her only the stiff obligatory note of an officer to his legal wife. "He was still in the north, near Étretat. Of course, they can't say where they are going."

"Well, it's bound to be very patchy, what gets through. I'm sure you'll hear soon."

On September 13, Julien came in, jubilant. "There has been a significant victory on the Marne. Really, the war could be over soon. The Germans are in retreat. Henri could be home for Christmas. Claude too."

Then there was Henri's telegram: the boy who brought it handed it to her, and she stood with her heart rocking her body before she read it. Then she made sense of the letters on the form—*Go slow, Pauline, pay attention, read what is actually there*—HAVE HORSE LIAISON OFFICER ALL WELL LOVE. He had been promoted, given a horse, and instead of leading his section in the front line, under fire, he was now a liaison officer, a position that was far less risky.

Oh, God who does not exist, thank you. She fell to her knees then, as Madame Fournier did, to thank this being whom the whole of France was petitioning as ardently as they were the minister of the interior. It seemed only polite. She went to the cathedral every day with Henri's mother, arm in arm. War seemed to demand this: a series of rituals to hold the worst at bay, a kind of sorcerer's thinking. *If I do this, or that, he will be safe. If I give alms to a beggar, if I cross the street now and not later, if I brush my hair a hundred times, if I do not eat even though I am hungry.* It was absurd, and yet necessary. So they went in together to kneel in the pews on the stone floor and pray to Henri's God that He would spare him. His mother was pious and sincere, she herself playing a kind of lottery in her head. That same God, whether Christian or Jewish, had not spared her father: prayers for intercession were useless. Yet now, what else was there to do? It was a sign of their weakness and helplessness, but it was also a sign she could make to and for Henri, to be there with his mother every day, to go through the motions demanded by his religion. It was also the role—everyone knew this—of women in a country at war.

In the cathedral, on the left side in an alcove, there was a statue of the Virgin Mary carrying her child. The locals believed that this statue, crowned in gold and pearls, had miraculous powers. It was surrounded by flowers, some dropping and dying, others fresh each morning; the flickering light of hundreds of candles lit the two marble faces, one serious, one smiling. Each day Henri's mother and she joined the crowd of people, kneeling, standing, elbow to elbow, faces bent in prayer or lifted toward the statue. To Pauline they seemed like people on a sinking ship, begging for mercy where there could be none. Weather and waves did not respond to fervent prayers, and neither did the abstract power of wreckage that was war. But it was worse to be here and not to believe; just as it would be worse to stand on that ship—she thought of the wretched passengers of the British ship, *Titanic*, sunk only two years earlier—and know oneself doomed. So she began to pray, to something, to someone, the words sounding clumsy and stupid in her head, absurd upon her lips, just because this was what Henri would have done. *God, you quixotic vengeful deity, will you exchange my lover's life for my conversion? If I say I believe—like the audiences in Barrie's* Peter Pan *in London who clapped to save Tinker Bell's life, showing that they believed in fairies—will you save my beloved?* Who knew? Perhaps someone, somewhere, would have his mind changed by the wind of prayer rising from all the churches and cathedrals of France, from the words spoken in desperation, the rosary beads rubbed between fingers, the tears shed, the hands gripped together. A command would be given, or not given. A bullet not fired, a sortie not undertaken; a change of wind, of weather, a sudden rainstorm, a general who overslept, who did not give a certain order. A soldier given a horse, to carry him high and safe through the danger of battle. These things, she could believe in. Human agency worked: humans made the decisions. There were moments, like the one when she'd burst into the dining room and confronted Briand over his dinner, when destinies could be changed, plans altered, and a man's life saved.

On September 16 she had a note from Briand asking her to see him immediately; he was back in Bordeaux. He looked even more exhausted than at their last conversation, and she saw how soiled his collar was and how unshaven his chin.

"Madame, I am extremely sorry, but in all the confusion of battle, I was unable to find the person responsible for organizing Lieutenant Fournier's transfer."

"Monsieur Briand, I am extremely grateful to you for trying. But in fact, he's been promoted, he's been given a horse and is involved in liaison work, so he is in less danger."

"Do you want me to go on trying to get him transferred as an interpreter? I know the English are short of good interpreters; unfortunately not many of our military men have a good command of their language. Think about it. Get back to me in twenty-four hours."

"I'll have to ask his mother and sister what they think." She, after all, was not his legal wife.

"Well, don't wait too long."

Henri's mother and Isabelle thought that since God had answered all their prayers by giving him a horse on which to ride high above danger, it would be ungrateful, even immoral, to question His decision.

She went back to tell Briand this, thanked him again, and saw his thick eyebrows go up in surprise. "Ah, well. Perhaps it will all be for the best."

Three days later, she went to the Ministry of Justice with a telegram to send to Henri. While she was in the office, she heard that the cathedral at Reims had been bombed and their dear friend Charles Péguy killed in the first wave of fighting after the German invasion, two weeks earlier. She couldn't help crying aloud at the news of Péguy's death, and she was struggling to control her tears when an attaché came to find her. "Monsieur Briand wants to see you immediately."

"Thank you. I'm coming." Pauline followed the young man down a corridor and into the room that had been taken over as a military map room, where Briand sat behind a desk.

"Madame Fournier."

She almost looked round for Henri's mother. "Monsieur Briand."

"Sit down for a minute."

If Péguy could die, so could Henri. Anyone could. The whole world, everything that mattered, was being destroyed. She wondered whether that confident statement that the French army would take the offensive and march into Germany was never accurate? Or, it had tried and been beaten back? Had the people who had said it would be easy, over in a few months, been lying just to make people like herself feel better? She held the arms of a gilt chair that belonged in someone's drawing room and looked at the minister, whose eyes above their bags of fatigue were kind and concerned. War was dirt, uncertainty, sleeplessness, at whatever level you were. Strangely, the memory came to her of the day after her first wedding, when she was only just eighteen and had first confronted Charles le Bargy in the breakfast room at the Ritz: like two generals facing each other across a map. *I want you never to do that to me again. I want a* mariage blanc*!*

Briand spoke gently. "Madame, I am sorry for the loss of your friend. It's only natural to worry about your husband. But I want to warn you against superstition. I know what a rational woman you are, and what a strong one. When I see the whole population of France weeping and wailing and on their knees begging God to save their one soldier, their son or husband or brother, I am sympathetic, but I also think it's sheer superstition and I believe you do too. I'm guessing that his family decided not to have your husband transferred, am I right? Now, if you would reconsider your decision, I will do what I can to have him transferred immediately. Contrary to what people think, the war is not going well, and it will certainly not be ended in a few weeks. The Germans may be in retreat, but I have intelligence that it's only in order to regroup. We are in for a long haul."

She looked into the square, rather ugly face—the bushy eyebrows, the bristly jaw—and saw an ally.

"It's very kind of you, Monsieur Briand, to take so much trouble. And thank you for telling me the truth."

"I read his book," Briand said. "And I know who you are. I saw you onstage, before all this craziness began, and I want you both alive at the end of it, so that I can read his next book and see you back on the stage. Enough said?"

"Thank you, Monsieur. I hope that what we both do, both on the stage and in literature, will be worthy of your confidence in us."

When she next went to church with Henri's mother, it was with relief at the power of human agency. One could do without the divine. She knelt before the fat, smiling Christ child and smiled back. *Just a Jewish baby,* she thought, *supposed to be killed at birth, only to die at thirty-three.* And what about the mother in blue, so patient and accepting? What had she thought of the sacrifice of her son's life? All around them, they heard the word *sacrifice,* as if the willingness to give up one's life were anything except the utmost folly. She wanted to tell him with her new fierceness: *Henri, don't write to me of sacrifice. Don't insult us both that way.*

She wrote to him and their letters crossed. She wanted to tell him about everything Briand had said, but she knew it would be censored. She told him how she had left Paris by train for Cambo just before the Germans began dropping bombs on it. How she did not have time to close up Trie or take the paintings off the walls before the Germans arrived. How she got out with only a day to spare, as the roads and railways were being blocked. He wrote to her of his confidence in the German retreat, and his increased piety since God had shown himself on their side. She wondered how many German soldiers believed this too.

Eighty wounded French soldiers had just arrived in Bordeaux. She'd spent the morning serving them soup. She knew nothing about God, only about wounds, how to try to treat them, how to feed men who couldn't swallow because they had no jaws. Ten women, including Henri's mother and herself, had volunteered at the hospital that had been a college before the war. They'd tied on long aprons as if they were cooks, and tucked up their hair. The soldiers had wounds that were oozing blood and pus through their bandages. Some of them might not last the day. They had not been expected till the following Saturday, and the hospital was missing medicine and equipment that still had to be delivered. There was a young man from the outskirts of Paris who had been shot in both arms and couldn't use his hands to feed himself. She brought the spoon to his cracked lips as if he were a baby, and his eyes blazed with fever. He'd been married one year, he said. He asked Pauline to write to his wife. Tomorrow, she told him. And told Henri, in her next letter, *You absolutely have to approve of me doing these things, it's my duty and it's all I can do.*

Every time she did something for a wounded soldier, she did it for Henri. It was what made it possible.

And he wrote to her: *All well, in spite of rough days and nights.* The Rasurel underwear, the silk cap, the sleeping bag, the scarf, and the bottle of Armagnac were doing their job. Ups and downs, he said, but basically all right. It was possible they might even see him before November.

She reread his letters. *It's raining, cold, the ground's soaked,* he wrote, *but the bad weather is slowing the enemy down. We seem to be holding them off since the victory on the Marne on September 10.*

And they told each other, like a talisman: *My love is with you always.*

36.

She goes on, telling him. Even if she wears herself out, he must know it all. "The whole mood of the country was swayed back and forth by the news that came in. The rumors, the false hopes. The victory on the Marne was seen as a miracle. People thought it meant a quick end to the war. Henri's letters were so optimistic, we longed to believe everything in them. He was, after all, at the front. But we also knew that news was censored, that no soldier was really allowed to write the truth. What is truth, in a situation like that? It would only ever be known piecemeal, through hindsight, long after many of those involved were dead."

Seb says, "So, you can never know the truth in the present? You have only a few clues to go on, and they may lead nowhere?"

"I think that is one of the hardest things about life. We walk in the dark, feeling our way. But we have to move ahead, anyway."

"You couldn't know how it would all turn out."

"Or even why it was happening. Do we know what will happen with all this business in Ireland, now? No. Do we know what is really going on at the moment in Chile? Or in Indochina? All we can know is from the past, from history. The future is invisible. History will try to make sense of it, years, even decades from now. We live in the middle of events we can never understand."

"Do you ever think that there could be other realities, other universes, parallel if you like, that run alongside this one, in which things happen differently?"

"I think there are many ways we can invent to console ourselves."

"So, to think like that would be only about consolation?"

"I do think so. I prefer to look the reality of what happens, what is actual, straight in the face. It's the same when I am invited to think about an afterlife, about heaven. It's all about consolation. People can't bear the facts. We live, we die, the world goes on without us."

He's silent, and she guesses he wants to smoke a cigarette, because he's feeling for the shirt pocket where he keeps his blue packet of Gauloises. "Go and have a smoke—I can tell you want one—and then we'll have something to eat. Yesterday's leftovers, will that do? I think we still have some wine."

Perhaps she has sounded too bleak. But parallel universes, afterlives, and alternative realities make her tired. She has staked her life already on what is. He gets up, apparently relieved. She sees him blink back into the present—his desire to smoke, the hunger that rumbles in his gut, and the present moment, here, now, halfway through this day.

37.

The real estate agent's smart car comes up the drive on the following Tuesday morning at eleven, a big white four-wheel drive following close behind it with English plates. A tug bringing a cruise ship into harbor. Both cars, small and large, park in the yard. Monsieur Destry has not been letting any grass grow under him. Seb looks down from his window, his shutters cracked open, sees Isa walking across the courtyard. Chloé is nowhere to be seen; has she been left out of this completely? A small chinless man in a white shirt and tie gets out of the smart car. Two people get out of the SUV, its doors held open like awkwardly unfolded wings. The new invaders, Seb thinks—people with money to burn. New money, IT or the stock market, property deals, even government. A man with blond hair thinning on top, a blue cotton shirt, chinos, deck shoes with no socks. A woman with light-brown hair tied back, a denim skirt, white blouse, sandals. She has red lipstick, red toenails, a shiny, expensive-looking leather bag. He slaps down the stairs, comes out from shadow to the bright light in the yard, is introduced, shakes hands.

"I'm the resident writer," he says. "Just here for a few weeks, to do some research."

It would have been more fun to say, *I'm the handyman*. His ladder is still propped outside the barn, waiting to be used again. The blond man looks relieved, perhaps to see another Englishman. His grip is painful. The woman looks anxious, shakes his hand in her small warm one, says, "Oh, hi. What are you researching? If you don't mind me asking?"

"Possibly a book." Immediately, he regrets having said it.

"Oh, how exciting. Will you put us in it?" The woman's ready enthusiasm makes everything she says sound bright and a little false. She wears big designer sunglasses pushed back onto her head. Wide eyes, a snub nose: not pretty, but good skin. Close to fifty, probably, with those fine little lines at her eyes, at the corners of her mouth. Hair pulled back like a teenager. A possessive curiosity, he sees. A collector, of things, places, people, amusing stories to tell in which she features well. People like to think they will appear in books, he remembers.

"Are you famous?"

"No," he assures her, "not at all."

"Well, good luck with it, anyway. I hope it's a novel. I love novels. I only ever read on my Kindle, these days, it's so convenient, and you save so much money. Oh, isn't this place perfect? It's really romantic." Her attention is gone from him; not famous, therefore to be let go. "Monsieur Destry told us about it in the nick of time, sent us the photos on the Internet. We have to go back next week, so we might have missed it, easily. We've absolutely fallen in love with the area, but we hadn't seen quite what we wanted till now. I suppose I shouldn't say that yet, should I? Now, who is going to show us round?"

Her husband just smiles and follows on, hands behind his back like a bodyguard, or the Duke of Edinburgh.

Susan Mottram, the wife, is using her hands to gesture prettily, as if she thinks this is how you communicate with the French. She darts out into the yard and back again. Could they pipe water there for a fountain? Oh, yes, there's the old pump, of course. She wants to see upstairs. And what's in all the wonderful outbuildings? Was it a working farm? What is the big tree in the courtyard? How far does the property actually go? Does it reach as far as the river? David Mottram walks close to the walls and examines everything, peering as if shortsighted: the portrait of Isa's grandmother, the fire bellows hung over the hearth, the books in the bookshelves, even the ones scattered about on the couch. He must have spent years, decades, being the sensible one, the male, the antidote to Susan's rash enthusiasm. The one who makes the money, who keeps the show on the road.

"Madame de Giovanni, may we look around upstairs?" Monsieur Destry says.

"What was that film? Darling, you know the one I mean. The house in the French countryside, the long alley of trees, the mysterious gateposts?" asks Susan Mottram.

Her husband only grunts, examining the mantelpiece with its jumble of old candles, creased photographs and pieces of string, and Isa's gardening glove, its curled fingers and palm like a severed hand, the other one of the pair lost.

"You know the one I mean? We saw it together, I'm sure we did. Anyway, this house reminds me of that one. It's perfect, really, it's just what we are looking for. We wanted something that hasn't been done up, so we can have a free hand. You know what I mean?"

The little red Mégane charges into the yard then, and brakes, Chloé at the wheel. She gets out and leans against the car. Seb sees her light a cigarette and stand smoking, her eyes narrowed against the sun. She watches, from a distance.

As the couple walk through the house—eyeing its cool rooms, its beamed ceilings, its promise of solidity—Seb feels the pressure of their casual assumption of the right to ownership. These two, if they see something they like, get it. It's being done in a very English way, a way he knows and despises. Americans would make a bigger deal about it, he thinks, would talk in dollars, not go in for this vagueness about actual cost. They would fill up the place with big strides and loud voices; the English only creep about it, touching things, marveling, reminding everyone of their fine taste. He feels an urge to protect the house, to have it remain unchanged. His countrymen irritate him as only one's countrymen can. He knows them, their money untouched by any financial crisis, probably invested offshore, their easy knowledge that they can have what they want, always. It's enough for them to "fall in love" with it. People give way to them. They give them what they want. It's a kind of entitlement that foreigners may not notice, they are so gracious, almost self-effacing, in their approach.

He sees Isa looking puzzled, as they move through the rooms as if they were in a museum, the wife leaning forward intently to examine objects, the husband still with his hands behind his back as if to prevent himself from grasping them. The agent, Monsieur Destry, follows them at a distance. Chloé is still smoking out in the courtyard, as if taking her time before moving into action. Isa herself moves outside, as if to remove herself from the couple in the house and stands a little apart. She avoids his eyes, looks up at the blameless sky. Her hair is like a helmet in the sun. Neither he nor Chloé, he understands, is to get in the way. He makes a small sign to Chloé and sees her shrug.

The Englishwoman stands at the kitchen door, a little flushed, her shirt-sleeves pushed up, the gold on her wrist shining. "I'm sorry, we've been here for ages. There's so much to look at. I just had to have one more look out here, you know, think where I'd put everything, I thought a fountain would be wonderful, what do you think? There's room to put a pool out at the back, but it would be fabulous to have the sound of running water out here, don't you think? Oh, sorry, I'm getting a bit ahead of myself, aren't I? But seriously, we do love it. It's just perfect."

Seb sees the rapturous teenager she once was as well as the sleek woman she is now, confident that her man can and will buy her the objects of her rapture. The hard bargaining, no doubt, will be going on inside. David the taciturn will know exactly what to do, how far to go, and when to straighten his back from leaning over the printed details of the house, glance at his beautiful watch, and retreat into a tactical absence from the scene. They will drive away with everything unresolved, in spite of Susan's enthusiasm, and she will grumble at him, *But you should have said, but why didn't you, why haven't you*, and he will drive silently and enjoy the knowledge that he has these French people eating out of his hand. Russians, thinks Seb, could have been worse. But when he sees Isa's expression after they have gone, and only the dust from car wheels—theirs and Destry's and Chloe's—is left in the air, he knows that the pain she is feeling does not depend on the nationality or even manners of the buyers. It goes deeper than that, and feels worse.

38.

Until that autumn, she had never let herself imagine that he could be killed. The numbers of the dead remained outside her—until Charles Péguy's death, when something was breached that could not be repaired. It was like letting in illness. As the first symptoms develop, you know you're getting a cold, then a fever.

On September 22, she had a severe headache all day, focused in a point in the middle of her forehead. There had been no news. She lay down in the rented room in the little house in Bordeaux that she shared with Henri's mother, who came in to see what was the matter. Pauline had pulled the blinds half-down, and the little acorn that hung off the string of the blind tapped against the window. She thought of blind Pew, in *Treasure Island*. She thought of the Black Spot. Tap, tap, death coming down the road.

"But darling, you've only just had a postcard. You can't let yourself be depressed like this; you'll hear from him again very soon."

Pauline fingered the rough edges of his last postcard, reassured by the date and the postmark. "These little bits of cardboard are all we are allowed to write on at the moment—otherwise nobody would be fighting, but writing long letters all the time!"

Henri's mother put a cool hand on her forehead and brought her chamomile tea. Her head throbbed and tears leaked from her hot eyes. At about four o'clock she decided to get up, fever or no fever, and go to the cathedral. She leaned on Henri's mother's arm as they walked up the street past the Chapeau Rouge, till at the end of rue Vital-Carles they could see the towers of the cathedral.

In the darkness, in among the murmurs and whispers, the sound of others sobbing, Pauline allowed herself to let go. She was at the end of her strength. The role she was playing was perhaps about to kill her. The pain in her head intensified and she thought she might vomit. It was impossible to imagine life without this pain. Had it been there always, just waiting to be felt—perhaps to kill her? She felt the cool stone of the floor with both palms, she crouched before the marble Virgin, and cried for everything: for Papa, for her loss of him, for Péguy's death, for her lost baby, and at last, for herself and Henri. For their lives, that had been small, and private, and their own.

Henri's mother held a hand at her back, between her shoulder blades. When Pauline had finished crying, she got up from her knees and found that the pain in the middle of her forehead had cleared and that she felt light, almost ethereal.

"We'll find a sign from him when we get back, I know we will," his mother said. "Come, let's go back."

They walked home quickly to the rented house at 4 rue Lafayette. Nothing had changed. The black front door with the metal grille across it, the damp, cool vestibule inside it, a steep stone staircase leading up to the second floor, everything was just the same. Pauline leaned against the wall before going into their rooms. Just for a second she felt it, a wing-beat, hope like a living thing: the existence of Henri, in this world.

Two more weeks later, that sensation on the stairs was just a memory. Her cousin Julien had telegraphed the colonel of the 288th and received a reply. *Lieutenant Fournier disappeared September 22.*

She cried out, "Then he's a prisoner! He must be! Otherwise they would have said he was dead!"

There was nothing to do now other than wait.

"Knit!" said Henri's mother. "That's what I do."

She tried, the needles slipping between her fingers, stitches dropping, a long woolen tribute to the waiting of women, an object with no shape and no point except to keep her fingers busy and her brain awake. She had to knit, she had to do something, or she would go mad; this long, straggling gray tube was her monument to hope.

Madame Fournier went to rejoin her husband, who was unwell. Julien went back to his apartment in Auteuil. Bordeaux was gradually emptying of its crowds, now the government had left to return to Paris. Pauline settled in alone, to wait, because if there was news, it would come here, to Bordeaux. In the room someone had left a new god for her, a bronze statue of David with his sling copied from the one by Donatello. A young man's body, slim as her lover's. She ran her hands over its smooth surface. She searched the bronze male body with her fingers to find the place where a bullet could have entered, and through which life might have leaked away. But he was not dead, not yet. He had simply *disappeared.*

V.

39.

The room where she had to go to wait for news had stained-glass windows like the kaleidoscope of her childhood, red, green, and bright blue filtering the light, the patterns flickering on the eye. The only patch of color, glass, turned the whole room into an illusion, a fiery vision in which she sat blinking. A small, stout man came in and told her that thousands of people had had letters from prisoners over the last three days, and only this afternoon had the flood of people wanting news begun to ebb.

"I am very sorry you have had to wait, Madame."

"Well, it will have been worth it if you have a message for me."

"But Madame, I am sorry to say there is no message."

"You may have one tomorrow, then?"

"No, Madame, we have received all the messages from prisoners that have been held up for three weeks now. There are no more, for the moment."

"Well, thank you. *Au revoir, monsieur.*"

She dragged herself home to her rented room. A letter had come while she was out, from one of Henri's comrades. It told her that Jacquot, his orderly, had been evacuated to the military hospital in

Mirande and would be able to give her the details of his disappearance and the last battle he had been in. Pauline thought, *I must go, at once. I must speak to Jacquot.* Now, there was at least this to do. She felt her energy return, once she had decided to act. Anything was better than just waiting.

She asked Marie-Louise, the young woman of eighteen who had been her chambermaid for the last month, to go with her. Marie-Louise wound her blonde hair in a roll and pinned it up, as if the request had immediately made an older woman of her. "Of course, Madame."

"It may be hard. We're going to a military hospital. You don't mind?"

"Madame, it is wartime. And it can't be any worse than here. Anyway, you must not go alone. I will take care of you."

Pauline looked at this girl, who was no more than a child. *We women grow up,* she thought, *in response to what is asked of us.* She went off to pack a few things and prepare some food for the journey.

They set off together by train toward the south, taking hardly any luggage. The train went incredibly slowly and the journey took all day. Their bread was stale, their water tepid. They chewed dried apricots that she had found on a shelf in a shop in Bordeaux. The train smelled of stale soot and old coins. It was already dark when they arrived. At the nearly empty station, a very old man wheeled a luggage trolley, peered at them. Pauline asked him the way. The hospital, he said, was over there, on the outskirts of town, near the army camp. It was as if he was the last man left here. Oh, she knew Mirande, in that other life, the one she had had with Henri, before this. Of course she did. It was where he had trained as a soldier, where he had set his novel *Colombe Blanchet*, where she'd driven with him only a few months earlier, the last place before Auch, when he was mobilized. Where she had seen him off with sweaters, scarves, and Stendhal, for a journey that neither of them could have imagined.

Outside the railway station, the old man abandoned his trolley with a sigh and waved the women toward a truck that was parked up at the roadside. "Ask him. He'll be going where you want."

The driver was a tall, dark young man with a Marseille accent. "Hop in. It's not very comfortable, I'm sorry."

It was Maman's accent before elocution lessons got to it. It reached far back into her childhood, as far as a shadowy grandparent in Marseille.

"It's fine," she said. Marie-Louise and she sat up in front next to the soldier, their thighs pressed together. Pauline felt the girl's youthful softness, smelled her girl-scent. Marie-Louise was someone who at another place and time could have rushed off on a jaunt with a soldier into the night. The truck roared through darkness until they saw the lights of the improvised hospital.

"Who are you looking for?"

"A Corporal Jacquot?"

"Is Jacquot a nickname? Corporal Jacquot could be anyone. Got a regimental number?"

Pauline said, "I don't know. I never thought. We just heard he was called Jacquot. But yes, the 288th." How stupid, not to have asked if that was his surname; otherwise it would be like asking for a soldier called Jack.

The man from Marseille went off and asked an orderly. He came back. "You said he was with the 288th?"

"Yes."

"Well, there aren't too many from the 288th here, it seems. They've been busy on the other side of France; they must be taking care of them nearer to the front. Wait here, I'll find out."

He went off again. She sat with Marie-Louise, the two of them hunched on the high front seat like runaways. Around them was the scenery of war as they had not yet seen it. Tents, fires, a lit building, men in groups, trucks, and the cold stars of a winter sky. The tall soldier came back to them, picking his way through mud.

"I've got him. Jacques Grevin, his name is, but everyone calls him Jacquot. Come on, I'll take you there. This can be hard if you're not used to it."

"Thank you, Monsieur."

"Oh, well, I'm hardly a monsieur anymore, but I'll accept it. Corporal Alfred Giono. Pleased to be of service."

The way in was through a long dormitory of occupied beds. Men on crutches, men with white bandages tying up destroyed faces, a man on a stretcher carried by two orderlies. Pauline was glad that she had at least worked in one of these field hospitals in Bordeaux. It was strange yet familiar, how the men went silent as they walked through, following the corporal from Marseille with his swinging gait.

"Corporal Jacquot?"

"That's me." A small man with a bandaged head lay with both his arms out over the sheet that covered him. Possibly nothing left of his legs, he seemed so short. She tried not to think about what was under the sheet. She heard Marie-Louise draw in her breath.

"I am Lieutenant Fournier's wife. My name is Pauline." She touched his arm, as she could not shake his bandaged hand. All these men, all over France, tucked in bed like babies, their missing limbs under sheets, their heads swathed in white, all of them waiting to be taken care of. Corporal Jacquot burst into tears. The parts of his face that were visible—one eye, mouth, nose—contorted, and he sobbed, "Oh, my God, Madame, Lieutenant Fournier, oh, why does it have to be me who tells you? They shot him, Madame. It was in September. In the Woëvre. Jesus, Mary, and Joseph. Oh, Madame. Oh, he was a good one, your husband. Oh, this is terrible, terrible." The tears ran down his one cheek into his bandages. She watched his mouth, a dark hole, most of his teeth gone.

"Did you see him? Did you see him dead?" Her whole body was shaking. Marie-Louise took hold of her arm.

"He was alone, Madame, he'd followed the captain, they were after some Boches. Him and another gentleman, another lieutenant. Just the three of them. God only knows what happened to their backup. Oh, it was a mess, Madame. It was an ambush. Couldn't have seen it coming. They walked right into it."

"But did you see him?" *Oh, tell me that you did not.*

"Well, no, Madame. But I heard. I was his batman, see. They shot him here. In the gut. Then in the head. So I heard." He gestured with a bandaged paw. "No, the last I saw of him was sitting against a tree."

"A tree?"

"Yes, like he was out in the country on a jaunt or something. We were on the opposite hill. We were too far away to do anything. There was some kind of ambush. They may have been behind enemy lines, him and his colonel, I'm not sure. Some said there was a stretcher party, a German one. I don't know for sure, Madame, I'm sorry."

She said it again. She had to. "You are sure he was shot dead."

"Yes, Madame, I am sorry to say."

"You don't know what happened to his body?"

"No, Madame, I don't. We had to run on fast after that. You see what happened to me, they got me, anyway. Oh, but he was a fine man, your husband, a fine officer."

She summoned her strength to say, "Corporal Jacquot, my husband told me a lot about you, and he said you were a fine man yourself. Thank you for telling me what you know."

"There was one more thing, Madame."

"What? Tell me."

"Like I said, I was on the opposite hill. We were stuck there most of the day. Later, a couple of hours later on, I saw a soldier stick a helmet on top of a rifle that was stuck in the ground. Like he was marking a spot."

"One of our soldiers?"

"I can't be sure, but I think he was a Boche. The helmet was one of ours."

So that was it. That was all. It was over. "Corporal Jacquot, you have been wonderful. Thank you again. And I do hope you will be better soon." The man was looking at her so sadly, she had to say it, the only thing he would want to hear. Nobody would be better. Nothing would ever be better. But you had to keep on, and say things, and be kind.

"Well, Madame, I've got one leg gone now, and one eye, and if you ask me, I'll be better off home with one of each than in that mess with two. I wouldn't say it if there was anyone else to hear, but that's how it is."

She backed away from him, because she thought she might vomit at his bedside. The sour taste in her throat rose and she swallowed, to choke it back, and Marie-Louise said, "Madame, some air, let's get some air." Air, darkness, the night sky. This bleak place, the makeshift buildings in the sea of mud and debris. The world emptied of Henri, the world that he had loved so passionately, that he had fought for—he had fought, didn't that make any difference, how could he be dead, how could she believe it. He was out there, surely, sending her a letter, laughing as he told her how he had worn his wool scarf, finished up his brandy. Pauline stopped, and the corporal who was leading the way, back to his waiting truck, paused to look back at her, worried; Marie-Louise put an arm up to pat her between the shoulder blades just as her whole stomach revolted and she vomited onto the path.

Her body refused to hear the truth, threw it back out in protest. She wiped her mouth. The soldier turned away. Marie-Louise handed her a handkerchief. There were no tears, not yet, just this refusal of the body to hold in what it contained. They made their way, following the corporal toward the truck, and were driven back to the railway station.

"Madame, I am sorry it was bad news," the soldier at the high wheel said, accelerating into darkness. But she couldn't answer. Perhaps she had said the last thing she was ever going to say.

They must leave, they must get out of this town immediately, this no-place that the war had ruined. Perhaps the whole world was now like this. Perhaps from now on people would only be able to stumble in darkness, lost under cold stars. She knew she must get back to Paris, see Henri's family, who were now all she herself had; surely, they were now her own family too. Marie-Louise and she sat to wait in the train station waiting room with no fire. The empty grate had paper in it, no coal available, and was surrounded by green tiles. A big clock ticked the minutes away on the wall. It was still impossible to speak. They sat next to each other, their hands in their laps. Knitting and prayer were the activities offered to the women of France, prayer and knitting: both of them utterly useless. She would never do either again. Marie-Louise's small, cold hand came out and found her own, and they sat side by side, holding hands tightly. The train came screeching in at last from Perpignan, reeking of coal smoke. They found a carriage, and sat opposite each other, the chill pane of the window, the emptied night between them. The night would begin earlier each evening, as the earth moved on from the equinox, the day on which Henri had been killed. After several hours, she heard her stomach rumble, and realized that she was now very hungry. Her body was making its own demands. But neither of them had anything left to eat.

The train shunted into villages and out again, slowly returning to Bordeaux. In the rented room she and Marie-Louise made hot chocolate, found some stale brioches, slept briefly in their clothes, lying together on the bed; then they piled their few belongings into suitcases, stripped the bed, and left the place with the window wide open and sheets hanging out of it to air. Only later did she remember that this was traditionally the sign of a death in the house.

"Marie-Louise, you've been such a help. If you want to stay here now, it's all right. I'll be fine." It was the first thing she had said in this new, pointless life.

"No, Madame, I want to come with you. I couldn't let you go alone now, it wouldn't be right."

"Well, all right. Thank you. We'll be getting the night train."

In the train to Paris, they sat opposite each other again, and stared out into the dark of another long night. Marie-Louise closed her eyes, but Pauline knew she was not asleep, just tactfully refusing to notice the tears that had begun to stream unchecked down her own cheeks. *He's dead. There's no more hope. He's dead. There's no more hope. It's happened. What I've known since that day when my head hurt so. We know, but we go on pretending, until we can't pretend anymore.*

Eventually, she slept. The train rattled on through the night. From time to time, there was the scream and rumble of another train passing theirs, the flicker of its lights upon their eyelids; the passage through a station, glaring yellow lights; a stop, people getting on, getting off; signs that there was a world out there that was somehow still able to function. At dawn, gray light reached into the carriage. Pauline woke, aching all over; she moved her head from side to side, stiff as an old woman, tasting the sourness in her mouth. Another day. They were crossing wide, flat countryside, cinder-gray under the lightening sky. All the others in the compartment were asleep, their heads tipped to one side or another, their mouths a little open. It was unbearable that the dawn light could be this unkind. They looked dead. Perhaps they all were already dead. Even Marie-Louise looked exhausted, her hair coming down, her mouth in a pout. Suddenly she sat upright and stared back at Pauline, aghast, woken out of a dream.

"We did hear it, didn't we?" Pauline asked her. She had to be sure. "In Mirande. We did hear him say that Lieutenant Fournier was dead."

"Yes, Madame. I am sorry. We did."

A streak of sun after a rainy sunrise woke all the other passengers; they stretched, yawned, started straightening their rumpled clothes and talking about food. The southern suburbs of Paris began rolling past. Pauline saw shuttered houses, rainy streets, a market where already someone was beginning to put up stalls. The sky over the city was mottled, held more rain. Marie-Louise and she looked at each other, and then the girl looked away, embarrassed, and rubbed her cheeks. There was a pink mark on her face where she had slept on a rope of hair.

"Thank you for coming with me," Pauline said to her. "I could not have done it alone."

As they drew into the station and the train slowed in a shush of wheels and a cloud of steam, she saw out of the corner of her eye a squat figure stumbling toward the edge of the platform: a short person, man or woman, impossible to say which. A bundle of clothes, gray-colored, indistinct. A hand outstretched, as if to beg, or accuse. Like the figure at the end of the street, when she had left the doctor's house after the abortion. Like the glimpse of a dwarf-like person she had seen on the way home from school the day her father died. There, there again, and then gone.

When they stepped out onto the platform at the Gare d'Austerlitz that morning, she gave Marie-Louise the money to go to a nearby hotel, to wait for her. Then she went by cab to rue Cassini to find Henri's family, as she must, and tell them the news.

Isabelle opened the door to her. "Simone! What on earth are you doing here?"

"I had to come. I'm sorry, Isabelle, I have—I have bad news. I had to come here, to tell you." There was no way to soften it. "I went to see Corporal Jacquot, who was with Henri at the front. He told me. Henri is dead."

Isabelle held the door open, but didn't let her pass. "My father's ill." She looked and sounded grim. Perhaps she, too, had hardly slept.

"I'm so sorry, I didn't know."

"How can you come here at a time like this to tell us such a thing! It's not true. We know he's alive. We had a telegram this morning from our uncle Feur, in the army. It said Henri missing, presumed imprisoned!"

Madame Fournier came to the door, a wool wrapper over her nightgown, and stood behind Isabelle. "Come in, my dear. Oh, you look worn out. What's happening? Do you have any news?" Pauline thought, *She has aged years since Henri left.*

Oh, God who does not exist, how could she say this? "I'm afraid I do. I went to Mirande. Marie-Louise came with me. We went to see Jacquot, his orderly. He told us Henri has been killed."

Isabelle moved aside and Pauline nearly fell into Madame Fournier's arms.

"Oh, my dear." The hall was full of Henri's family, his father struggling downstairs still only partly dressed, his mother clinging to her, Isabelle screaming, "It's not true, it's not true, how can you say that? Why did you come here to torment us?"

"I had to come." She did not say, *You are my only family now.*

"I don't understand," the father said slowly. "We heard from my cousin Feur that he has probably been imprisoned. He'd heard from another officer who had seen Henri, that he'd been wounded, propped against a tree. He said, 'Please don't leave me.' Those were his words, apparently. You don't make up something like that." He held himself up by the newel post of the stairs.

"We have to believe that he's still alive! We have to!" Isabelle shouted.

Madame Fournier said, "Come in, my dear, we can't all stand here in the hall. Tell us what you know. We hear all these confusing accounts. Nobody can be sure what's true anymore. Isa, stop shouting, it doesn't help. We all need to sit down."

They went into the salon. The parents in their shabby nightclothes held on to each other. Isabelle stared at Pauline, her eyes hard under her straight black brows. Pauline sat down on the edge of a chair. She didn't know what to say. She was exhausted beyond belief. She should not have come. Could Corporal Jacquot possibly have been wrong? But Henri was dead; she felt it in her. It was this total fatigue, this heaviness inside, as if she had swallowed lead.

"Why do you want to deprive us of hope? We must hope!" Isabelle stood close, glaring at her, her black eyebrows drawn down in a line over her brown eyes—Henri's eyes.

"Isabelle, don't be so unkind." Henri's mother intervened.

"Well, she comes in here claiming to be his wife and to know exactly what happened to him, and she's still married to le Bargy in the eyes of the Church, not to mention Casimir-Perier; she isn't even free to marry anyone, and then she says—I've heard her, Maman, so have you—the war is useless, is doing nothing for France, only gets millions of good men killed! Maman, she's not one of us, can't you see it? She doesn't understand him—she never has!"

Pauline felt as if she'd been slapped. She'd begun to believe that Isabelle accepted her. What had happened? Surely Henri's mother was still on her side? Did it count for nothing that they had shared rooms, talked all night, been to church together, cried together? The damage was from way back. It felt like her father's death, and the hopelessness of her childhood afterward.

Henri's mother reached for her hand and held it in her cold one. She said gently, "You see, there is so much contradictory news, it's hard for us. Isabelle and I have not slept for days. Monsieur Fournier is not at all well. Perhaps, my dear, you should leave us alone for now."

She managed to say, "I just thought you would want to know. I'm so sorry."

"I know, my dear. But it's hard at the moment. Isabelle is so tense about Jacques too."

"But Jacques is alive!"

"I know. But we only recently heard that."

Pauline thought, *You cannot destroy someone's hope and not be hated. I should not have come.*

"My dear, this is not a good time," Henri's mother said. She heard the firmness in her schoolteacher's voice. "I'm sorry, but I think you had better go."

So she gave up, and went away. *Oh, God who does not exist, what will become of us? Will we all become monsters now, with the damage that is being done?*

40.

Sebastian says to her. "That was terrible. How could they be so mean, after what had happened?"

"I discovered then that when people are suffering, they are not kind. They draw in, close ranks, and protect themselves. At that moment, that morning, the Fourniers all needed to protect themselves. Against me. I was the outsider. No, it was not my fault, but I was there. I had thought they would console me, or I them, but I was wrong. I saw the reason that wars happen and people are hounded out of countries, because they are the wrong people at the wrong time."

"Did you ever go back?"

"I went back to ask for Henri's papers. My letters to him, that was all I requested at that time. Isabelle had put them all in a yellow leather suitcase, after she had finally accepted that he wasn't coming back. She went on believing he was only missing, not dead, right until the end of the war. She told me that since Henri was still alive, the papers were his, including the letters, and his family had to keep them for him. It was a sort of fixation with her that he would come back. And, it was the one power she could have over me, I saw that."

"So she wouldn't let you have them, even the letters you had written to him?"

"No, she said that they were Henri's property. In law, that was true, if he was alive. Then, after the war, she eventually let me have some of them back. Those are the ones I have here." She gestured to the covered trunk in the corner. "The rest, the letters to his family, she kept of course. And I knew she had read everything we ever wrote to each other when she brought out her awful book saying that I was an immoral woman and I'd ruined her brother's life. I did see his mother again, after the war. She apologized for that dreadful morning, and for Isabelle. But they had lost too much. They could not forgive me."

"But why you? You loved him too. Why did they blame you?"

He's young. He has not experienced anything like this.

"Because they had to blame someone. They couldn't blame the army, the politicians, the whole idea of patriotism. Nobody could. I was the scapegoat for everything they were feeling. It often happens, I know that now."

"So, what did you do?"

"I went home. To quai Debilly, to Claude's house. He wasn't there, as he'd been called up too. He was killed only a few months after Henri. It was such a dead time. I remember the cold. I remember snow. I remember death being so close for all of us that it was as if it waited at the corner of the street. Like a beggar. Like a beggar who would not go away."

41.

Later, after the English people have gone, he finds her crying at the sink. He has come down to pick up yesterday's copy of *Le Monde*. "Isa?"

"Oh, Sébastien, look, I broke a cup." The green porcelain pieces are on the counter.

"That's not why you're crying?"

"Just, the last straw. It was my grandmother's." She paused. "No, really, it's selling this place. When it comes down to it, I have such mixed feelings. Yet I have to sell it. And Chloé is still so furious with me about it."

Long married, he finds he still has the habit of taking someone who is crying in his arms. She lays her head briefly upon his chest, allows herself to sob for a moment, then sniffs, "I'm sorry. Excuse me."

"No need to be sorry."

Seb says nothing more for the moment. His hand moves across her back. It was what he would have done, has done, for Annie. A wife trains you, he thinks. Just let it out, let it be. He has stopped trying to be the man who solves problems long ago; as well as being impossible, this is not what women want. A shoulder to cry on is usually all that is needed, and maybe an attempt later at gluing the broken object back together. But he has not, for months, held anyone who was crying. His daughter, Laura, after the funeral, yes. But not a woman his age, not like this. He feels, as she cries, that his own ribs are cracking; he can't bear it, that she feels this hurt. *Is this what has been happening to me,* he thinks, *is this what grief does, lets you feel others' pain this sharply?*

He feels her relax against him. She lets herself sob for a moment longer. He looks down at the white skin of the top of her head, the shining reddish whorl of hair that grows from that center. His hand rubs her shoulders, first one, then the other, and his fingers press at her nape. He feels the warmth of her breasts against him. Just breasts, all women have them.

"Thank you, Sébastien. You're a kind man. I'm sorry to burden you with all our family problems."

He is a kind man. He feels as if she has pinned a medal on him that he neither wants nor deserves. He feels raw with a sensation that seems to come from a heart that fills his chest. No, he doesn't want to be just a kind man, he wants to be the man he is. Enough with being kind, attentive, polite. Enough of being bereaved. He wants to be here for her; to fill that space.

She leans into him still, as she has probably not dared to lean for a long time. His fingers make small circling movements on the bone of her shoulder but don't enlarge their circles or change their pressure; she stays there, against him. Then she pushes him away a little—just inches, but enough.

"You couldn't talk to her, could you? Chloé, I mean?"

"What could I possibly say?"

"No, no, of course not. I can't expect that of you. Forget I ever said it."

"Isa," he says, "what is it you really want?" He hears the rough edge to his voice. Feeling his way, trying to guess, it's like pushing through cobwebs.

She takes a full step back from him, rubs her cheekbones with the heels of her two hands. "Oh, God. What do I want? I want to be free of all this, the house, the obligations, the family heritage, the time it all takes, the effort, the way I have to think about it all even when I'm in Paris, and Chloé's obsessions about it all, and being responsible for everything. I want to live in Paris and paint while I still can. I just don't want the burden of it, you understand, the burden of a fucking country estate I can't afford. I don't want to be drained of all my energy, the way I am." She sniffs and stands straighter. Her own voice grows louder, angrier. "The vegetables don't grow themselves, you know, the fruit doesn't bottle itself, the drains and the roof don't look after themselves, it all takes energy—more energy and more money than I have. I don't even want to think about Uncle Henri's damn papers, if you want to know. I want a life. But when those people were here, I just felt so— furious. I felt like Chloé. I know, it doesn't make any sense."

Seb thinks of the way the English couple walked about, confident that they could have what they wanted.

"You know, I still feel my mother and my grandmother here, and Hugo when we were first married, and now there's Chloé, who thinks the past is what she needs to ground her. I thought I wanted to sell it. I do. But when it comes to the point, I just feel so angry that I should have to."

"Chloé will be all right, whatever you do."

"You think so?"

"She's mostly in Paris too, isn't she? She'll be back at work?"

"Yes, but she has all these theories about *le patrimoine de France*. She sees herself as some kind of custodian of it all."

He thinks, *I don't want it to be sold either. It would probably make sense for her to sell it. But again, perhaps this is not the point. Perhaps we are talking about something else here. Perhaps we are talking about our own lives?* Again, he says, "If you do sell it, she will be all right. Her bark is worse than her bite, isn't it? I know, you probably don't want my advice." He's given it, in spite of himself. "In fact, I'm thinking of selling my house in England too."

"Really? Why?"

"Well. It's too big, and my marriage of forty years was in it, and if you want to know, I can't bear it. Everything about it makes me too sad. I don't want to be sad anymore."

"You think you won't get over it?"

"I don't know. I see myself alone there, getting old, living with my memories, and I want something else. I want life, not memories, not cold north Oxford and the same work I've been doing forever. I'm only sixty-three, and I promised Annie, if she went first, I wouldn't just sit there and be sad. I don't even want to do any more research, or write the sort of thing I've been writing, or see students, or old friends. I want to be somewhere new. Somewhere where people don't know me as who I was, part of a couple. I want—oh, this is probably far more than you ever wanted to hear, but I want companionship, warmth, love even. I have to believe it's there for me still, or I might just as well die too." He's set out to listen to her, and now here he is, spilling his own feelings; he's held back long enough. He feels the extraordinary relief of it and doesn't apologize.

She listens. She doesn't even look surprised. She doesn't try to make it all right.

"Love?" she says. "Can you just choose it? Doesn't it have to take you by surprise, knock you sideways?"

"Do you want that sort of love again? The sort that knocks you over?"

"No. It was hard enough when I was young." She makes that French mouth-pursing face, a little shrug. "Hugo the hurricane lover. I've avoided it ever since."

"There's been nobody else? Don't bite my head off for asking, please. You said it was none of my business, and it isn't. But Isa, surely we can talk about it?"

"A few. But not long-term. I had a hard time trusting anybody."

He nods—*yes, I get it.*

"I'm sorry I was rude to you the other day. I suppose you could say, it's a sore point. I've had a few lovers, okay. But not anyone that lasted."

"It's not what it used to be, is it?" he says. "It's not the Lost Domain anymore, the romantic place you long to go back to. We don't have those illusions."

"For women, it always seems to end up being about houses, domesticity, you know; we get sick of them, though. They take up too much of us; they wear us out. Really, I want a small flat in Paris, with white walls and very little furniture—the one I have, in fact—and my studio."

"But what about all the rest?"

"Love, you mean? Companionship?"

"Yes."

"I don't know."

"But you might decide to trust somebody again?"

"Possibly." She looks down. "But what I do have to do is sell Les Martinières before it swallows me up."

"How much do you want for it?"

"What?"

"How much? In euros? Just, theoretically. Just so that I know."

"Are you going to make me an offer?"

"I might. If you don't want the other one."

"Which is what?"

"Well. Look at it this way. This may sound really crazy, but I don't think it is. We combine our lives. I buy half, you keep half. You come and go to Paris as you want, I live here, and Chloé lives where she wants. I could probably manage five or six hundred thousand euros, maybe more, when I sell mine. House prices are high in Oxford."

"Sébastien, this is all far too sudden. It sounds as if you've got it all worked out."

"Not worked out, not really. Just, I've been thinking about it. Wouldn't it make sense?"

Is it always a bargain, he thinks, *at the age we are? My house for your house, my loneliness for yours, my impossible situation for your impossible situation; life as a joint project, when you cannot bear to go on alone? Life is for making, and remaking, surely. At our age, it is for the bold.* "As for being sudden, I have discovered that death is sudden, change is sudden, and life takes us where it wants us. So sometimes we have to make sudden decisions. Actually, I think the important decisions we make are always sudden. Now, do you want to throw that broken china away before you cut yourself? You can buy coffee cups, you know. You don't have to inherit them."

She stands there in tears again, the broken cup abandoned, and he puts his arms around her and feels her lean in against him. A woman's weight, more solid than Annie's, yet without Annie's inner tensile strength. He thinks, *Give up comparisons. Do it now.*

Isa pulls back from him, though. "It won't do," she says. "It's ridiculous. You can't just move into my life because you're lonely and you don't know what to do next. You haven't got over her, Seb. It wouldn't work."

He feels at this moment that whatever has been choking him, that tightness in his throat, that inability to breathe properly, is beginning to break up; that he might begin to cry himself. He says, "I haven't got over her, and I probably won't. But I want to move on. I think I want to do it with you."

"You mean, it isn't just about the house, and money, and things?"

He doesn't know what's true anymore; he's feeling his way. She is a few inches away from him still, looking at him critically. Oh, God, let him not say the wrong thing now, he thinks; let some grace intervene, so that even if language fails, the sense of it all may survive.

"No, it's not just about the house. Sorry, I always seem to put things backward. It's about us. Me and you. Our lives." He stops, takes a deep breath. "I feel, well, I don't want to leave you." There, it's out. He feels its truth, at last, the raw fact of it.

"But we hardly know each other, really."

"But isn't that always true? Nobody knows another person completely. But we could begin to find out."

"You mean, you would really want to be with me?" She sounds disbelieving, still. "It's not just about being lonely?"

"Well, being lonely's part of it, isn't it? You can't separate it all out, loss, loneliness, the circumstances of life, happiness, unhappiness, wanting another person to do it all with? Oh, I'm losing myself here, I can't do this in French, it's coming out all wrong probably, but Isa, I'm happy with you, I'm happy here, I've been happy these last weeks, and you have a problem with the house, and I could help with that. I can do the handyman stuff, and contribute some money, and that isn't nothing."

"A handyman?" She's laughing at him, but close to tears, he sees. "You think I need a handyman?"

Oh, Isa. "Well don't you? Someone to keep the gutters unblocked, cut the grass? Apart from anything else?"

"Well, yes." She's still laughing, "But Seb, if this is a proposal, you're doing it all backward. The gutters, the grass, really."

"I know. I'm out of practice. I'm sorry. Nothing too sudden," he says. "Just, shall we give it a try? I'm not going to ask you if you can love me, not yet."

"All right, I won't answer that."

"But, it's not impossible for you, I mean, with me?"

"I don't think it's impossible. But don't ask me, not yet." She grins at him and tosses back her hair, with that new, freed gesture he's been noticing, and tucks the red strands behind her ears, that he sees for the first time are small and close to her head, like neat white shells. Her ears make him want to cry too; they fit her so perfectly.

42.

Pauline was alone at home at quai Debilly. Cold had moved inside her like an illness. There was little fuel to be had and the streets had not been swept of snow. She couldn't differentiate now between cold and grief. It all seemed to be the same; it had invaded her. The loss of Henri, her particular loss in a country of loss, a century of loss—how could it be hers alone, how could she be living with it locked inside her? Everywhere, people were feeling it. But somehow this made no differ- ence. Loss was always particular, always personal. Perhaps if Henri had died when the country was prosperous, normal, in a mood of celebra- tion, it would have been worse. She had no means of telling, no way of imagining anything worse. But in situations like that, young, healthy men did not just die. It took a war. It took organized slaughter.

    She took her copy of his book to bed with her and read and reread it, as if there were some secret mechanism in it that could unlock history and bring him back. She read about Franz in the forest with the gypsy Gavroche, Franz mad with regret and love, wearing his bloodstained bandage around his head, wounded by his own hand. She read about Meaulnes going to Paris to find Valentine, Franz's lover, and bring her back to him so that the wedding could take place. She found François

Seurel, adult and now a teacher himself, waiting for his friend and companion to return.

She read, *Weeks, months passed. A whole era, gone. Happiness, lost . . . I had no memory but the one that was almost wiped out already, of a handsome, gaunt face, and eyes whose lids lowered slowly as they looked at me, as if they only wanted to see an interior world now.*

That was François, writing about his lost friend. If Henri were to come back, would he look like this? Would he be able to see, not her, not life, but only a remote interior world? It was perhaps crazy to peruse his novel for the key to his life and death, but it was all she could do. It was Henri, as she had felt when she first read it; it was his essence. But now it seemed to her less like a boyish adventure than a vision of doom and loss. If Henri was Meaulnes, she was by turn François, with his endless vigil, and Franz, roaming the forest with the gypsy, and Valentine, running from the whole scene to Paris to become a seamstress and put the past behind her. She was never Yvonne. She had renounced being Yvonne when she had given up Henri's child.

She sat in the evenings in a deep armchair, reading him. She fingered the pages as if they were marked with invisible signs. Remembered a book with herbs placed as bookmarks in it: bay leaves, a sprig of mint. A young man walking in the orchard with a little black notebook and pencil, stopping to write, moving on. It was very nearly unbearable, to remember Henri reading, Henri walking, Henri marking the place. She moved backward and forward through the story. Sometimes she seemed to come upon a paragraph or sentence that she had never read before. If the book was capable of renewing itself, then so must he be. Madness to think so, she knew. But it was all she wanted to do. He had written these words and they were all she had of him, apart from the letters with military stamps that he had written to her from the front. All the rest of his letters and her own to him were in a yellow suitcase at rue Cassini, and she did not dare go back there to ask for them.

On one of these winter evenings, someone knocked and then immediately jangled the bell. It was dusk. Wrapped in a big shawl, Pauline went to open the door. Outside, the sky was ripe with more snow to come, and the way to the front steps, dug out this morning, was already blurred. It was her cousin Julien, belted and hatted like a Russian.

"Julien! Come in. I'm so glad to see you." She hugged him on the doorstep. The cloth of his coat, his cheeks, and his moustache were cold. "Come in, oh, how lovely, I can't think of anyone I'd rather see." It was strange that the arrival of another person brought her close to tears. Alone, she couldn't cry. She was afraid of the animal of grief and outrage in her. If she began, she would not be able to stop.

"You're alone?"

"Just Marie-Louise, my maid from Bordeaux, and the cook, and me." She shuts the door to the cold outside, leads him into her salon.

"What are you doing? Have I interrupted you?"

"I was reading Henri's book."

"Pauline, darling, you don't look well. Are you eating?"

"Sometimes. I won't die. I know that. Though I sometimes feel I want to."

"You must live, you must eat! Henri would have wanted it."

"But you know, I can't see any point in going on without him. I can't even talk to him, Julien. How can I know what he'd want? I can't hear his voice, let alone hear him telling me to eat some soup or make a cup of chocolate."

"It's a bad business," he said, "and the people who said we'd have them running back to Berlin by Christmas, well, they got it seriously wrong. I was sorry to hear about Claude too."

Pauline straightened her spine. No more talk of Henri, then. "I last heard from Claude in December. I've only just had the news that he was killed on January 12. You know, after a while you lose the ability to feel anything anymore." It was like talking to Julien through a fog, or a drug. Words didn't mean what they used to; they all seemed to have been drained of meaning. As her life had been. She was thirty-six; she had more ability to protect herself than she'd had at thirteen. But she felt thirteen years old again. Twice in a lifetime, this agony. How much more, oh, God who does not exist?

She poured him cognac, from Claude's supplies. They stood in front of the miserable little fire made with sea coal, all they could get these days. The blue flame guttered low, and very little heat came off it. Henri's novel lay facedown upon the chair arm and Julien picked it up, leafed through it, and laid it back again.

"You lost my place. Not that it matters, really. I go back and forth through it, looking for something I'll probably never find."

He looked at her. "Pauline, you should stop that."

"I will. But it's all I have of him."

"François Porché is in the hospital at La Courneuve," he said after a silence. "I heard it from Jean Cocteau. I thought you'd want to know. François is very ill, pneumonia I think, but I know he would love to see you. I'm going to see him tomorrow. Will you come?"

"You really think he would want to see me?"

"Yes, I'm sure of it. He's been evacuated from Diksmuide, in Belgium. He was in a Red Cross hospital there. Apparently they had no real equipment. But he's strong; there's a good chance he'll survive. All those Russian winters, remember?"

Henri had called him the Russian Bear. He had been her friend since she was young, in that other life. Poetry in black ink on Japanese paper, a musical voice reading aloud poems that reminded her of François Villon. Walks round the pond in the Jardin du Luxembourg. A blonde woman he'd been in love with, a name like something out of Tolstoy. Then, Russia, he had been in Russia, he had been ill, there had been that woman, a breakup, something tragic that had sent him back to France. A child, someone had said. Her own life seemed pointless to her now, but François Porché's did not; and if he wanted to see her, she would go.

It was too much like going into that other hospital. The smells, the sounds, the eyes of the men were the same. But this was a hospital for people whose lungs were affected. Some of them had been gassed and their lungs bubbled and oozed. The coughing and spitting went on as if they would never stop. They were alive, that was true. But wouldn't it be better not to be alive than to be like this? She walked with Julien, looking for François. Looking at these men in their beds, as men were in beds all over France, she thought, *Is anyone left whole today?* François had had double pneumonia and had been brought in almost unable to move. Her father's asthma had started when he was an officer in the Franco-Prussian War. Men's vulnerable bodies were not built for war. These terrible chemicals, the gas, the cold and damp, the freezing water of the trenches were all enough to maim and injure any human body without a single enemy shot fired. She thought of the waste, the suffering, the lies that it would all quickly be over; the absurd hopes and wishes that people passed on to each other, the little glimmers of optimism. She had heard the news about Claude only months after Henri's death. All their anxieties, divorce, bankruptcy, scandal, everything that had seemed unavoidable, had been wiped out by something they could never have imagined. A clean slate—but at what cost.

She had bought a small bunch of early snowdrops for a few sous from an old woman sitting on the street outside the hospital, wrapped in a filthy blue shawl, wearing men's boots, singing out her messages: "Flowers, lovely flowers, buy them for your sweetheart!" She laid them down on his sheet. "François."

His broad face was bony, grayish, hollowed from within. His eyebrows stood out and his mouth was marked at the corners with deep lines. His beard had grown thickly all over his jaw. But his brown-eyed glance was still that of the young poet who had walked in the Jardin du Luxembourg with her when she was still married to le Bargy, joking about the expressions on the stone faces of the queens of France. She had seen him at Trie, and in Paris since then, but only briefly. It was Henri who'd told her there had been an unhappy love affair and it was why François had come back from Russia.

"Pauline! Julien! How incredible to see you! How did you find me?"

"It was Jean Cocteau. He knows everything."

"My dear, I am so, so sorry to hear about Henri." He wheezed, gasped a little for breath.

"Yes. It's unbearable. Well, you must know."

"Hmm. It's a tragedy. Him of all people. Excuse me. I have to cough."

"François, where were you? What happened?"

"I was in Flanders, near the front line. It was those freezing nights in the trenches. I got a cold, then influenza, then pneumonia, or so it seems." He paused, to cough up phlegm and spit behind a napkin. "I was coughing my lungs up. Still am, as you see. Not gas, thank God, like some of these other poor fellows. The Belgian Red Cross picked me up. I was in Belgium in a hospital where they had almost nothing in the way of medicine and we even had to sleep on straw, and then they brought me back here." He spoke very slowly, with pauses for breath, to control the cough that contorted him from time to time. "Excuse me. You shouldn't have to see this."

"We shouldn't have made you talk. How long will you be here, do you know?"

"Nobody ever tells you things like that. They just throw you out one fine day."

"Have you anywhere to go?"

"Well, there's a place that belongs to my family, in the Jura. I thought I might go there. I can't be anywhere damp. Paris is awful at the moment; it seems to be wrapped in a sort of permanent miasma. When it's not snowing, it's thawing, and that's even worse." A breath in, then out. "What about you?"

"I have to leave Paris. I'm still at home, surrounded by all Claude's things. I seem not to be able to do anything about them. I long to go somewhere I've never been before. I just don't know where."

Julien said, "You could do worse than convalesce together, don't you think?"

43.

It was already nearly a year after Henri's death. They were in the Jura, near Domblans in eastern France, in a small sixteenth-century château with thick walls and a tree growing out of its ruined tower. The land all around was vineyards, fields, and low houses belonging to the peasant farmers and workers in the vineyards. Everything was so green. A Russian vine grew all over the walls, spreading unstoppably almost as they watched it. The vineyards were full of grapes for the harvest that would start in a week or so.

François was still struggling with the effects of the double pneumonia that had nearly killed him on the Belgian front. He was thirty-eight now, tall, good-looking still, with his Valois beard trimmed back. A beautiful face, marked by death, as so many men's were these days. When Pauline had seen him in the hospital, he had looked as if he had been too close to death ever to come back completely, but he had been given oxygen and put in a steam tent, and had regained strength. He was writing a poem about the Battle of the Marne. He dreamed of getting back to sculpture, modeling clay and cutting marble, his other passion. He sat with a rug over his knees, a notebook on the rug and a pencil in his hand. The poem was the first he had begun to work on since he was invalided out of the war. She was glad to be useful: to bring him soup and make the strong Russian tea he liked, to straighten his bed. It was like being a nurse again, like doing it for Henri.

Outside, the corn was already cut; the haystacks stood like cottages in the stripped blond fields. September. Only a year since Henri's death. Julien sent a wire to say he was coming to visit them. Pauline sent a carriage to pick him up at Lons-le-Saunier. The aching beauty of September in the country. Henri had fallen on a day like this. When Julien arrived, they didn't talk about him, not yet. She showed him to a room on the second floor with a view out over the valley. She watched while he unpacked his things, spread his papers out on the table in front of the window, and immediately handed the two chambermaids a bundle of dirty clothes.

"Don't philosophers do their own laundry? I can't believe you traveled with all that dirty linen."

"I had to leave Pau in a hurry."

"What happened?"

"I had to escape from an elderly lady who wanted to marry me."

"Ah, Julien!"

"She is a good person, you understand, but too romantic. She wanted me to sit holding hands with her in the moonlight, can you imagine? She isn't of my intellectual stature, so she would have not made a good companion. And, she is at least forty."

"I'm surprised she didn't throw you out along with your dirty clothes!"

"Well"—he gave his childish giggle—"she almost did."

He paced up and down on the terrace looking at the view across the valley. Pauline noticed he was still wearing his white shoes. "I put them on for the summer, July 1, and wear them until September 15. Never wear white shoes after mid-September. It is just not done. But we are not yet quite there."

With the country at war and half their friends injured or dead, he was worried about the color of his shoes? Still, he was Julien, he was her dear cousin; she had to forgive his eccentricities. François was on his chaise longue, his eyes half-closed, dreaming or thinking of poetry or perhaps just hiding from Julien and his white shoes.

Julien cleared his throat, staring at the shoes as he spoke. He was elegant, compact still, with his pale fringe of hair. "I think it's time you two got married. It would do you both good. François, you need to be looked after. Pauline, you need cheering up. Why don't you get married?"

"I've been married twice, Julien. Neither was a good experience. Why would we want to get married? We're fine as we are."

François closed his eyes.

"Well, my friend here seems depressed to me," Julien said.

Pauline laughed. She saw François's hat, tipped over his eyes, twitch slightly.

"I think you're confusing thinking with depression. Not everyone chatters on like you," she said.

"What do you think of war poetry, Julien?" François's voice came from beneath his hat. "Do you think anything worthwhile can come from such a mess?"

They went in to lunch, the two men talking about literature, and the difference the war had made to French writing, and what would come of it all in the end. Pauline walked behind them, still fuming.

Two days later, on September 22, she woke sweating from a dream. Her mouth was full of earth. She had been buried alive. She was also with Henri, who was spitting earth that had filled his mouth, wiping saliva away.

It was the first anniversary of his death. Still, nobody had found his body. He had no tomb, no place on this earth where she could go to speak to him. He was lying decomposing in earth, trodden by passers-by, marched over by armies. The body she had so loved was as good as refuse. It was unbearable. She got up, and decided to go into Domblans and at least lay some flowers on the altar in the church there, because he had believed in the Christian God, even if she could not.

On the way, in the carriage, she saw Julien walking toward her. He raised a hand, and his hat. His shoes were now brown, and as highly polished as horse chestnuts. He simply waved absentmindedly as she passed, and walked on back to the château. When she came back from the church, where she had left a bunch of wildflowers and grasses before the altar, he was sitting on the terrace. He got up and came to meet her, as if he had some news.

"Oh, Julien."

"Sit down, darling. You must be tired. Lie down on the chaise longue, why don't you?"

She sank down, took her hat off; she was half lying down when she heard him say, "It must be a hard day for you, Pauline."

She sat up, wary, warned by his tone.

"Apropos, I know you'll be interested. I read the report on the German atrocities in the Woëvre that man Joseph Bédier wrote. Did you know about it? You knew that they had just executed some of our troops in cold blood? I wonder, are you sure that those eight corpses of French officers that were found in the Calonne trench last September were not those of Fournier and his fellows? Because really, the trench lies along the side of the wood at Saint-Rémy, so I thought it possible . . ."

"Julien, I can assure you that they were not. An uncle of Henri's went to see Bédier, and no officer of the 288th was among the men who were buried that evening."

"Are you sure, though? Bédier could have told him a white lie, after all."

"I am sure."

"Well, I really hope you are right. But in your place, I'd be worried about it."

Silence. She sat hiding her face from him. It was too much, even to be asked to think about the men dug up and reburied in that place.

She was so angry she could hardly speak. She got up from the chaise longue and walked past him and into the house. How dare he, how could he, today of all days, how could he be so cruel and thoughtless and not even realize it?

She met François on his way to his room. He stopped her in the corridor, took hold of her wrists, and said, "What happened? You look terrible. Come in for a minute."

She told him what Julien had said.

"I can't believe he could be so crass. Pauline, listen." He took her hand between both of his and held it. She felt the dry warmth and the size of his hand, enclosing hers. "Why focus on that? What matters most was Henri's wonderful life, all he wrote, all he did, your life together; you are connected forever. We all are, don't you see. We're like an ocean with no boundaries, where all the rivers of our lives flow and mix; there's no containing that and no ending it. Pauline, he lives on in you, and in all your memories of him. Nothing Julien can say changes that. Henri's everywhere. He'll live forever."

He pulled her to him and held her close and let her cry on his chest. "Sleep now. Stay here with me. I'll wake you in time for dinner. I'm with you. I'll never be anywhere else."

At dinner, and during the next few days of Julien's stay, she managed to be calm and polite to her cousin. Julien knew her so well, he could not possibly have missed how cold she was to him. None of them mentioned what he had said. François was firm and friendly, she quiet and aloof. He left after a few days, to find out if his woman in Pau had become less absurdly romantic.

"Well, goodbye, you two. Don't forget to invite me to the wedding. I may even be marrying before long, if she'll have me. You have quite inspired me. And keep in touch, as much as one can these days. You are both close to my heart. You know that."

The Russian vine began to lose its leaves. Dusk grew chilly; they no longer sat outside. From three in the afternoon on, François moved indoors to work in his room, where he sat at a white wooden table in front of the window to write. The poem grew. His health seemed to improve; he was hardly coughing. Their first round against his illness was won. While the war went on, playing ninepins with the lives of the best men of their generation, here was one, at least, who still had permission to exist. October arrived, and the air was pure, cold, transparent. Pauline closed the windows and shutters as soon as the sun began to go down behind the hill opposite. Together they sat in one room, warmed by the old-fashioned round white porcelain stove. Silence came with the early night: it leaned on the walls and shutters, enclosing them. Sometimes hours passed, with only the sound of ash shifting inside the stove, or the turning of a page.

One evening she went down into the garden in the dark and cried for as long as it took. It was time. She howled like an animal and didn't hold back. François knew, she was sure; he'd seen her go out. She thought of Henri's young body, decomposing in God knew what clay mud of the Woëvre, as the final communiqué had brutally put it a year ago. Mist rose from the valley below the château. Through a crack in the shutters she could see the light of the lamp on François's table, where he was still working. He was alive and writing, and Henri was dead and would go on being dead. The shock of his death had not allowed her to take in the long reality of him remaining dead—his being gone forever. He was dead, as her father had been dead all through her adolescence and the rest of her life. There could be no reprieve. The war went on. He had gone; it was as if he had never been.

Out in the darkness she felt the damp evening air on her skin. The humid breath of the earth that had swallowed him. She bent over, her fists to her stomach, as if she might vomit. There would always be this absence, and with it no explanation, no consolation. She would live with the gap of it inside her as she had lived with an emptied womb after the child was gone. Nothing could give him back to her. All his writing was powerless to do so, as was all her longing. She sobbed until she was hollow, until there was no more anguish left.

Then she walked back to the house, straight into the room where François was working. He looked up and Pauline saw from his face that he had heard her out there like a fox in a trap. In silence, he moved a low chair toward his writing table so that when she sank onto it, her shoulders were at the level of his page. He put a hand on her shoulder, and went on writing. She laid her head down on the page he had just written.

"Pauline, would you like to marry me?" His hand firm on her shoulder, the paper cool beneath her cheek. "It may not be the right time. You don't have to answer. But, think about it?"

After a moment, she sat up. Time moved on, whether she did or not. It always would.

He said, "I think I'll finish this by Christmas, with any luck."

"François, did I ever tell you that Henri once told me that you would be the perfect person for me to marry?"

"No! Did he really? I wonder why."

"I think he said it because he knew how good you are."

"We all knew that we could be killed. When I was in Belgium, I thought I was going to die in that field hospital. I couldn't breathe. My whole body was shutting down from lack of oxygen. My extremities seemed to have gone already. I couldn't feel my legs at all."

"But you didn't die."

"No, I was terribly dehydrated; that was why my muscles were not working. Once they got me to Paris, I started improving. But this cough still goes on, and apparently my lungs are very scarred. So I'm not much of a catch, really; but at least I'm here for now."

"François, you're going to live."

"Now you're here, I believe I will."

"I think there is something that is set, about our death. I see it now. And I think now that Henri knew he would be killed. I think he knew, too, that we would console each other."

"What I wanted to say, my dear, is that it can be a *mariage blanc*, if you like. It might just make it easier for us to live together. I mean, this is very soon after Henri. If you don't feel you can love me physically, it's all right."

She stood and took his head and held it against her chest, her fingers in his thinning hair. They knew each other very well. She felt the warmth of his breath. She felt him waiting. The lamp's circle of light, the pages with his handwriting, the dark night outside. *At such moments,* she thought, *you have to choose life, and go on choosing it. Otherwise you have died too.* "No, François, that would never do. I want to marry you. I want us to have a married life."

"You're sure?"

"Sure."

They looked at each other and she thought, *He knows, it's like that for him too; we need each other as we need life. We are like people staggering toward each other in no-man's-land, astonished to be able to move at all.*

44.

You act, Seb thinks, *and something happens as a result. You speak out loud, voicing something that was just a slight and private idea only hours earlier, and the world takes it up and believes it, and the future begins to happen. You touch somebody, and ask a question, and she does not pull away.* Only once before in his life has he been so impulsive: the night he came back from Paris in 1975, threw gravel up at Annie's window, and shouted out that he loved her, for anyone to hear.

She'd shushed him, laughing, and come down and let him in. It was in a rented flat in Putney and some other girls lived there too, but either it was so late that they were all asleep, or they were away, he can't remember. She brought him into her room, because it was the only private space she had, and made him a cup of hot cocoa on her little gas burner, and he told her, incoherent and fast, about Paris, about the house on rue du Bac, about Madame Simone—Pauline—who had let him read her love letters, who had told him that if you loved someone, you must let that person know. They lay down together on her narrow bed, fully dressed, but somehow after an hour or two they were struggling out of their clothes and holding each other hard on the narrow bed, and it was there, as the dawn began to rise behind the roofs of south London, that he first made love to her. Their love affair began that became a marriage, and a lifetime. He'd thought about nothing else on the brief flight from Orly to London. If he hadn't been with Pauline, he wouldn't have dared.

And then what happened? In a long, happy life with someone, you hardly ever need to be impulsive, to make rash decisions. He's avoided the wars that his contemporaries have been caught up in, and he's never been seriously tempted to have an affair, or even think about divorce; his children were born easily, he has always had work. The challenges of being human that the rest of the world experiences have hardly come up for him. He has counted himself lucky, yes, but has taken it all for granted just the same. He is a pure product of his generation, born after a major war, given all the advantages both of the welfare state in Britain and of the booming economy of the USA. He has skipped between worlds, between societies, taking the best of everything as his right. And then, Annie collapsed, and his world with her.

He didn't know of the twist of vein and artery in her head that the doctors at the Radcliffe told him, forty years later, had probably been there all her life. No, he knew only her smile, her tastes in food, the parts of her body that even she could not see. He knew her against him, around him; he knew how she brushed her hair, cleaned her teeth, plucked her eyebrows in front of a mirror, how she rolled on lipstick and turned her lips inward to make it even; he knew how she came smiling toward him when he came in at the door, how her flesh had softened as she aged; he knew her in every way you could know a person, her perfectionism, her self-doubt, her calm love of her children, her cry when she came, the way she sat on the toilet, the faces she made when talking on the telephone to someone she didn't like; her whole way of being in the world. He knew that she swallowed aspirin and then codeine against her occasional fierce headaches, and did yoga positions on the living room floor, and insisted on healthy food. But he did not know anything of that fatal combination that was tightening inside her head, maybe for years—who knew, maybe since that first night in Putney—the prepared explosion that would kill her as surely as a placed bomb. You can't know these things. Life is an experiment with the outcome hidden. It's a dauntlessness in the face of such things. It's going forward, anyway, against the odds. You shout under a window, you take that risk, and you win and lose it all at the same time. Now, he remembers that moment of risk—that existential moment, even—when he told young Annie that he loved her, laying himself open, not knowing what the outcome might be.

He doesn't know if he can love Isa de Giovanni, or she him; or really, even what that means anymore. What is the connection between knowing and loving? Where is the seam that knits it all together? Is it chance, decision, or a kind of grace that comes when you have allowed both chance and decision their turn? It's not about beginning on a whole life, it's about rescuing the lives they both have. It's finding out what they can make together. It's coming out of the ruins, hand in hand. It's a gamble, yes, but people gamble on each other all the time, on Internet dating sites for widows and widowers, for God's sake, through meetings in bars and at other people's weddings and even funerals. Life, as he sees it now, is entirely different from how it seemed in those early days, when the urge to marry Annie consumed him. Now, he does not want to be alone, because alone is a kind of extinction; it is giving up. He wants to wake in the night and find someone there: a hand to hold in the darkness, a voice that speaks to him, a bodily presence, another human. Not just comfort, but exploration: knowledge of the other. To go on for all the rest of his life, able to love, to ask, to listen. To be there. To be up for it, whatever it is. He wants to know that this is possible. To find out who she is, this woman who drew him with such a patient hand and assessing eye, whose simple invitation to wash some lettuce made him feel deeply at home. She will never be Annie. He doesn't want her to be Annie. He wonders what she wants, and if she will tell him, and where they will go from here.

Yet perhaps Isa guessed before he said anything. He wonders. When she was drawing him, her eye was perhaps not entirely professional. Her slightly flirtatious comment, you're really—what was it, lopsided? Her kiss on both cheeks, slowed down, deliberate, that evening. The fact of her changed hair, even. He's known something for weeks. The glances, the moments when neither has known quite what to say. Only now can he see, in hindsight, and recognize it. Chloé brought him to feel, uncomfortably, the old sudden burn of sexual feeling—that moment at the kitchen table, that moment in the church—but it was Isa, standing ungainly on that chair to bring down the little case with Fournier's writings in it, who touched his heart even then with her clumsiness, her rucked-up shirt and dusty trousers, her young laugh. At this age, the heart must have its way. He has loved the way she moves about her kitchen, knowing where everything is; how she hands him a plate, fills a glass. He has already loved the way she is with him, in this most banal of situations: he, a man waiting to be fed, she providing. Is this shamefully sexist, he wonders, or it simply real, and to be accepted? He has already loved her shyness and bravado, coming home with her new hair. He has loved the seriousness with which she talked about painting. He has loved watching her cross the yard with her basket of vegetables. He has loved her presence, already, and he hasn't known it, till now. Where he's believed that absence—Annie's—filled him completely, there has been this slow accretion of presence—Isa's, almost unnoticed.

That first evening, when she took him to the concert and he fell asleep for a moment on her shoulder. That long evening, the children in the dark garden, the tables laid, the music; did she know then what she was doing, drawing him in to a kind of dream, from which in all these weeks since he has not really woken? Was it deliberate? Did it matter? Now he thinks, *She wanted to go there with me for a reason, as she wanted to draw me, as Chloé wanted to feed me strawberries and take me to that church with the paintings. She knew that I would go along; they both did. I went willingly, and I will continue to do so, because whatever we used to seduce each other has now done its trick. It has worked, and we have moved on, closer together. We have allowed each other into the place of hope, and dream. Henri Fournier, my old companion, have you been telling me this all along? As I read your love letters, labored over your plots and their flawed endings, followed the flow of your handwriting till the last word you wrote? Was this what you risked everything, finally, to say?*

45.

December 1915, Jura–South of France

Snow fell, and intense cold wrapped the château. They had been there for five months.

"We have to find somewhere warmer. This isn't good for you."

"But where can we go?" He was huddled in blankets, even with the big porcelain stove lit, and she dreaded the return of his cough.

"South. *Le Midi*. We'll find something cheap. What about Cavalaire? I know a little hotel there, a family hotel, and from there we could look for something to rent."

"We'll come back here for the summer, though, won't we?"

The château, which belonged to his family, would be empty until their return. They set off for the Var, installed themselves in a little hotel at Cavalaire with its own beach and the dark-blue Mediterranean only yards away. Once again, François spread out his writing materials on a table in front of the window. Blue sea, blue sky, the smells of orange blossom and tomatoes cooking; red earth, rocks, and sand; the glitter of winter sun. Here, he would write the last stanzas of his long poem on the Battle of the Marne. Every time Pauline saw him lay out pens and paper and smooth his paper flat with both hands—that peculiar tenderness of writers for their materials—she would think of Henri.

Henri with his papers and notebooks at Cambo, at Trie. That gesture: smoothing a sheet of paper flat, tipping back his head for a moment, his pen poised, then straightening his shoulders, leaning forward slightly, making that first mark. It was Henri and now it was François. Perhaps, as François had said, they were all rivers that found their way to the same sea. The Mediterranean Sea, that she now saw daily as she walked down from the little hotel past the oleander and mimosa bushes, under the pine-thick hill.

46.

September 1975, Paris

Our last morning, she thinks on waking. The light's different, and she wakes late, because of it. Outside, the steady drip of rain on the streets. Gray sky at the windows when she opens the shutters to the day. She aches, as she always does when it's raining; in fact, if she'd paid attention yesterday, she would have known the weather was about to break. She's slow to get her breakfast tray, a little more shaky than usual as she carries it through to place it on the round table; her hand upon her coffee cup gropes for the handle before it can grasp it. All the little vagaries and caprices of the body—how accurately, when you are old, it tells you what is going on. She dresses slowly, carefully, when she's had her breakfast—the brioche from yesterday scattering more crumbs than usual as she lifts it to take a bite, the coffee more necessary than ever. She chooses a blouse and a pair of loose silk trousers, as it isn't yet cold, and the touch of silk is almost like a second skin. Materials matter. She thinks of Henri and his unashamed passion for the clothes women wore. He loved the fall of skirts, the swish of materials as women walked; he had first noticed it in his mother, he'd told her. He even wrote about it: how a clothed woman was more seductive than a naked one.

Seb is punctual, but wet. She hands him a towel for his hair, hangs his jacket up on the door. "You don't have an umbrella?"

"I didn't think I'd need one. Besides, one always leaves them behind somewhere. And I like walking in the rain. Paris in the rain is so lovely." He rubs his wet dark head, and the skin shows white on his scalp. He sniffs and pants like a young dog.

"You must be a romantic." She pours him coffee, strong as she knows he likes it. "It's too wet to go out to smoke. You could always stick your head out of the window, if you like."

"No, I'm all right for now. Later, maybe."

The little tape recorder, the new tape inserted; his hands busy, shoulders bent.

"Shall we go on?"

"Of course."

He asks her, surprising her with his bluntness, "Did you ever discover what happened?"

They have only a limited amount of time; that must be it. She plunges in. "You mean, how Henri died? No. Not entirely, though there were some clues. Jacques Rivière was nice enough to tell me about going to the place after the war. He went there in 1919. You know who he was—the director of *La Nouvelle Revue Française*? Henri's brother-in-law and oldest friend. He wrote about going to the battlefield. I did appreciate Jacques sending his account to me first, though I don't suppose his wife wanted him to."

Seb is looking at her through his eyelashes. She wants to reach out and feel the shape of that young head through its damp rough hair, as she wanted to towel it dry for him earlier, but of course does not.

"There was fighting all around Verdun that September. It seems that Henri was in the woods northeast of Vaux-lès-Palameix, in the forest of Saint-Rémy, right up near the front line. There was a lot of argument afterward about what happened, but it seemed that Henri's captain was enthusiastic about just going in and shooting Germans, and the last anyone saw was this captain leaping out from behind a tree, followed by two lieutenants, all of them with their revolvers in hand and running toward a trench. The trench was full of German soldiers, it seems. It was a kind of ambush. Jacques thought that Henri was one of the lieutenants and that he was certainly wounded, if not killed. He could well have been taken prisoner, as Jacques was. Anyway, Jacques went back to the battleground on foot in 1919 to try to find out what had happened to his brother-in-law. He said it was still a ravaged, empty landscape, scarred and battered. He went from the empty village of Ranzières to Vaux-lès-Palameix. Again, flattened, razed. A dead place. Blackened, stripped trees. But further on, into the woods, vegetation had grown back, and he found little graves marked with German inscriptions, *A French hero*, *A French warrior*, and so on. Nice of them, eh? Wooden buildings here and there with corrugated metal roofs, with torn, ripped mattresses in them. Everything moldy and rotten. An old car, like a wrecked ship. The Americans had camped there in 1918, and had left a great heap of shells, rusty tins of preserves, old clothes even. I remember him saying that next to a heap of shells, there was the whitened skull of a horse. That somehow brought it home to me like nothing else. The war killed millions of horses; tanks attacked men on horseback—the end of an old order. Crosses here and there, stuck in the ground. Silence, desolation. Wind in the trees. Old broken chairs set out there in front of the buildings, as if waiting for guests. Jacques said he sat down and felt Henri's presence—he talked and wrote about souls and spirits, but I knew what he meant; when you have been that close to someone, they can indeed come back to you. I could imagine him sitting there, listening to the wind in the trees, thinking of Henri. He thought about what it would be like to be young and alive and to run toward certain death, and what you'd think about at that moment, and whether you would even have time to think at all. What was in Henri's mind, when he leapt after that captain as instinctively as he would have thrown himself into a rugby scrum? We'll never know. Sorry, I can't talk about it without—thank you, my dear."

He snaps the tape off. She takes his large, rather dirty white hand-kerchief and dries her eyes, then sips her water. "I haven't talked about it for a very long time. For Henri, everything in a place like that would have reminded him so vividly of life. Trees, grass, mud, the smells of the countryside. A forest. It was somehow right that he died in a forest. But what did he think? What did he feel? Maybe when the captain called out an order to him, it was just as if Frantz de Galais in the book had called out to Meaulnes, and he simply had to follow him."

"Just what I was thinking," Sebastian says. "Do you want to keep the hanky? We needn't record anymore."

"No, no, thanks. I'm all right now."

"You know," he says, "I think at a time like that you'd just do the next thing. He probably didn't have time to think. Easier to run forward than to hold back. Especially for a man who played a lot of sports. You'd just be part of the team. I often think about it, actually. Men my age being asked to go and commit suicide, more or less, by some old geezer sitting in an office somewhere. But what I think is, in the situation Henri was in, death would be so quick, you'd hardly feel it. It's harder for you. I mean, all these years later, still not knowing."

She says, "I heard, a couple of years later, that his last words were 'Tell a woman in Paris whose name is Perier.' A soldier heard that before he died. So he didn't die immediately. I don't know whether that makes it worse, or not."

"His last thought was of you."

"Yes. And, I've so much wanted to know where he was buried. It's been an unanswered question for so much of my life. I don't think it's ever going to be answered. If you don't believe in an afterlife, the body matters. The soul is in the body. There isn't any separation."

47.

What had it really meant, to survive this war? She and François lived on into a different world, one which Henri would never know. They took walks, wrote plays, ate meals, saw friends, talked about money. They were leaving him behind. She was leaving him behind. She cried for him less often, thought of him perhaps once a week, then once a month, when once it had been every single day. He had stopped living as the people in his novel had stopped living: there was no more Meaulnes after he had walked out that night with his daughter wrapped in his coat. The trail had gone cold. Yet, as Meaulnes lived on in readers' imaginations, in the life of the culture, so must his creator. Nobody would ever forget Alain-Fournier the writer; and yet she, his lover, was beginning to forget Henri Fournier the man. It was not humanly possible to go on remembering every last detail: the sound of his voice grew faint, as did the smell of his skin, the touch of his hand, the sound of his laughter.

Yet, she would not really be able to accept Henri's death until she knew where his body was: it was as simple, as incontrovertible as that. His body had been her reality. His voice was in his books—but his body, lost in the mud of France, lost to her, lost to everyone who had loved him. Where was that, and how could she accept its disappearance without trace? A religious person might find relief in believing that his soul had been transported elsewhere, and was in some blissful state, awaiting her own arrival. But she was not that person. Her shaky connection to Henri's faith had died with him. She could not accept a God who would let this outrage happen, this war persist. Heaven was an empty concept: it could not match up to the happiness she had known with Henri under the trees and in the bee-loud gardens on earth.

In early November, she and François drove back to Paris on an unseasonably warm day, to arrive at rue du Bac at about six o'clock. The city was extraordinarily calm. A place had been reserved for them on a balcony at the corner of boulevard de la Madeleine. They would have to be in their places by four in the morning for a parade that wouldn't start till ten; otherwise, the barriers would be up and they would be on the street, behind eight or ten rows of pushing, curious people.

Her house on rue du Bac, bought after she had sold Claude's house on quai Debilly, seemed stopped in time. The shutters all closed, the air stale, no sign of the extraordinary changes that had taken place on the outside. She threw open windows and shutters to let the evening air move through. She unpacked a cold chicken, some cheese, and some wine for them and urged François to go to bed in her own big bed, to catch a little sleep before they had to leave again. She stretched out beside him and thought she wouldn't sleep, there was so much to think about. The war that had defined her life had ended. What would life be like now? Side by side like two carved people on a tomb, they lay there. She wasn't sure if François was awake. How strange it was to have spent these years with him, when she and Henri had believed so fervently in their own life together; life, love, survival were all different paths through the same forest. She heard from the change in François's breathing that he had fallen asleep, that little rasp at the end of each breath; she felt his temperature rise at her side. Then there was the jangling little hammer on the bell of the alarm clock. Then, silence. Then, little by little, between the gaps in the curtains, behind the closed shutters of the bedroom, a sound that became a noise. Dim lights moved across the window's narrow gap; a pale stripe moved across the ceiling. It was still dark outside. Henri had told her of the night between All Hallows and All Saints, when Christians believed the dead were mysteriously close and could even visit the living; when the thin veil between death and life was said to be its most transparent. Tonight was like this. The other world was close, out there approaching in the streets before dawn; perhaps it was in this time that the dead from this war would be allowed a moment's grace, to come back for just an instant, take their earthly form again, the flesh that had been so much loved; to call their lovers by their names, just once, so that those names never sounded the same afterward. She had renounced the name that Henri called her. Now she heard it whispered in the near-dark: *Pauline!* She waited. A grumbling sound, a faint distant roar, the accumulated stamp of marching feet; were these the armies of the dead, come back alive from the burial grounds of France? No. The marching feet came closer; the voices were those of a vast approaching crowd of the living, shouting out the relief of having won this war. She sat up, longing all at once to be with them, elbow to elbow; to march, shout, lose herself in the crowd. She went to the window. They were down there; they must be filling the street, overflowing the pavements, a single flow with a single aim and a single thought, but she couldn't see them, only hear them pass the house, and go on, and on, an unending procession, invisible because of the courtyard and the big gates that separated the house from the street. These people had come from where? Had they been up all night? Had they crossed France, or simply Paris, to get here?

"François?"

He was awake in the half dark. "It's time to go." They fumbled to dress in the dark, neither thinking to turn on a light. She pulled the curtains wide, opened the shutters, and gray light filled the room.

They reached the house on boulevard de la Madeleine after a long walk, crossing the river by the Pont des Arts to take a different route from the marching crowd on the boulevards. At the crossroads in front of the church of La Madeleine and on the steps of the church, people were sitting and lying; Pauline and François had to step over them, as if walking over the bodies of people in bed, people who had been there all night, waiting. Men and women lying embraced, children in heaps, still asleep. Some men with bottles, laughing, poking each other in the ribs; others sitting rapt, their arms around their knees, stoically waiting out the night. Men with one leg, men with a stump for an arm, men with bandaged heads. Blind men, led by nurses. Women who sobbed, women who embraced the nearest man at hand, women who bashed saucepans and sang the Marseillaise.

The house had a high balcony; they couldn't have had a better view, just above the leaves of the plane trees, but close enough to see the least change of expression, the slightest tremor of excitement, in the people down below. Then the formal procession began: two horsemen led the way, each one with a dark-blue baton held to his thigh, the color of the night sky; one rode a quiet horse used to crowds, with a high pommel to the saddle, the other was on a dancing bay stallion. Marshals Joffre and Foch. The clash of cymbals and the thunder of drums. The horses pricked their ears. The two victorious generals sat them easily; Foch, François commented afterward, looked as distant as he would later sound in his books. The long-sighted stare of a man who had outmaneuvered his enemies, fought them in a long war of attrition, and sent them home. Behind them, the marching men of what was left of the armies of France. The blue, white, and red of banners. The cacophony of sound that was more relief than joy.

Oh, if Henri could have seen this day. She stood with tears in her eyes that then ran down her face, and she did nothing to stop them. Her throat ached. The memory of that other balcony, on which she had stood with Henri less than five years ago, that night in late May when he stretched his arms wide to take in the whole starry sky, and together they had looked down on Paris and smelled the grassy smell of an early summer night, and finally spoken of their love. The sound of marching men, at the camp, at Auch. Marching away, perhaps forever. Now, marching back. He was down there, he must be, Lieutenant Fournier, coming home with his regiment, even if missing an arm, an eye, it would be bearable if he were still just alive. To be here. To march or ride beneath the watching eyes of Paris, to hear the cheering, yelling crowds, to notice that young woman who jumped up to throw flowers before the feet of the prancing horses, to laugh with her at the sleepy children who were hoisted on their parents' shoulders and were told, *You will always remember this.* To be part of this world, not in exile from it. The extraordinary relief of this day was the exact mirror of her sadness. François stood close at her side. He handed her his handkerchief. She took it, and his hand, grateful that the war had spared her this thoughtful, gracious man.

Yet 1918 was not 1914. Henri would have been different, if he had survived these four years of war. He wouldn't be the idealistic enthusiast who had left from Auch that day. Nobody was that way anymore. Nobody who had survived the slaughter and understood the underlying reasons for it—the venality, the unreadiness of France to fight, the uselessness of sending men against machine guns, horses against armored cars, the pointlessness of patriotism as they had felt it in 1914—could possibly feel anything but relief today that it was over. The war to end all wars, they called it; fighting for peace, dying for your country, a beautiful death, glory, sacrifice, all these concepts had no meaning now. Hundreds of thousands of young Frenchmen, as well as Englishmen, Germans, Americans, Russians, Hungarians had died—for what? For this day? For bashing saucepans and singing and watching men on horseback parade through the streets of Paris? *Bread and circuses,* she thought, *how we all love them, how we all love to stop thinking and gloss over the horror and then probably do it all again.* Nobody could end all war unless they understood what made men want it. She had seen in Henri the passion and naïveté that created that kind of courage. If he were here now, would he be cynical? Would he even watch this performance? What would he have written, in his book about the war? What difference would he have made, if he had only lived?

48.

Around them, the steady pelt of rain. The room is like an aquarium, water streaming down. In here, they move slowly toward each other, she feels it, like fish; perhaps it is to do with a drop in her blood pressure. Today is a day for quiet, and she has already talked too much.

She laughs. Crying, laughing, all this talking; she's exhausted, but she wants it to go on, still. It. Life. To go on till it stops.

"Let's take a break," he says. "I'll go down for that cigarette, I can stand outside the concierge's lodge and stay dry. Don't worry about me. Back in a minute."

She remembers Henri's mother telling her about his first trip to England as a teenager, how he bought cakes and ate them in the street, the way the English did. He'd been working in some wallpaper factory, in London, in 1905, and living with people called Nightingale; strange, people with the name of that bird. He'd written to his parents to ask for more money, and they had worried that he wasn't getting enough to eat. How these details came back to one! She thinks of him, eating cakes on the streets of London, free and alone and slightly homesick and excited by the strangeness; a boy called Augustin Meaulnes perhaps already part of him. Now, here is this English boy with his wet hair and his French cigarettes and a look of loneliness that sits on him like a cloak. Here, and about to be gone. She thinks, *Love is no respecter of person, or age. It comes when it will, and all we can do is recognize it. Greet it and let it go, as Blake so wisely said.* But the letting go, that never gets any easier. The blank of days after Seb's departure is something she doesn't want to contemplate. At this age, more than ever, you need people, talk, exchanges. You need the warmth and vigor of love in one of its many forms, the only one that is left to you now.

He comes pounding up the stairs and through her door. His hair stands up from the wind outside, which has begun to blow stray yellow leaves down to the pavement.

She watches him walk about her room, sit down on the sofa without being asked, stretch out his long legs, and tip his head back, making himself at home. She smells the sharp tobacco smoke mixed with his own fresh sweat when he comes close to her. *Oh, God who does not exist, thank you for this boy.*

He sits back on the sagging sofa and sighs. "It's great being here. I feel as if we've known each other for ages. Thanks for making so much time for me."

"It's been my pleasure. I look forward to the book. You will send me a copy?"

"Of course. Simone, what matters most in the end? You must know, being the age you are?"

She meets his gaze. It's as if there is no distance at all between them, no difference of generations, no lapse of time or space. "That you're here. That I'm here. We're contemporaries. This is all that matters. Being alive, in the present."

"Not the past?"

"The past is just another present. You and I, sitting here in my apartment, will become the past. Tomorrow, even in an hour. There isn't any past, not really, just another time when we were here, in life. And I do think you have to love the time you're in."

"It feels hard to, sometimes."

"Well, what is the alternative? We're here. It's not chance that brought you here. Or we can call it chance, we can call it anything, but the important thing is that it happens. You'll remember. I'll die. You're Henri's age, but you'll have a long life. You'll have the life he never had. But you'll always be here, now, sitting here with me. We've met. That is what really counts."

He blows air between pursed lips as if after running a race, and looks at her, and blushes.

"We've done our best to kill off everything that's sacred in this century," she says. "But there's still this. The truth of being human."

She telephones to order their lunch. "How about some cassoulet for today? I know they do that on Wednesdays, and presumably they can send some up."

"Great."

She thinks, *I could get him to come back. This need not be the end. I have something that he wants. When you are old, do you have to bargain for love? Or is it simply a straight and honorable exchange, my memories for your presence; your need for information, mine for human warmth?*

She lays out their plates, their cutlery; she places the wine bottle at the center, straightens napkins, lays their table like a freshly made bed, and the two chairs, tucked in to the satisfying curve of the table, await them.

Later, when they have eaten the hot, filling dish she felt they needed, she asks him, "What time do you go tomorrow?"

"I'm flying back to London midmorning."

"You will tell me how you get on with your book?"

"Of course."

"Well, my dear, I'm going to have my siesta now. Don't go out, you'll get wet. Under the rug, there in the corner. Take as long as you like. You can read them all, if you have the time. They are the essence of him and me. They will tell you what you want to know. I hope they tell you what you need to know about love. And, if you ever need a room to work in, I have room here, as you know, and it would save you the cost of a hotel. You could read them here and write your book. Think it over."

"You mean, your letters, yours and Henri's? Really?"

"Yes. Take your time. I'm feeling a little tired, so I may sleep for some time. You can see yourself out?"

He thinks, *So, this is goodbye?* It's as if she is abandoning him half-way through a story. But she has said he can come back. That makes a difference. He wants to thank her. He wants to know what to say, to do. One day, he thinks, he will know, but it will be too late. All he can do now is mutter, "Yes, sure, thank you," and then he embraces her, or she him; there are two clashes of cheekbones, a softness of old skin, a scent of roses, and neither of them says another word. She goes into her bedroom and closes the door, and he sits down on the floor, the patterned Egyptian rug lifted, the steamer trunk opened, and takes from its tray the first small packet of envelopes with Henri Fournier's handwriting on them, unties the faded ribbon on them, and begins to open them, where they have already been slit with a paper knife, one at a time.

He sits and reads, during that whole rainy September afternoon. Reading someone else's love letters probably always feels like an intrusion, and the fact that one of these people is actually asleep in the next room is weirdly inhibiting. But he reads on—they seem to have been put in order—until he begins to feel the warmth in his body, the arousal, the effect of these words on him, here, now, at this moment in his life.

He pauses, puts down the letter in which Henri asks Pauline, *Will you wear your red nightdress?* He thinks of Annie. Why was he prepared to give her up so easily? What was wrong with him? Why, when they first met, did he not pursue her with his own certainties, as Henri Fournier did, like a tracker in the forest, like a spy, like a true lover? Why on earth has he let her drift off with Giles into a boring round of London pubs and crowded parties? The last time he saw her, she was dancing with Giles, her hair bouncing on her shoulders, at a party somewhere off the Fulham Road, and he saw her glance over Giles's shoulder at him, and even lift her fingers off Giles's shoulder in a tiny wave. Now, he thinks, someone who was madly in love would not have done that. She isn't in love with Giles. There is a chance. There is a chance that he will take, tomorrow, when he gets back to London, hot from Paris and these letters and with a new certainty, even if it's borrowed from the letters of a man who has been dead for decades: a certainty that you can catch like a thrown ball, and pass on, from one generation to another, one person to another; like a secret, like a story, like a word blown on the wind.

49.

In the early evening of his last day, Seb sits down at the outside table to slice and stone the damsons they picked from the tree by the river that afternoon. Isa has pushed the basket into his hands, handed him the short-bladed knife. "You don't mind?" It's going to rain, he hears; they have been picking all afternoon.

A big basket full of small bluish dusty fruit, some leaves still among them. He, who has never sliced damsons before, cuts and pushes the stones out with his thumb and lets the fruit fall in halves into the copper pan for jam-making. Chloé comes and sits down opposite him, and begins to cut with a sharp Opinel knife, not speaking. Their hands work the split yellow damsons into the copper pan, the stones into a plastic tub, juice running between their fingers. Seb does not look up. His hands work on. He sees the speed of her hands, her short nails, the curves of her thumbs. She has forgotten to be provocative, for days; has her mother told her something about him, about the house? Now, she is simply allowing herself to be busy and silent in his company, as they share a task.

She looks up just once, with a grin for him. "You know, she really likes you." And that is it.

Isa is inside, cooking dinner. He's heard it is to be jugged hare. Someone from the village brought them the long body of the animal that was shot yesterday. Chloé skinned it in the barn, simply stripping it of the pelt that lies out on the woodpile now, a small fur shirt. This is what the house has been for, during all those centuries of its life: people growing food, processing it, storing it, cooking it, eating it. Everything else is peripheral. A deep silent peace has imposed itself with the afternoon's activities. He has been up ladders to grasp the handfuls of blue damsons; Chloé has gleaned the ones dropped. Isa works with her copper pans and wooden spoons, creaming froth from the surface of the jam that was already cooking on the stove; *prunes bleues*, the beautiful names of fruit. Harvest times, food stored for the winter. The rhythms of the land, for nearly seventy years now uninterrupted by war.

She has said nothing more about his proposal of yesterday; yet somehow it has not been refused. This is today: the house, the damsons, jam-making, skinning and cooking a hare.

When their basket is empty, Chloé glances up at him and smiles again. "Fast work, eh?"

The plums, or his courtship of her mother? He doesn't know. She seems lighter; she doesn't even scowl as her mother calls from the kitchen window to bring the fruit indoors. He sees Isa lift her arms and pour a long white chute of sugar from a bag into the sliced fruit on the stove. Chloé carries a tray of glass jars. This is what they do, what they know how to do: when life snares them in its complications, they go back to it. The English couple might just as well not have been here at all.

Clouds pile up in the western sky at sunset, and the sun goes down in a yellow stain. Isa walks round the house closing windows. The air is still and heavy. He can smell the rain coming. There's the grumble of thunder getting closer, the horizon lit with sheet lightning. The air smells metallic, then the rain comes down, and it's rich with a vegetable tang. Seb walks down with Isa to the gate to watch, rain jackets held over their heads. The country lies flattened by the storm. He feels old, in the way of being part of something old, and as she stands beside him watching the rain soak the land, it's like being part of a couple again, part of something larger than himself, a family, a place, a way of life, a future, even an acceptable death.

He imagines people saying to him, once he's home, *Oh, so you're running off to rural France? You know it's not what it was, everyone's moved to the cities, all the cafés are closed. It's getting terribly right wing too.*

He imagines raised eyebrows. *So, you found a French woman, did you? That was quick. Are you sure it isn't just on the rebound?* But who are these people, this imaginary public? They don't exist. Or if they do, he does not need to listen to them. Only Annie, in her silence, in her absence, pushes him on into the next moment, the next choice.

They come back, still holding raincoats over their heads, feet splashed, striding and hopping across the suddenly flooded courtyard. She reaches to hold his arm before they reach the house. She says to him, "You'll come back soon, then?"

"If you want me to, Isa. Do you?"

"If it isn't too soon after Annie? Really?"

"No," he says, "it's not too soon. It's time. What about you?"

"I told you I've hardly been with anyone since Hugo. I feel as if I don't know how to. I think I may need more time."

"What will you do with it?"

She laughs. "I don't know. Miss you, maybe?"

"It won't take me long to miss you, Isa."

"You don't mind waiting?"

"Yes, actually I do. So, when you've missed me enough, what do you think you'll say?"

"I don't know. I can't tell you yet. But I'll think about it, *d'accord?*"

He sees the gleam of her teeth in the near-darkness, a smile that nobody has seen, he imagines, for years. *It's now. Life is now, Isa. Let's live it.*

AUTHOR'S NOTE

For those readers who are interested in the facts as well as the fictions of history:

I have taken a few liberties, as novelists do. Isabelle Fournier did not have a granddaughter called after her. Her daughter Jacqueline became a nun.

The rift between the Fourniers and Pauline Benda (Madame Simone) was mended when their descendants, Alain Rivière and Colette Pennin-Siglitz, allowed the publication of their correspondence after Pauline's death in 1985. The novel *Colombe Blanchet* was never finished, or published.

Henri-Alban Fournier's body was found in 1991, when a farmer drew attention to a grave on his land in which two skeletons were found, one exceptionally tall. Jack Lang, the minister of education at the time, organized Henri's reburial in the cemetery at Rémy-la-Calonne. Pauline wrote several novels after she left the stage, founded the Prix Femina, died in 1985 at the age of 108, and is said to be buried under the name of Madame François Porché in the cemetery at Montparnasse. I looked for a long time; it was raining; I did not find her.

ACKNOWLEDGMENTS

I would like to thank the following for their invaluable help with this novel.

First, Paul Savatier for finding the manuscripts and out-of-print works of Pauline Benda (Madame Simone), at Gallimard and in many Paris libraries, that made this book possible; also for Les Patrières, where I began work on it.

Ellen McLaughlin for her total and professional attention to its structure during the time I stayed with her in Nyack in 2012.

Gillian Stern for her great editorial expertise and insights.

Felicity Blunt at Curtis Brown, London, for her belief in the project.

Simon Eine of the Comédie Française for allowing me into their archives.

The College of William and Mary, in Williamsburg, Virginia, who gave me time, as creative writing fellow, to work on the book.

Thad Carhart for his thorough reading and suggestions.

My husband, Allen Meece, for his constant support and encouragement of me and my writing.

Kathryn Kilgore, for my room in the writers' and artists' house in Key West.

The writers of Key West who have encouraged me, especially Alison Lurie, Harry Mathews, and Marie-Claire Blais.

And, most importantly for any writer, my wonderful agent, Kimberley Cameron, who believed in this book from the start and never gave up, after our initial meeting in 2015 at the San Miguel Writers' Conference in San Miguel de Allende, Mexico.

I would also like to thank the team at Lake Union for their enthusiasm for my work and their professional expertise in bringing it into the world.

ABOUT THE AUTHOR

Photo ©2014 Nancy Spiewak

Poet and novelist Rosalind Brackenbury is the author of *Paris Still Life* and *Becoming George Sand*. A former writer in residence at the College of William and Mary in Williamsburg, Virginia, she has also served as poet laureate of Key West, teaching poetry workshops. She has attended the yearly Key West Literary Seminar as both panelist and moderator. Born in London, Rosalind lived in Scotland and France before moving to the United States. She spends part of each year in Paris. Her hobbies include swimming, reading, walking, travel, the cinema, and talking with friends. For more on the author and her work, visit www.rosalindbrackenbury.com.